MW00639661

IDENTITY

KATHLEEN HELMS

ZZYYZX PUBLISHING

Identity / Kathleen Helms - 1st ed.

Ebook ISBN 978-1-7361836-4-9

Paperback ISBN 978-1-7361836-3-2

Library of Congress Control Number: 2022920085

For my brother, Mark Palmerton.
When dreams become reality....

PROLOGUE

The package sat on the kitchen counter for just over one week. She knew what was inside, she was the one who had ordered it after all. The prospect of actually using it both frightened and excited her. The secrets this product could reveal were deep and mysterious. There were doors it had the potential to open, relationships it could bring into the light. On a Saturday evening in January she finally opened it. She read the directions carefully and followed them exactly.

Step one: Create an account

Step two: register your kit

Step three: agree to privacy policy (but don't read it she told herself. You can't proceed without accepting their terms)

Step four: No food, water, cigarettes, chewing gum, or mouthwash thirty minutes prior to taking the test

Step five: fill the vial with saliva (no bubbles) to the fill line

Step six: combine buffer and saliva; shake well

Step seven: Seal in box and send in mail
Step eight: Review results in your account

She dropped the package at the post office on her way to work Monday morning. Her hand trembled as she slipped it into the drive-through box.

Simple, easy, and fast. Who could it possibly hurt?

1

LEISEL TIMMERMAN

L eisel pulled into her parents driveway at 5:05. She slid quickly out of her Toyota Highlander and hurried to the front door. Sunday dinner began promptly at five o'clock and lateness was frowned upon by her mother, a nervous woman who worried incessantly and startled easily. Leisel and her brother Tyler had learned at a young age not to sneak up on their mother. Leisel entered the house, slipped off her shoes in the entry way, and hurried to the dining room. Her father and Tyler were sitting at the table.

"You're late," said her father glancing at the Patek Philippe Platinum on his left wrist.

"Five minutes Dad," she said. "I hit a lot of red lights on the way over."

"Leave earlier," he said, but not unkindly. "Early arrival is acceptable, late is not. Your mother worries." He paused then added, "She's in the kitchen."

Leisel walked into the kitchen. Her mother was at the sink,

her back to her daughter. Leisel crossed the space saying, "I'm here mom, sorry I was late."

Her mother turned from the sink. Her eyes were red as if she had been crying. Leisel gave her a warm hug then stepped back to look at her mother.

"I'm fine Mom," she said. "If I'm ever going to be late again I'll call, okay?"

Her mother nodded and Leisel folded her into another hug.

"It smells great in here mom," she said.

Her mother, who loved to cook, smiled. "Teriyaki and maple salmon, ginger rice, and fresh baked cheesy garlic rolls," she said. "Help me carry everything to the table."

Dinner conversation was light and easy. Leisel's lateness was forgiven and everyone enjoyed a glass of white wine with their food. After dinner Leisel's parents, Charles and Daisy, sat in the den with a second glass of wine while Leisel and Tyler cleared the table and washed the dishes. Her parents had a state of the art dishwasher in their kitchen which Leisel was sure they used throughout the week. On Sundays, however, Leisel washed and Tyler dried by hand.

Leisel was handing a serving platter to her brother when he said, "Have you ever heard mom or dad say anything about them having a baby when they were in high school and giving it up for adoption?"

Leisel nearly dropped the platter.

"What?" she said. "No, never. What makes you ask that?"

"I did a direct to consumer DNA test and it came back that I have a full sibling somewhere."

"You have got to be kidding me," said Leisel, "there's no way." She paused a moment then added, "I can't believe you did one of those tests Tyler."

"Jolene got them for us for Christmas. We did them together."

"Jolene is an idiot," said Leisel. "You need to dump her."

"I like her,"said Tyler, "she's fun."

"Well you are both fools for giving your DNA away. Does she have a long lost sibling too?"

Tyler shook his head. "I want to ask mom and dad about it."

"No way," said Leisel. "It has to be a scam. I bet the company has an algorithm that scans submissions for people like us."

"What's that supposed to mean?"

"Our dad is on the list of the 500 wealthiest people in the world Tyler. Someone is trying to get money out of you."

They were both quiet for a minute then Tyler said, "The person reached out to me through the company's messaging system. Her name is Jane Gray and she says she was born to teenage parents in 1990 and adopted as a newborn."

"Did you respond?"

"Not yet," said Tyler.

"Good," said Leisel. She turned so that she was facing her brother. "Don't respond Tyler," she said. "It has to be a scam. Mom and dad would have told us if we had another sibling out there somewhere."

Tyler pulled his phone out of his pocket, tapped some keys, then handed the phone to his sister.

"Here," he said, "read the message."

Leisel dried her hands and took the phone from him. The message was short.

Hello,

My name is Jane Gray and I believe I am your sister. I was born in 1990 and adopted at birth. All I know about my birth parents is that they were 16 and 17 and that their families were unable or unwilling to help them raise me. I live in Escondido, Ca. I'm hoping to be able to talk to you, or perhaps meet, depending on where you live.

Looking forward to hearing from you,

Jane Gray

LOYAL TRUESDALE

L oyal slipped his shoes on his feet and stood to check his appearance once more in the full length mirror. He didn't look great. He hadn't been taking the best care of himself since his return from New Mexico in December. He'd lost about ten pounds and his clothes hung loosely on his frame. His thinner face made him look older, and his hair was longer than it had ever been. He had combed it back from his face and the wavy ends touched the collar of his Tommy Bahama. His complexion was dull and his eyes, normally bright and sparkling, were somber. He'd always taken care with his appearance when he was, first, an officer and then a detective with the Carlsbad Sheriff's Department. In the year since his retirement his looks had faded a bit. Mostly because he was mildly depressed.

Loyal had reasons to be sad. Trinity, his girlfriend of nearly one year, was still insisting they take a break. They had talked on the phone only two times in the past three months and he missed her more than he could believe. Additionally, his friend Chris, who he had met a year previously through Maggie, had passed away on New Year's eve. And today he was attending a memorial for Bruce Meyers. He still found it hard to believe that Bruce was gone. Loyal had met Bruce in August of 2019 and they had become good friends. The loss was hard to take.

Loyal patted his cat, Boo, on the head and told him he would be back in the evening. He closed and locked the front door of his Carlsbad home, walked to his truck, and slid in. He was heading to Valley Center to meet up with his friend, and fellow buggy club member, Maggie. She was catching a ride with him to the memorial being held at a campground in the desert. Many attendees had brought motorhomes and spent the night in the desert. Maggie and Loyal were only going for the day.

He pulled into her driveway about forty-five minutes after he left his own. The front door of the house opened and Maggie stepped out; hobbled out was probably a better description. A black knee brace was wrapped around her jeans on her left leg and she carried a cane in her left hand. She had told Loyal on the phone that she had tripped over her dog, Storm, when she had gotten up to use the bathroom in the middle of the night and had suffered a torn ACL. Fortunately surgery had not been needed. She was wearing the brace and receiving physical therapy. Loyal slid out of his truck and walked quickly to the passenger side. He opened the door and helped Maggie slip inside then walked back around and slid into the driver's seat.

"Thanks for picking me up Loyal," said Maggie.

"Happy to," said Loyal.

"I wish this day wasn't happening," said Maggie.

"Me too," said Loyal, "but Bruce did have an amazing life. He lived every minute to the fullest."

Maggie brushed a stray tear off her cheek and nodded.

MAGGIE MACPHEARSON

The drive to the memorial was mostly quiet. Loyal and Maggie were each lost in their own thoughts and memories. They pulled into Stagecoach Campground and parked near some buggies. They slid out and spent the next half hour mingling and saying hello to friends from the buggy club. When Mike and Lori Ann Dario started suggesting that people move toward the large open-walled building where the actual memorial was taking place Loyal appeared beside Maggie with two folding chairs in his arms.

"Come on," he said, "let's find a good spot and make you comfortable."

The memorial was supposed to start with a slide show of pictures from Bruce's adventurous life but technical difficulties changed the order around and people were encouraged to share personal stories about Bruce with the crowd. Maggie watched and listened as people, some she had known for many years, spoke about their relationships with Bruce. When she saw the opportunity Maggie eased herself out of the chair and walked toward the front of the room. Her injured knee slowed her progress. When she reached the front, Maggie turned and looked at the crowd. She took a deep breath in and began to speak.

"Bruce," she paused, "and Winnie, have been such amazing friends. Ed and I had so many fun adventures with them. And after Ed died they were such a source of support for me. They would show up on my doorstep and take me to Fat Ivor's for lunch or dinner. One of them called me almost every day for that first year." She felt the tears filling her eyes. "I wouldn't have made it without them."

The tears burst out. Maggie's face crumpled and she stood there crying. No one in the audience moved for about ten seconds, everyone hoping she would be able to regain control. When it was clear that she could not, Winnie stood and walked to her. She pulled Maggie into a close hug and whispered, "He loved you. And I do too." Winnie released her and, with an arm over Maggie's shoulders, walked her back to her chair beside Loyal. A few more people spoke after Maggie and then the slide show was finally ready to go. Maggie watched it numbly. When the slideshow ended Lori Ann and Mike Dario passed out small, shot glass sized, plastic bottles of Fireball whiskey. It had been Bruce's new favorite drink. Anyone who wanted to could raise a toast and take a shot in Bruce's honor. Maggie drank three.

LOYAL TRUESDALE

Loyal was shocked to see Maggie, who rarely drank hard alcohol, take three shots. He stayed close by her and was not surprised when, after less than ten minutes, she hobbled to the nearest bathroom. When she came out she was wiping her face with a paper towel. Loyal gathered the chairs, said goodbye to the people nearest him, then grasped Maggie's arm gently and led her to the truck. As he drove he began to tell her the story of what had happened to him in New Mexico the past December. He was just explaining about his visit to a gravely wounded private investigator named Arnie Crenshaw when he heard a slight snore. He glanced at Maggie and saw that she was asleep, her head resting lightly against the passenger window. Loyal smiled. Sleep was just what she needed.

As Loyal was navigating the roundabout at the base of Palomar Mountain he made an impulse decision and continued west rather that turning south toward Rincon and Valley Center.

Instead he drove about 200 yards then turned left and parked in front of The Lazy H restaurant. He turned off the truck and tapped Maggie gently on the shoulder. She opened her eyes slowly and looked around as if trying to remember where she was.

"I thought maybe we could use some food," he said.

Maggie smiled and sat up straighter.

"That sounds like a great idea," she said.

They each slid out of the truck and walked into the restaurant. It was almost 5:30 and the dining room was nearly full. Loyal and Maggie found an empty table in the bar and sat. When the bartender, Henry, approached they ordered drinks. Beer for Loyal and 7up for Maggie. The waitress, Sybil, brought them menus, water, and rolls. When she returned they placed their orders; fish and chips for Maggie and barbecued ribs for Loyal.

"So how is the physical therapy going?" asked Loyal.

"Painful," said Maggie, "but my therapist is really gentle so that helps. And we get along great. She's actually got a pretty interesting life story."

Loyal leaned back in his chair and took a sip of beer.

"Yeah?" he said.

"She was adopted as an infant by a single man," Maggie said.

"That's kind of strange," said Loyal, "especially since it was probably in the '90's or earlier. I'm surprised a single man was allowed to adopt."

"Yeah," said Maggie, "I don't know the backstory on that part. I do know he raised her on his own with some help from his mother. They all lived together. When she was twelve she and her Dad were in a bad car accident. He died and she required a lot of physical therapy. That's when she decided to become a physical therapist herself."

"Twelve is a hard age to lose a parent," said Loyal. "I lost my dad when I was eleven."

"Yes," agreed Maggie, "it is. Her grandmother raised her after her father died. It sounds like she was a pretty stern woman. She died during Jane's sophomore year of college."

"She should do some DNA testing," said Loyal, "see if she can find her birth family."

At that moment Sybil appeared with their food. The conversation stilled while they ate then Maggie said, "She actually did do DNA testing. She just found out that she has a full sibling but they aren't responding to her email attempts to contact them." She took another bite and when she had chewed and swallowed she said, "Do you think you could help her find out who they are? Trace them through the email address?"

Loyal shook his head. "I don't know how to do that sort of thing."

"But you must still have contacts at the Sheriff's department," said Maggie.

Loyal wiped his face with his napkin. "Yeah, I do have contacts, but I'm not going to ask them to do something like that."

Maggie paused for a beat then said, "She's been all alone for so long Loyal. Now she knows that she has a relative out there."

"Maggie, I really don't want to get involved in this."

"Please Loyal," Maggie said, "at least just meet her and hear her story. What harm can that do?"

"You'd be surprised how much harm can come from small,

seemingly innocent, actions," said Loyal. "I've seen it first hand."

"As a favor to me, Loyal," said Maggie, "just listen to her story."

Loyal let out a long breath and despite his misgivings said, "Ok Maggie, as a favor to you."

MAGGIE MACPHEARSON

Maggie removed her phone from her purse.

"I have her cell phone number," she said. "Why don't I call her and see if she is available to meet with you?"

"While you do that," said Loyal, "I'm going to grab another beer."

Maggie nodded and stood.

"It's loud in here," she said, "I'm going to step outside."

Maggie went out the door and turned to the left where there was a large lawn. Several giant avocado trees rose out of the green fringe and reached towards the sky. Hummingbird feeders, populated by dozens of tiny green birds, hung from the western edge of the restaurant. Maggie spent a moment watching their frenzied flying then turned her attention to her phone. She pulled up Jane's contact information and tapped the blue home key.

Jane answered on the third ring. "Maggie," she said, "is everything ok?"

"Yes," said Maggie, "I'm fine. I'm actually calling because I know someone who might be able to help you locate your sibling and I was wondering if you want to meet up with him?"

"Oh my gosh!" said Jane. "Yes please. When and where?"

"Do you have any time tomorrow?" asked Maggie. "Want to meet for coffee?"

"There's a place on Grand in Escondido that's good," said Jane. "It's called Kettle. It's three or four blocks west of the old hospital."

Maggie walked back inside the Lazy H as she said, "Let me just make sure that works for him."

She sat back at the table and asked Loyal, "Coffee tomorrow in Escondido?"

Loyal nodded.

"He says yes," said Maggie. "9:30 work for you?"

"Absolutely," said Jane. "I'll see you there."

Maggie disconnected the call and smiled at Loyal.

"This is really nice of you," she said.

"I'm not making any promises," he said, "but I'll listen to her story."

"Thanks again for today," said Maggie. "I don't think I could have handled it alone."

"Me neither," said Loyal.

When Sybil approached with the bill Loyal reached out his hand.

"Dinner's on me," he said with a smile.

He pulled out his wallet, slid some bills into the check presenter, then stood and reached out his hand to Maggie.

"Come on," he said, "let's get you home.

JANE GRAY

J ane saw that her hands were trembling as she set the phone down. She ran her fingers over her face and through her shoulder length black hair. She walked to a bookcase in the living room and lifted a framed picture off one of the shelves. It was a picture of Jane and her adoptive father, William. It had been taken just weeks before the car accident that took William away from Jane and forever changed her life. Occasionally Jane still had dreams about the accident. It had been her father's fault. They had been driving to the market, both of them laughing and singing along loudly to the latest Taylor Swift song. William, distracted by the laughter and music, failed to notice a traffic signal turn from green to yellow to red. He drove straight into the intersection and their car was hit on both sides. William's side was hit first and less than a second passed before Jane's side was hit as well. The car folded in on itself, the two sides pushed together like an hourglass. Jane and William were pushed together in the center, much like sand that had become clogged in the narrow opening. William's head lay on Jane's left shoulder. He didn't move. The right side of Jane's body was a mass of white hot pain. They remained in this position for what felt like hours but, in reality, was only minutes. The first responders used the jaws of life to free them from the crushed vehicle. By the time she was lifted out and placed on a gurney Jane already knew that her father was dead.

Jane had been severely injured in the accident. Her right side was a mass of broken bones; femur, wrist, three ribs, and collarbone. She had stitches that ran vertically down her face starting at her temple, running down her cheek, and ending near her chin. When the bones healed she began physical therapy. The sessions were excruciating and there were times when Jane actually threw up or momentarily lost consciousness because of the pain. Her therapist, Eden, was her salvation. Eden had skin the color of dark chocolate, kind brown eyes, and a brilliant white smile. Her hair was long and braided in what looked like hundreds of braids which she tied behind her head in brightly colored ribbons, the braids cascading down her back like a twisting river. They worked together for months and gradually Jane's body healed. The only outward reminders of the accident were a slight limp and a scar that tracked down the right side of Jane's face.

William had always been open about the fact that Jane was adopted. Looking at the picture of the two of them it was obvious. William was 5'6' and slender. He had bright red hair, pale skin dotted with freckles, and light blue eyes. At twelve Jane was already taller than her father by two inches. Her skin was olive, her hair was black, and her eyes were dark brown. They looked nothing like each other. The only thing about them that matched was the joy in their smiles. Jane spent a moment looking at the picture. She ran her finger across her father's face and felt tears well up in her eyes. She blinked them back and returned the picture to the shelf. She turned and walked to her small kitchen. She lived in the house she had grown up in. Her grandmother had left everything to Jane when she had died. The house was a three bedroom two bath on Highland Street in Escondido. She stood at the kitchen sink and gazed out at the small backyard. Her eyes were open but she wasn't really seeing anything. She was thinking about the fact that she had a full sibling somewhere. That meant one of two things. The first thought that had occurred to Jane was that she might have a twin brother or sister who had been adopted out as well. The second thought, which Jane didn't like to think about, was that her birth parents had stayed together and had another child. If that was the case then why had they given her up and why hadn't they searched for her?

The only thing that William had told Jane about her birth parents was that they were young, both still in high school, and that their families had not been well off. They had given Jane to him in the hopes that he could provide more for her than they would ever be able to. The adoption was a closed adoption. William had explained to Jane that her birth mother's parents had insisted on this. If they were going to cut ties with their grandchild they wanted to cut them completely. Over the years Jane had often wondered if her birth mother had regretted the decision that had been made for her. Jane imagined her growing older, marrying, and having a family. In Jane's imagination her birth mother longed for her first child. And now, tomorrow, Jane was going to meet someone who could potentially make that imagined reunion a reality.

LOYAL TRUESDALE

L oyal woke early on Sunday. He slipped on a pair of elastic waisted shorts, a gray Meyers Manx Big Bear Bash T-shirt, socks, and tennis shoes. He put out some dry food for Boo, did a few stretches, then went outside for a short run. He jogged the half mile to Cannon Park, did two loops around the small park, then jogged the half mile home. The short run and the cool spring air were invigorating. Loyal loved springtime on the coast. The month of March had been mild so far this year. December and January had been some of the wettest months on record. Loyal was enjoying the feeling of the springtime sun on his face.

When he got home he started some coffee in his Mister Coffee machine and showered while it brewed. Once he was dry and had dressed in tan slacks and a button-down he poured a mug and sipped while Boo ate a can of wet food. Loyal was not looking forward to meeting Jane. While it was true that he didn't have much on his plate at the moment, he wasn't very comfortable getting mixed up in this Jane woman's business. Still, Stella, his daughter, her partner Mitch, and their son Mason were out of town for the week. His grandson was five months old now and Loyal spent as much time as he could with the little guy. It might feel good, he thought, to feel useful again.

At 8:00 Loyal left his Carlsbad home and headed toward Valley Center. Because of her knee injury Maggie preferred not to drive so he had volunteered to pick her up. She stepped out of her house when he pulled into her driveway. Like the previous day, he exited his truck and helped her into the passenger seat.

"Thanks for agreeing to meet Jane," said Maggie.

"Sure," said Loyal. "Like I told you yesterday, I'm not too keen on getting involved in all this."

"It would just be so great if she could meet her birth parents," said Maggie.

"Yeah," said Loyal, "except what if they don't want to meet her? That's one of the things that concerns me."

Maggie was silent for a moment. Loyal supposed she was thinking about it from the birth parent's point of view.

"You make a good point," she said at last. "There is always the chance that they don't want to be found."

JANE GRAY

Jane was up early on Sunday. She spent the morning reading information and testimonials from the Genomcestry website. It amazed her how many people had submitted their DNA to the five direct to consumer DNA sites. She loved reading about people's positive experiences. She was aware that some people had negative experiences, but she made it a point never to read what they wrote. Her hope was that she, too, could write a positive testimonial for genomecestry.com.

According to a Consumer Reports Survey as of October 2020 1 in 5 Americans have taken a direct to consumer DNA test.

genomecestry.com testimonial : Anna
    Submitting my DNA to genomecestry was the best thing I have ever done. I was adopted as an infant. My upbringing was a happy one and my relationship with my adoptive parents is very close, but I

always did wonder about my birth parents. Through genomecestry I have been connected with my birth mother and three half siblings. We communicate regularly and have met in person two times. What a blessing this has been...

genomecestry.com testimonial : Gordon

My son gave me a genomecestry kit for Father's Day. I was raised by my mother and maternal grandmother (who were both wonderful people and did an amazing job) but I had always wondered who my father was. I didn't want to hurt my mother by searching for him, but after she passed away the urge to find him got even stronger. I submitted my sample and found him. He didn't even know I existed. After he got over the shock he agreed to meet me. I wouldn't describe our relationship as close, but we do exchange emails and text messages on occasion. I'm glad I took the plunge

.

genomecesatry.com testimonial: Erica

My sister got everyone in the family DNA kits for Christmas last year. We all submitted them at the same time and received our results within days of each other. There weren't any real surprises or skeletons in the closet, but it was interesting to learn more about where our ancestors were from. We also learned more about our genetic health risks and potential for certain diseases.

Jane arrived at Kettle at 9:15 and secured a table for four in the back. She was both nervous and excited. She had tried on half a dozen outfits before choosing the khaki chinos, navy and white striped T-shirt, and navy blazer that she was wearing. She hadn't wanted to dress too formally, but didn't want to look like a slob either. She sat at the far side of the table so she could see the entrance to the coffee shop.

At 9:25 Maggie and a man walked into the shop. He was about 5'10" with sandy brown hair that reached his shoulders. He wore tan slacks and a Hawaiian style button-down short sleeved shirt. Maggie was in her usual jeans and had on a green T-shirt that matched her eyes perfectly. Her long dark hair was pulled into a ponytail and she wore sunglasses that she was in the process of removing as she entered the coffee shop. Maggie paused, looked around, then smiled and waved when she spotted Jane. She said something to the man and pointed toward the back of the shop. Jane stood when they reached the table.

"Jane," said Maggie, "this is Loyal. Loyal, Jane."

Jane reached out her right hand and Loyal shook it with a smile.

"Nice to meet you Jane," he said.

"You as well," said Jane.

"Have you ordered yet?" asked Maggie.

Jane shook her head. "I was waiting for you guys." She paused then said, "Please sit down guys. Coffee's on me. What can I get you?"

Jane ordered the coffees and waited at the counter until they were ready. She carried them back to the table and sat down. Each person took a few appreciative sips than Jane looked at Loyal and said, "Maggie said you might be able to help me locate my sibling?"

Loyal shook his head. "I agreed to listen to your story as a favor to Maggie. I'm very hesitant to get involved in this."

The smile faded from Jane's face.

"Why don't you tell me your story and let's go from there," said Loyal.

"Well, I was adopted as a newborn," Jane said. "I remember the day my dad told me I was adopted. I was four. He made the whole situation so special and just reinforced how much he loved me. He was a wonderful man," she paused and took a deep breath, "but he died when I was twelve. My grandmother raised me after that. She died when I was nineteen."

"What do you know about your birth mother?"

"My dad said that she wanted to keep me but was only sixteen and knew that he could give me a better life," said Jane. This was not exactly what her father had told her, but it was what Jane truly believed.

"I find it hard to believe that a single man could adopt an infant in the 1990's," said Loyal. "Things were very different then. Do you know how the adoption came about?"

Jane shook her head. "My father never said anything about that and I never thought to ask."

Loyal was silent for a moment while he considered her answer.

"Maybe your dad knew the family," he said, "I guess that's one thing you might never have the answer to."

"Maybe not," said Jane.

"Maggie said you found a full sibling through DNA testing?"

Jane nodded.

"That means your birth parents had another child," said Loyal.

Jane nodded. "Maybe," she said. "Another thought is that I have a twin."

LOYAL TRUESDALE

L oyal thought about this possibility while he sipped his coffee. The theory about a twin had actually occurred to him.

"So, you have reached out to this person by email and have not gotten a response?"

"Its not actually email," said Jane. "It is a messaging system through the company that processed the DNA. Its designed to keep people anonymous."

"Your sibling might not want contact," he said.

Jane nodded again. "I've thought about that. That's why I hesitated on reaching out. But my results also identified several genes in my DNA that indicate the potential for certain diseases. I'm hoping to get some medical background as well."

Loyal considered her response for a brief moment. He folded his hands on the table in front of him. "Ok," he said, "the fact that it isn't an actual email address is going to make this more difficult, but I do have one person I can ask to help. He's likely to be as resistant as I am, possibly more so." Loyal paused and Jane could see the indecision clearly on his face. Finally he said, "I'll need your log in and password for the messaging board and your contact information. I'll see what I can do."

Jane wrote the information on a napkin and slid it towards Loyal. She then reached out and clasped his hands in her own.

"Thank you Loyal," she said with tears shining in her eyes, "thank you so much."

Loyal, Maggie, and Jane left Kettle less than ten minutes later. Loyal had found parking to the right of the coffee shop. Jane said her car was around the block to the left. She shook Loyal's hand again then gave Maggie a hug and said that she would see her at physical therapy the next day. Jane then turned and walked around the corner and out of sight. Loyal helped Maggie into the truck and started toward Valley Center.

"You need anything while we are in town?" he asked.

Maggie shook her head.

"Do you think she's sincere?" he asked.

"I think so," said Maggie.

"I was surprised by her height," said Loyal.

Maggie smiled and nodded. "I was too the first time I met her. She's six feet tall. Unusual for a woman."

Loyal nodded his head. "She carries herself well. Lots of tall women sort of hunch over to look smaller. She stands tall."

Loyal dropped Maggie at her house and headed back towards Carlsbad.

His plan was to reach out to Pat O'Keefe for help with connecting the messaging information with its owner. Pat was a friend and a detective with the Carlsbad Sheriff's Department, Loyal's former employer. Pat specialized in computer forensics.

Loyal had thought that tracing an email address backwards to its owner would be a simple task for him. The fact that it was through an anonymous message board would make it more difficult, but Loyal believed if anyone could accomplish it, it would be Pat. The problem for Loyal was that he had involved Pat in cases outside of the department in the past and the last one had nearly gotten Pat killed. Pat had a wife and three young children to support and had made it clear that, while he wanted to maintain their friendship, he had no interest in helping on any more of Loyal's "adventures". Loyal had made a point of stopping by Pat's house frequently over the past three months and spending time with the family without asking Pat for any favors. Olive, Pat's wife, was gradually starting to trust him again.

Loyal thought about Jane as he drove through Escondido. He had noticed the limp when she went to order the coffees. He had also seen the scar that tracked down her face, nearly invisible under the make up she wore. Her hands had a slight tremor. Having been a detective for many years, Loyal was good at reading people. He felt that something was slightly off with Jane. He also didn't appreciate it that she had arranged the seating in the coffee shop so that he had his back to the door. Loyal always chose a seat that faced the entrance of an establishment and he had been uncomfortable the entire time. Still, he trusted Maggie's judgement. That was the only reason he had reluctantly agreed to help.

Loyal left Escondido and merged onto Highway 78 heading west. As he neared the exit for Pat's San Marcos home Loyal said "What the hell" out loud, crossed two lanes of traffic, and took the exit. He pulled up in front of the O'Keefe's house ten minutes later. The minivan and the truck were in the driveway. The family was home. Loyal glanced at his truck's clock. 11:16. Not too early to risk waking them, yet early enough that it was unlikely they were sitting down to lunch. Loyal picked up the napkin with Jane's username, password, and contact information written on it and considered one last time if this was a good idea. With a small sigh he slipped the napkin in his shirt pocket, slid out of the truck, and headed for the front door.

LOYAL TRUESDALE

Loyal knocked on the front door but got no response. He rang the bell and waited a moment but no one opened the door. He pulled his phone out of his pocket, intending to call Pat, when he heard the laughter. He turned and walked around the side of the house and peeked over the back fence. Pat and his family were in the backyard. Pat held five month old Ava in one arm. With the other he pushed 3 year old Piper in a swing. Sullivan, now 6, was in the other swing generating his own motion by pumping his legs. Olive stood beside Pat watching the activity.

Loyal unhooked the gate leading to the backyard and stepped through. Olive must have sensed his motion because she turned and looked in his direction. She waved a hand in greeting.

"Hi Loyal," she said.

Loyal waved back and crossed the yard.

"Hey guys," he said. "I was just driving home from Valley Center and thought I would stop by. Hope I'm not intruding."

"Not at all," said Olive. "I'll be making lunch in about half an hour if you want to stay."

"I'd like that," said Loyal.

Loyal stayed outside with Pat and the kids when Olive went inside to prepare lunch. When Sullivan's legs got tired Loyal pushed him on the swing. He and Pat chatted about everyday things. Fatima, the main receptionist at the Carlsbad Sheriff's Department had gotten engaged and was to be married in September. Pat told Loyal to expect an invitation. When Olive called out that lunch was ready Loyal helped Piper out of her swing and they all walked into the house.

Lunch consisted of tuna sandwiches, apple slices, and homemade lemonade. Ava sat in a soft chair and drank formula from a bottle. Piper and Sullivan sat at the table with Pat, Olive, and Loyal.

"So what took you to Valley Center today?" asked Olive.

"I was dropping my friend Maggie off," said Loyal. "We had coffee in Escondido this morning. She tore her ACL tripping over her dog in the night. No surgery thankfully, but she wears a brace and has physical therapy." He paused a moment then added, "We actually met her physical therapist for coffee. She has a pretty unusual story."

Loyal spent a few minutes telling them Jane's background.

"So she has reached out through the message board to a full sibling but they aren't responding?" Olive asked.

"Yep."

She turned to Pat and said, "Can't you reverse engineer that and go backwards to find the name?"

Pat nodded. "I probably could," he said. "I don't think its illegal but I'm sure it's not an ethical thing to do."

"That's true," said Olive. "Still, with her father and grandmother dead Jane's all alone. And with the potential for disease she really needs to know more about her birth parent's medical histories. "

Loyal kept a straight face during Pat and Olive's exchange but inside he was smiling. Olive had actually just asked Pat to do the very thing that Loyal had been hesitant to ask. He stood when Olive did and helped carry the plates and glasses into the kitchen. He returned to the table and sat. Pat was clearly thinking about the situation. Loyal sat quietly and let him think.

LOYAL TRUESDALE

After about five full minutes Pat turned to Loyal and said, "Before we do anything you are going to run a background check on this woman." Pat reached out his hand. "I'm going to need a credit card and your phone."

Loyal handed Pat his phone, then pulled out his wallet and removed a credit card. He watched over Pat's shoulder as the young man pulled up a site called truthfinder.com. Pat entered Loyal's credit card information and ran a check on Jane Gray. He simply entered her name and city of residence. The results came back quickly and indicated that there was no criminal activity in Jane's past and she had no aliases. The report also included phone numbers, social media accounts and email addresses associated with Jane Gray. Also revealed were qualifications, work details, assets, names of relatives, and acquaintances. Pat emailed the report to both his own and Loyal's email addresses, then logged out of the site and handed Loyal his phone and credit card.

. . .

"I guess we could find out the identity and then make the decision about giving the information to Jane."

Loyal nodded. Pat stood and left the dining room. He returned a minute later with his laptop. Loyal pulled out the napkin with Jane's username and password on it and slid it over to Pat. It took Pat over half an hour, but eventually Loyal heard him say, "Got it."

Pat turned to Loyal. "I found him. It was easier than I thought it would be," he said. "The security on this site is pretty weak. His name is Tyler Timmerman." Pat ran his hand through his closely cropped red hair. "That last name sounds so familiar," he said. "Let me see if I can find some information on him." A few minutes passed then Loyal heard Pat say "holy shit" under his breath.

"What?" asked Loyal.

Pat turned the computer so Loyal could see the screen. There was a picture of a family of four on the display. The father and son were both quite tall. They had dark hair and olive skin. The mother and daughter were smaller with light brown hair and fair skin. It was hard to guess their actual heights because there was nothing in the picture to give any perspective, but the men towered over the women. What struck Loyal immediately was how much Jane looked like the father and the brother.

"Who are they?" he asked.

Pat placed his finger on the image of the father. "He's Charles Timmerman," he said. "Designed a micro drone back in the 1990's. Sold the design to the DHS for millions. He still works on secret projects for the government." Pat paused and looked directly in Loyal's eyes. "He's loaded Loyal, like really rich. I'm talking billions."

Pat leaned back in his chair and let out a deep sigh.

"I'm not sure I'm on board with sharing this information," he said.

"This could be a game changer for Jane," Loyal said. "I mean if this guy Charles is her dad I'd imagine he would share some of his wealth with her." He paused, then added, "She looks just like the dad and brother, Pat."

"I'll give you the contact information," Pat said. "What you do with it is up to you."

JANE GRAY

J ane was washing her lunch dishes when her phone rang. She rinsed and dried her hands then picked up the phone.

"Hello," she said.

"Jane, it's Loyal Truesdale."

Jane felt a shiver of anticipation flow through her. Was it possible he had found the information this quickly? She took a long slow breath in.

"Hi Loyal," she said.

"Listen Jane," he said, "I have the name and address of your sibling for you." He paused a moment then continued. "He's a very private guy. No social media, low internet exhaust. If he doesn't want a relationship you promise to respect that, right?"

"Absolutely," said Jane.

"Ok," said Loyal. "His name is Tyler Timmerman. He lives in Carlsbad. Do you have a pen and paper handy?"

Jane walked to the kitchen counter and opened the top right hand drawer. She pulled out a scrap of paper and a pencil. Her hand was shaking.

"Ready," she said.

Loyal recited an address on Brava Street. Jane wrote it on the paper along with Tyler's name.

"Thank you Loyal," she said in a trembling voice. "I can't tell you what this means to me."

Jane set her phone on the counter and looked at the scrap of paper for a long moment. She picked up the paper and walked to the dining room table. She sat in front of her laptop and opened it. She googled Tyler Timmerman. There wasn't much. She searched images and found a picture of Tyler with his family. The resemblance was uncanny. Jane looked just like Tyler and his father.

"My father," she said under her breath. The picture had been taken May 19, 2018 at the Jewels of San Diego Annual Gala to benefit adults and children with disabilities. The Timmerman family foundation was being honored for their generous support. Jane ran her finger over their faces. The father was listed as Charles Timmerman, his wife's name was Daisy, and the children were Leisel and Tyler.

Jane googled Charles Timmerman and found a Wikipedia entry about the man. In 1995 he had developed cutting edge new micro drone technology that he had sold to the US government. This had earned him millions. Although the entry was short, it did include the fact that he and Daisy had been married in August of 1991, Leisel had been born in 1993, and Tyler in 1995. Jane closed the computer and thought about the dates. She had been born in May of 1990. Charles and Daisy had married in August of 1991. Jane thought it was unlikely that

Charles had met someone and married them in little more than a year. Could Daisy be her mother? She opened the computer and looked again at the image of the family. Liesel looked very much like her mother, petite and fair. Tyler was the spitting image of Charles, tall and dark. He looked very much like Jane.

Jane opened a new window and googled Tyler's address in Carlsbad. He lived in a residential community off La Costa Ave. According to Google maps his house was about halfway between Hataca Road and Verde Ave. The back of his property butted up against a small community park. Jane plugged the address into google maps on her phone. If she left now she could get there around 4:30. She brushed her teeth and hair, gathered her purse and keys and stepped into the garage. She slid into her sky blue Nissan Rouge, hit the remote to open the garage, and backed down her driveway.

13

JANE GRAY

Jane followed Google's directions and arrived at Tyler's house less than an hour later. She drove by the house slowly, noting that there was a white truck parked in the driveway. Jane continued past his house, turned right on Verde Ave, then right again on Carlina Street which ran parallel to Brava Street. Carlina turned right and became Hataca, which bisected Brava. Jane turned onto Brava again and found street parking a few houses west of and across the street from Tyler's house and pulled her car to the curb. She sat in her car and looked across the street at her brother's house. It was painted tan and had a cement driveway that had small patches of neatly mowed green lawn on either side of it. There was a large window in the front of the house that Jane assumed was the living room window. The blinds were closed.

Jane sat in her car and thought about what she was doing. She thought about the many testimonials she had read, written by people who had located relatives using DNA. They were so positive and joyful. Many were adoptees, like herself, who were searching for siblings, birth parents, and cousins. As she read these happy tales Jane had pictured herself in the same scenario. She had seen the picture of Tyler and his family so she knew what they looked like. It was easy for her, in her imagination, to insert her own image into the family picture. She and Tyler had such a strong resemblance. She would fit right in.

Jane's intention had been to walk right up to Tyler's door and ring the bell. Now that she was here, however, she was beginning to have second thoughts. She had messaged him three times over the past two weeks. She had tried to keep the messages light, but knew in the last one there had been an air of desperation. Jane had no idea if Tyler had even accessed his account on the DNA site. He may not have even seen the messages. She felt her anxiety growing. She was sweating. It wasn't the kind of sweat produced by exercise, rather it was the type produced by stress. Despite the application of deodorant earlier Jane could smell her sour body odor. Tyler would certainly smell it too.

Jane started her car, intending to drive home to Escondido and shower. She would, she decided, approach Tyler tomorrow evening after work. Just as she was shifting into drive Tyler's front door opened and he stepped out. He was wearing jeans and an untucked button-down shirt. His brown hair was combed away from his face and he wore sunglasses. Jane watched as he walked down the short walkway and slid into his truck. When he backed out of his driveway Jane released the emergency brake and pulled out behind him.

14

TYLER TIMMERMAN

Tyler drove toward his parent's house in a daze; he was practically on auto-pilot. Had he been more aware of his surroundings he would have noticed the sky blue Nissan Rouge that stayed two car lengths behind him all the way to the Timmerman property on Lone Jack Road in Olivenhain. While he drove Tyler thought about several things. The first was his sister, Leisel. He hadn't communicated with her since their disagreement at last Sunday's family dinner. She had called twice and texted a dozen times but he had not replied. Tyler wasn't necessarily angry at Leisel, she was entitled to her opinion after all. Disappointed was a more accurate word to describe his feelings. He just wished that she would have listened to his thoughts on the subject of DNA testing and Jane Gray.

The second thing he was thinking about was Jane Gray. She had sent two more messages over the last week and the last one had included a picture of her. Tyler had no doubt they were related, the family resemblance was uncanny. She had also mentioned some medical concerns relating to her DNA analysis and that she was hoping to learn more about the family's medical history. Tyler had nearly responded to her. In the end he had decided to take the issue up with Leisel when he saw her at Sunday dinner.

Tyler pulled up to the gates of his parent's 15 acre ranch. He punched in the code and the gate opened slowly. His parent's property was named Tall T Ranch. The house was a 7 bedroom 9 bath ranch house. It was a single story with wood floors and an open floor plan. The house had three fireplaces. In the backyard an outdoor kitchen was adjacent to a flagstone fire pit and a vanishing edge pool. There was a lake with naturally occurring fish on the property as well. The water was kept at an optimal level by one of the two wells on their land.

Tyler paused his forward motion to make sure the gate closed properly then continued down the driveway towards the house. He saw Leisel's Highlander parked on the right and steered his truck towards her car. When he pulled up next to her he could see that she was still sitting in the driver's seat her head tilted down as if she was on her phone. She must have sensed the motion of his truck because she looked up and to her right as he parked. She slid out of her car as he stepped down from his.

"You've been ignoring me," said Leisel. Her arms were crossed tightly across her chest and her eyes were hard.

"I needed some space and time to think," said Tyler.

"Think about what?" asked Leisel. "Jane Gray is a scam Tyler, there's nothing to think about."

Tyler pulled his phone out of his pocket and brought up the last message from Jane. He turned the phone towards Leisel.

"Here's her picture," he said. "You still think it's a scam?"

Leisel took the phone from his hand and studied the picture for a moment then handed the phone back to Tyler.

"It's a fake," she said, "photoshopped or something."

"Well I'm going to ask Mom and Dad about it tonight," said Tyler as he turned toward the house. Leisel grabbed his upper arm with surprising strength and turned him back to face her.

"Don't you dare, Tyler," she said in a low hard whisper spitting the words out harshly. "Don't you dare."

15

JANE GRAY

When Tyler pulled into the gated property Jane continued past and executed a u-turn about 50 yards down the road. She drove back and parked on a small dirt patch across the street from the gated entrance. The name of the property, Tall T Ranch, was engraved in a boulder just to the left of the gate. Jane considered the idea that perhaps this was the Timmerman family home as she watched Tyler park near a Toyota Highlander and hop out of his truck. The door of the Highlander opened and a woman slid out. She was much smaller than Tyler and had honey colored blond hair. Jane was a bit less than a football field away from them and couldn't see the woman's face clearly, but could see that she wore tan slacks and a loose untucked lilac colored blouse. She approached Tyler with her arms crossed tightly across her chest. Even from this distance Jane could tell the woman was angry. She watched as Tyler and the woman exchanged a few words. Then Tyler pulled his phone from his pocket, tapped it a few times and turned it so it faced the woman. She removed the phone from his hand, studied it a moment, then handed it back. Tyler took it then turned toward the house. The woman's hand shot out and grasped his upper arm. Jane couldn't hear the words the woman said but her body language was screaming anger.

Jane watched as the two people walked toward the house. She couldn't see the entrance from her vantage point. They simply disappeared behind some foliage. Jane sat and thought about what she had just witnessed. Surely the woman was Tyler's sister, Leisel. It was clear that they had been having some type of disagreement. Jane wondered if it could possibly be about her? Had Tyler actually read her messages and told his sister about them? She felt a tingle of excitement run down her spine at the thought.

Jane had not had an easy time of it after the accident. Witnessing her father's death, coupled with unrelenting pain and a brutal scar down the right side of her face that she was unable to conceal left her angry and prone to outbursts. Her grandmother Edith, who was nearly 90, did not have the tools to deal with a sullen teenager and soon gave up trying. She provided Jane with everything she needed to survive but was unavailable emotionally. Jane's friends, who were trying to deal with their own teenage angst, gradually distanced themselves from her. Eventually Eden, the physical therapist, was Jane's only friend.

Despite the loneliness and depression, or perhaps because of it, Jane excelled academically. She graduated from high school near the top of her class and was accepted to UCSD. To keep her student loans at a reasonable level, Jane commuted from Escondido. Her grandmother passed away in her sleep during Jane's sophomore year. Although they had not been close Jane still felt Edith's absence acutely. With her grandmother gone she was truly alone.

Jane found herself thinking about her father and grandmother as she sat in her car looking at the Timmerman's gate and driveway. Lost in thought, she only became aware of the sheriff's car pulled in behind her when he tapped gently on the window. She flinched, composed herself, then rolled down the window. The officer was older, probably close to retirement. His hair was gray and a bushy gray mustache filled the space between his nose and upper lip. His eyes were blue-gray and kind looking.

"Are you ok ma'am?" he asked.

"Yes," said Jane, "I pulled over to take a call."

"You are parked on a horse path," he said. "We received a complaint call."

"I'm sorry," said Jane quickly. "I'll move right away."

"I'm going to need to see your license, registration, and proof of insurance," said the officer.

"Is that really necessary?" Jane asked. "I'll move immediately."

The officer's eyes narrowed a bit. "Yes ma'am, it is necessary." His voice had hardened a bit and his tone had become much less friendly.

Jane sighed and found the items he had requested. She watched in the side mirror as he returned to his vehicle. She knew he wouldn't find anything, she didn't even have a traffic ticket on her record. She just found the fact that there would be official documentation about her being parked outside the Timmerman family home a bit disquieting.

The officer returned and handed her documents through the window. "Thank you," he said, "have a nice evening Ms. Gray."

TYLER TIMMERMAN

In honor of the new horse she had purchased the previous day, a chestnut colored Arabian, Daisy prepared what she called a "cowboy" themed dinner. Big juicy burgers, baked beans, corn on the cob, and sourdough biscuits fought for room on each diner's plate. The drinks were whiskey sours. Conversation was light and easy. Daisy, usually quiet and reserved, was in a talkative mood. About halfway through the meal Tyler said, "Dad, I have a question for you." Leisel kicked him under the table, hard, a clear warning not to proceed. Charles raised his eyes toward his son.

"I want to know more about my extended family," said Tyler. His father's eyes narrowed slightly but he said nothing in response.

"I know you cut both your families out of your lives a long time ago," Tyler said. "I'm just curious about my relatives. Have you ever thought about reaching out to them?"

. . .

Charles gave Tyler a long look. His jaw was tight, a sure sign of barely suppressed anger.

"I've told you before," he said. "Your mother and I purposefully chose to walk away from those people. I changed my name and began a new life with your mother."

"But they might have been looking for you all these years," Tyler began. His father cut him off before he could complete his thought.

"They aren't looking for us. There's no room for discussion on this Tyler."

"I've been thinking about doing some DNA testing," Tyler said. His father's face darkened, while at the same moment his mother's face went completely white. Charles slammed his palm on the table. It shook from the force and some of Tyler's whiskey sour splashed out of his glass.

"You do that and you better be prepared to stay with whoever you might find," he said. "You certainly won't be welcomed back here and you can forget about any inheritance when I'm gone."

Charles stood, pushing his chair back roughly and turned to Daisy who was crying quietly. He reached out his hand and helped her up from her chair. Together they left the dining room without a backwards glance.

The room was silent for a full thirty seconds before Leisel spoke.

"I warned you Tyler," she said. "Are you going to let this go now?"

Tyler nodded. "He's not giving me much choice is he? I think I have to," he said. "I'll cancel my account tonight when I get home."

He leaned in closer to Leisel and said, "I don't think Jane Gray is a hoax though. I think they did have a kid. I think they had to give her up and that's why they hate their families. I think Jane Gray is our sister."

JANE GRAY

J ane drove west on Lone Jack Road until she came to the intersection with Rancho Santa Fe Road. The sheriff was directly behind her. At the intersection she turned right. The sheriff turned left. Jane drove one block then executed a u-turn and returned to Lone Jack Road. She knew now, following her interaction with the sheriff, that the residents of this particular neighborhood were suspicious. She needed someplace inconspicuous to park while she waited for Leisel. Jane had decided that she wanted to know more about her "family" before she introduced herself to them. She found the thought of performing surveillance on them to be an exciting prospect. She already knew where Tyler, Charles, and Daisy lived. Following Leisel was the next obvious step in her burgeoning plan.

She had seen a sign for Little Oaks Equestrian Park as she followed Tyler on the drive to the Timmerman home. She found the entrance to the park and pulled into the dirt parking lot. She backed into a parking space in the corner of the lot and turned off her car. She felt giddy with excitement. She imagined she was feeling much like the protagonists she loved to read about in novels of mystery and suspense. It no longer mattered to her whether or not Tyler had read the messages she had sent. For the first time in a very long time she felt she was in charge of her life.

Jane picked up her phone and navigated to Amazon's website. She typed *magnetic vehicle tracker* into the search bar and scrolled through the results. After reading multiple reviews she decided on the Spytech GPS GL300. It cost $59.99 and gave results in real time. One of the reviews included the information that the battery lasted approximately 12 days and the gps was accurate to within ten feet. Jane ordered two trackers and was pleased to see that they would arrive to her house on Tuesday. She then placed a call to her work and left a message that she would be out for a week. She apologized for the late notice and said that a personal matter had come up suddenly. That done, she settled in to wait for Leisel and her Highlander.

18

LEISEL TIMMERMAN

Leisel didn't know quite how to respond to her brother's accusation against their parents.

"At the very least they are keeping secrets from us," Tyler added when she didn't say anything.

"They have that right, Tyler," she said. "Everyone has secrets. They aren't obligated to tell us everything."

Tyler blew a huffy breath out of his nose and leaned in towards Leisel again.

"Don't you want to know?" he asked.

Leisel considered her response carefully then said, "No Tyler, I don't think I do want to know."

Tyler's eyes grew wide and his mouth dropped open slightly. He looked at Leisel for about thirty seconds. She kept her eyes locked on his, her gaze even and steady. Eventually Tyler looked away. When he broke the eye contact Leisel stood up and started clearing the dining room table. When Tyler didn't move she turned to him and said, "Are you going to help?"

. . .

They cleared the table, packed up the food, and washed the dishes in silence. Tyler left without saying goodbye to his parents. Leisel went into the living room to say goodbye. Charles and Daisy were sitting on the couch. Daisy was curled up against Charles, her head on his shoulder and her eyes closed. Charles' arm was wrapped around Daisy and his eyes were closed as well. Leisel paused and just looked at her parents for a long moment. She had never known two people with such a close relationship. She knew her parents loved her and Tyler deeply, but she had always had the impression that all her parents truly needed was each other. She approached them and leaned down to kiss Charles' cheek. He opened his eyes at the touch.

"The kitchen is clean and the food is packed away," Leisel said. He gave her a small smile. "Just wanted to say goodbye and I love you."

"I love you too Leisel," said Charles. "Tyler?" he added.

"He left," said Leisel.

Charles nodded but said nothing more. Leisel gave him another kiss on the cheek and left. She exited her parents property and drove towards Rancho Santa Fe Road. Her thoughts were dense and heavy. So preoccupied was she that she never noticed the blue Nissan pull out of the equestrian park and fall in behind her.

19

CHARLES TIMMERMAN

Charles watched Leisel walk out of the room then turned his attention back to his wife. The light and even way she was breathing told him she was asleep. When he looked at her face he still saw the fourteen year old girl she had been when they had met. All these years later she was still as beautiful to him as she had been the first time he had seen her in their pre-algebra class at San Pasqual high school in Escondido. In 1988 Charles' name was Jason Davis. He was the oldest of four boys born to a mean tempered hard drinking man and a frightened woman. Jason tried his best to protect his brothers and stay out of his father's way. In 1988 Daisy's name was Amy White. She was one of five siblings, smack dab in the middle of two older brothers and two younger sisters. Her parents were very strict and very religious. Jason and Amy dated on the sly, neither one telling their family they were seeing each other. That all changed in the fall of 1989 when Amy told Jason she was pregnant.

.   .   .

Daisy stirred in her sleep, rolled slightly to the right, then settled down again. She still refused to talk about that time in their lives. It had been extremely traumatic for both of them, but Amy had suffered the most. When Jason told his father about the pregnancy he was expecting a beating. Instead his father said the last four words Jason ever heard the man say. "Get the hell out." Jason packed his belongings into a back pack and left without another word. He walked to the neighborhood 7 Eleven and used the pay phone to call his friend Kent. Kent's parents allowed Jason to move into their giant house on Mary Lane until graduation the following June. Amy kept the pregnancy secret until the sixth month when she could no longer hide it. Her family didn't kick her out of the house, but they viewed her as a disgrace to the family and a disgrace to God. The unborn child they considered to be an abomination. Amy suffered intense emotional abuse during the last three months of her pregnancy. If not for Jason's constant reminders that their love was good and true she might have come to believe the things her parents said to her. In spite of all the words Amy's parents hurled at their vulnerable daughter there was never any discussion about keeping the child.

Although Amy's parents forbade her to see Jason, the two had brief contact at school each day. The child was born in May of 1990. Jason was not allowed at the hospital. Amy told him later that she became so hysterical after the birth, screaming that she wanted to keep the child, that she was sedated. Neither Jason nor Amy ever held their daughter.

20

JANE GRAY

J ane stayed a few car lengths back and followed Leisel as she turned right on Rancho Santa Fe Road, left on Olivenhain, then right onto El Camino Real. Traffic on El Camino Real was heavy, as usual, and Jane felt confident that Leisel was unaware she was being followed. When Leisel turned left onto Kelly Drive Jane became concerned. They were the only two cars on the road. When Leisel made a quick right turn onto Hillside Drive Jane drove past the street then made a quick u-turn and turned onto Hillside. She caught up to Leisel just as she was turning left onto Skyline Road. A sign on the side of the road informed Jane that this was not a through street. Jane drove past Skyline Drive and pulled to the curb. Leaving her engine running she Google mapped the area and quickly saw that Skyline dead ended into a street called Sunburst Road that was shaped like a comma. Jane zoomed in and counted the houses. There were 27.

Jane didn't think it wise to drive down a quiet residential neighborhood in the evening searching for Leisel's house. She made the decision to come back at a different time. She let her car idle by the curb for another minute. She rubbed her eyes and realized that she had not eaten since the ham sandwich she had made for lunch. She put the car in drive, made a quick u-turn, and headed back to El Camino Real. She drove north until she reached highway 78, then turned east and headed towards home. It was just past 8:30 when Jane pulled into her driveway. She activated the remote control and the garage door slowly opened. She pulled into her parking space and pressed the remote once more. The garage door reversed its motion and closed quietly.

Jane sat in the quiet of her garage and processed her day. She had found her birth parents, a brother, and a sister. She knew the locations of their homes and what kind of cars the siblings drove. She had ordered the trackers which would arrive on Tuesday, and she had called out of work for a week. She slid out of her car and went into her house. She made herself a cup of Earl Gray tea, plucked a package of shortbread cookies from the pantry, and carried them and her lap top into her home office.

Jane still slept in the bedroom of her youth. Her father's room remained the same as it was prior to his death. Her grandmother had refused to get rid of or change anything. It was neat and tidy and could have been used as a guest room if Jane ever had a guest stay over. When her grandmother had passed away Jane had changed Edith's room (the largest of the three) into a home office. She had purchased a sturdy L shaped desk which sat in a corner by the window. She had also splurged on an ergonomically correct chair that had actually cost slightly more than the desk. There was a bookcase to the left of the desk that held textbooks from her college days, novels of mystery and suspense, and a few small potted cactus plants. The rest of the room was bare.

Jane placed the lap top on the desk and set the tea and cookies to the left of it then sat heavily in the chair. Emotions were swirling through her brain. She felt like laughing and crying at the same time. She took a few calming sips of tea then opened the lap top. She pulled up the Wikipedia page she had seen earlier and read through it again. It was sparse, but did contain a link to the Timmerman Foundation. Jane clicked that link and read the foundation's history and stated goals. It had been founded in the year 2001 and focused on health and education for children and adults. Jane found a wikipedia entry for the foundation. Its endowment was listed at 3.6 billion dollars. Jane blinked, rubbed her eyes, and looked again. She printed the page and highlighted the endowment amount. She took a red pen from the desk drawer and underlined the b in billion. She then googled the Forbes list of the 500 wealthiest people in the world. Charles Timmerman was number 496, with a net worth of 8.2 billion dollars. Jane printed this page as well, highlighting her father's name and underlining the b in billion.

21

TYLER TIMMERMAN

Tyler's mood was dark as he drove home. He loved his parents and wanted to respect their privacy, but he felt very strongly that they owed him the truth about a possible sibling. It affected his life as well. And now his dad had thrown the possibility of losing out on his inheritance into the mix. Tyler couldn't just throw that money away. Charles was generous with his two children, but both Tyler and Leisel held full time jobs within the family foundation. His inheritance was Tyler's retirement plan.

Tyler parked in the driveway and slid out of his truck. He used the ring app on his phone to unlock his smart door lock on the front door and entered his house. He set his keys down on an end table in his living room and settled himself on the couch. He spent a few minutes reviewing footage from his ring doorbell cameras, one in the front of the house and two in the back yard, to make sure he hadn't missed anyone and that no one had been on his property. Satisfied, he logged into his Lg thinq app and checked inside his fridge to see what beverages were available. He was disappointed to see that his fridge was pretty empty and set a reminder for himself for the next morning to go grocery shopping after he went surfing. Tyler loved smart devices and had nearly every one available. He was able to control all his appliances from his phone.

Tyler logged onto the DNA testing site and checked to see if there were any more messages from Jane. There was nothing more. He spent some time looking at the picture she had sent. The resemblance was startling. He wondered why, if his parents actually had given a child up as teenagers, they had no interest in finding her now. It didn't make sense. And now, because of his father's ultimatum, Tyler would never know the answer. He logged out of the messaging section and called the 24 hour customer service number. After following multiple prompts Tyler was eventually connected to a human being.

"Hello," said the woman, "my name is Susan. How can I be of assistance?"

Although the woman said her name was Susan, her accent was strong enough for Tyler to know he had been connected to a call center in India.

"I'd like to delete my account," Tyler said. He proceeded to give her his account information and answered a few security questions.

"You understand that by closing this account you will no longer receive updates or notifications and will not have access to the messaging center?" Susan asked.

"Yes," said Tyler.

"Ok, I've closed the account," said Susan. "If you ever want to reactivate it just give us a call or go online."

"I want the account deleted," said Tyler, "like it never existed. And I want my sample destroyed."

The silence on the line lasted long enough for Tyler to think the connection had been broken. Finally Susan spoke again.

"I'm afraid I can't do that sir," she said.

"Why not?" Tyler asked. "It's my DNA."

"You agreed to our privacy policy and terms of service when you submitted your sample," Susan said.

"I had to," said Tyler.

"Did you read them sir?" Susan asked.

"Nobody reads those," Tyler said.

"Genomecestry owns your DNA sir. For the next 35 years. You agreed to this when you accepted our terms of service."

"I want to talk to someone above you Susan," Tyler said. "Someone in the United States."

"I can arrange for someone to contact you tomorrow sir," said Susan, "but I'm afraid they are going to tell you the same thing."

Susan verified Tyler's contact information, assured him someone would call the following day, then thanked him for being part of the Genomecestry family and disconnected the call. Tyler set his phone down and turned back to his lap top. He went to Genomecestry's website and began reading the privacy policy and terms of service. It took him two and a half hours.

22

CHARLES TIMMERMAN

Charles remained on the couch holding Daisy for several hours. She was not sleeping deeply and any movement would surely disturb her. As he held her, he thought back to the days and months after the birth of their baby. Jason and Amy, as they were known then, still saw each other at school each day. They were both traumatized by the pregnancy and birth, but remained devoted to each other and sure in the love they felt for one another. In June Jason had graduated from high school and Kent's father had helped him get a job as a nighttime janitor at the Space and Naval Warfare Systems Center in San Diego. He had also loaned Jason enough money to buy a used truck and rent an apartment in Santee. Jason picked Amy up each day after school and drove her to the bus stop several blocks from her home. One day he picked her up and drove her to Santee. She moved in with him and neither of them ever looked back.

They married when Amy turned 18 and Leisel was born a year

and a half later. Jason only had a high school education but he was extremely intelligent and very driven. He developed an interest in drone technology and in 1995, just after Tyler's birth, patented a novel innovation in micro drone technology. Through contacts at work he was connected with people at the Department of Defense. He sold the patent and earned his first million. At that time they legally changed their full names and their children's last names. They moved from the apartment to a small house in Santee. Charles continued to innovate and sell his products to the DOD. After the horrific events of September 11, 2001 federal money was pouring into the DOD and the newly created Department of Homeland Security. Charles continued to develop and the government continued to pay. In November of 2001 they purchased their property on Lone Jack Road.

With the exception of her description of the traumatic birth, Daisy refused to discuss the child they had given away. Occasionally Charles would be woken in the night by wrenching sobs coming from his wife. "My baby," she would cry. Charles simply held his wife until the sobbing stopped. He did not believe in God, but he did consider it a kindness from somewhere in the universe that Daisy never woke from these dreams or remembered them the next day. Over the years, with DNA testing becoming mainstream, Charles had occasionally brought up searching for the child. Daisy refused to consider this and eventually Charles stopped asking. He thought he understood why she did not want to search for their child. By refusing to discuss or look for her, Daisy somehow kept the guilt that had taken up permanent residence in the depths of her soul at bay. Daisy meant more to

Charles than anything or anyone. If she said no, then the answer was no.

Charles opened his eyes and brought himself back to the present. The arm he had around Daisy was aching and his fingers were tingling. He had to move. When he removed his arm Daisy woke slowly. She turned to him and he knew the question he saw in her eyes.

"He left without saying goodbye," he said, "but don't worry Daisy, he'll make the right choice."

23

JANE GRAY

J ane was certainly not a hacker, but she knew how to search for information on the internet. She started with Charles and Daisy, scanning for any tidbits of information while she nibbled her cookies and sipped her tea. Information was sparse. There was the wikipedia entry, which she had printed and highlighted. She searched for a wedding announcement in the local papers for 1991 but found nothing. She paid a fee to use vitalsearch.com but still came up empty handed. She searched for articles on micro drone technology and found a few that mentioned Charles' name. She printed and highlighted these. Jane pulled up the picture of the family at the gala in 2018 and printed that as well.

Next Jane began her search into Leisel and Tyler's histories. She used vitalsearch.com to search for their birth certificates and was surprised to find no results. She scanned the local papers from 1993 and 1995 but found no birth announcements. She did find a few articles in the local papers from their high school years. Apparently Leisel was an accomplished equestrian. Jane found a picture that accompanied an article about Leisel coming in first place in a dressage competition. She was on a podium, dressed in knee high black riding boots, white pants and shirt, and navy blue jacket and helmet. She held a bouquet of roses in her hand. Jane printed everything she could find then moved on to Tyler.

She found several articles from his high school years. He had been a star player on the lacrosse team. Pictures accompanied two of the articles. In one Tyler was racing down the playing field. The helmet he wore obscured his face but his legs were long and lean. The image captured his speed and athleticism. The second photo had been taken when his team had become CIF champions. It was a team picture and the helmets were off. Jane could see Tyler's excited face and the joy in his eyes. Again, she printed everything she found.

When Jane finally looked up from the computer it was nearly two o'clock in the morning. She wasn't tired at all, rather she felt strangely energized. She gathered all the pages she had printed and began methodically taping them to the wall just to the right of her desk. She arranged everything in chronological order. When she was done she took a few steps back to admire her handiwork. There wasn't a ton of information, but she was pleased with what she had found. She washed her tea cup, showered, and lay in bed. She closed her eyes and took in slow deep breaths. She had decided surveillance on Tyler would be her priority the next day and a few hours sleep, if she could manage it, would be beneficial.

24

JANE GRAY

Jane managed three hours sleep and was up with the rising sun. She dressed in black leggings and a dark blue sweatshirt, placed a black ball cap on her head, and fortified herself with two strong cups of coffee and a bagel. After her breakfast she packed some water bottles, granola bars, an apple, and a banana in a small cooler. She placed a backpack containing binoculars and a camera with a zoom lens on the passenger seat, started the Nissan, and backed out of her garage. She took highway 78 west. Heavy Monday morning traffic slowed her progress and frustrated her. She exited the highway at Rancho Santa Fe Road in San Marcos. After exiting the freeway, she headed west on Rancho Santa Fe until she reached La Costa Avenue. She followed the same steps she had taken the previous day, passed by Tyler's house and noted the truck in the driveway, then turned right on Verde and Carlina and found curbside street parking on Hataca. She was facing Brava Street. Tyler would have to pass by her if he left his home.

. . .

Jane glanced at her phone. 8:17. She had discovered through her research that Tyler worked for his family's foundation, but was not aware of the type of hours he kept or if he worked in an office or remotely. Jane had no idea how to conduct surveillance. She read frequently, mostly novels of mystery and suspense, so she tried, again, to imagine what her favorite protagonists would do. She thought about her current favorite, Tracy Crosswhite, author Robert Dugoni's plucky Seattle homicide detective. She was thinking about what Tracy would do in this situation when Tyler's truck passed in front of her. She could see surfboard fins sticking up in the bed of the truck. She pulled out behind him and followed as he made his way to La Costa Avenue and turned right. Traffic was fairly heavy and Jane was able to keep one car in between her vehicle and Tyler's truck.

She followed Tyler west, running through several stale yellow traffic lights, until he turned left on the Coast Highway. They passed through the tiny city of Leucadia, then through Encinitas as well. Just past the Self Realization Temple Tyler turned into the parking lot for Swamis seaside park and beach. The parking lot was tiny and Tyler got the last parking spot. Jane circled several times and was ready to give up when a man, hair wet and carrying a surfboard, walked up to a black jeep. Jane swung around the lot, took up a space behind him, and turned on her turn signal. He saw her, gave a quick wave, loaded his board, and backed out. With a small sigh of relief Jane slid into the spot.

Jane adjusted her hat and sunglasses. She grabbed the backpack, and slipped out of her car. She walked by Tyler's truck. It was empty. She took the steep wooden stairs down to the beach stepping carefully as they were sandy and wet. When she reached the bottom she looked around for Tyler. There were quite a few surfers in the water and several on the sand. Tyler's height is what gave him away. He was standing on shore, his surfboard placed carefully on the sand beside him, and wearing a black full body wet suit. Jane stared for a moment, then was startled by the words "excuse me" coming from behind her. She turned and saw a young woman standing behind her. She was wearing a full body wet suit and carrying a board. Jane gave a quick smile and moved out of the way. The woman returned the smile and eased past Jane. She made her way across the sand and ended up standing next to Tyler. He turned when she approached and leaned down to give her a quick kiss. Jane felt an unexpected flare of anger and jealousy flow through her as she watched this. It disappeared as quickly as it had materialized. As Jane watched they both carried their boards into the ocean.

Jane found a spot on the sand about 20 yards away from Tyler and the mystery woman's towels. She sat down, opened the backpack, and removed the binoculars. They had been her fathers and were old, but still worked well. She brought Tyler and the woman into focus and watched as they waited for the perfect set of waves. They were talking while they waited. Jane kept her eyes on them, wondering what they were talking about. It wasn't long before an acceptable set of waves approached and both of them turned their focus to the water. They surfed for nearly an hour. Jane was no expert, but it appeared to her that they were both quite good. She watched for a while, then traded the binoculars for her camera and took a few pictures of each of them.

After the binoculars and camera had been returned to the backpack, Jane spent the rest of the time watching them surf and analyzing the burst of anger and jealousy she had felt when they had kissed. According to the DNA test Tyler was her full sibling and Jane absolutely believed this to be true. Tyler was her brother and she was not attracted to him in a romantic way. So why the strong emotions? She eventually settled on the fact that he had so many things that Jane did not. The jealousy and anger, she realized, was directed at Tyler not the woman he had kissed. He had a family, a romantic relationship, and money. She had none of those things.

25

LOYAL TRUESDALE

L oyal woke just after 7:00 on Monday morning. He stretched and jogged to the park, circled it a few times, then jogged home. He had set up a Total Gym Apex G5 machine in the room he called his office, but only used at tax time. Loyal had not been able to bring himself to continue to work out at JK Gym following the violent murder of his trainer, Lacey, and the subsequent investigation into her death. Loyal had been on disability following a heart attack while he was on a one month suspension from the Carlsbad Sheriff's Department at the time of her death. He had investigated anyway and eventually solved the case, but he had ruffled enough feathers during the course of the investigation that he had been asked to resign his position as Homicide Detective. The only good thing to come out of the whole mess had been meeting Trinity. That wasn't working out so well at the moment but Loyal was keeping his hopes up.

Loyal spent 40 minutes on the Total Gym, then showered,

dressed, and brewed some coffee. It was nearly 9:00 and the day stretched out in front of him. He stood at the large window in his living room and looked out at the clear blue sky. It was a perfect spring day. The temperature was in the low 70's, the sun shone brightly, the air was still. Loyal decided a buggy ride was in order. He pulled on a jacket and a beanie, told Boo he'd be back in a few hours and stepped outside to move his truck from the driveway to the street so he could get the buggy out of the garage. He opened the garage door and rolled the buggy into the driveway then placed a piece of wood he kept in the passenger seat footwell behind a tire so the buggy wouldn't roll away. He closed the garage, checked to make sure the house was locked, then removed the wood and rolled the buggy into the street. He slid into the driver's seat and started the engine hoping the loud noise wasn't disturbing anyone. After idling for a minute or so Loyal shifted into first and drove away.

Loyal merged onto Coast Highway 101 and headed South without a concrete destination in mind. That was the beauty of the buggy. Simply driving it was often the destination. The wind was cold on his face but the beanie and the jacket kept his head and body warm. The ocean air was crisp and salty. As he drove Loyal felt his sadness about Bruce, Chris, and Trinity slip away into the breeze. When he reached La Jolla Loyal decided he was hungry and stopped at one of his favorite breakfast restaurants, The Coffee Cup, which was located on Wall Street. He ordered an avocado scramble, which came with rosemary potatoes, rosemary bread, and fresh salsa. As always, the food was delicious and Loyal ate every bite. Full, and feeling happier than he had in the past three months, Loyal slid back into the buggy and pointed it north.

26

PATRICK O'KEEFE

P at was at his desk in his computer forensics office at the Carlsbad Sheriff's Department, head bent over a suspected drug dealer's computer, when he heard a knock. He looked up and saw Detective Hammond leaning against the door frame of the open door. Pat wouldn't describe their working relationship as friendly exactly, but each had earned a grudging respect for the other during a case they had worked the previous December. Pat had been forced to admit that Hammond had some good instincts and Hammond had reluctantly acknowledged Pat's stunning computer skills. Skills that had ultimately produced the proof that solved the case. Frederick Young's prosecution for murdering his wife was set to go to trial two weeks from now. Pat and Hammond would both have to testify. Pat wondered if that was why Hammond was at his door.

"You got a minute?" Hammond said as he eased his 5'10"

slender frame into the room. Pat waved him towards one of the chairs on the opposite side of his desk.

"Sure," he said, "want to sit?"

Hammond dropped heavily into one of the chairs. He looked tired.

"Been up since 4:00 am," he said. "Called out to what looks like a murder suicide on Oxford Street. Neighbor heard the gunshots and called it in." Hammond ran his hands over his face and through his light brown hair. Pat noticed a few stray gray hairs mixed in among the brown along Hammonds temples. "Young married couple," Hammond said. "From the initial analysis of the scene it looks like the husband shot the wife while she slept then turned the gun on himself. You have any time to take a look at their phones and computers?"

Pat nodded. "I'll make time," he said. "You request the warrants yet?"

Hammond nodded. "They are pretty straightforward. Don't think they'll take much time to get a signature. I'll get everything to you as soon as they are approved." Hammond stood and turned to walk out of the room, then turned back. "Thanks O'Keefe," he said.

Pat was just finishing the last of the lunch his wife, Olive, had packed for him when Hammond returned to his office. He was carrying a bankers box which he placed on the corner of Pat's desk.

"Warrants are signed," he said, "phones and computers are in the box. They had a ring doorbell which you will see is included in the warrant."

Pat nodded then said, "I have a few loose ends to tie up on

the case I'm working for vice. I'll get started on your case as soon as I'm done."

Hammond nodded then walked out of the room without saying anything else.

27

JANE GRAY

After nearly an hour of surfing Tyler and the blond woman walked out of the ocean. They carried their boards to their towels and set them down. Jane watched as they peeled off their wetsuits. Tyler wore board shorts under his suit. The woman had a skimpy bikini. She had a slender athletic figure and what Jane was sure were augmented breasts. There was no way someone that slim had boobs that big naturally. They were talking and laughing as they dried themselves off, gathered their things, and walked up the steep stairs to the parking lot. Jane followed at a discreet distance but thought she probably could have walked right beside them. They were oblivious to anything but each other.

When they reached the parking lot Tyler placed his surfboard in the back of his truck then helped the woman slide her board onto a roof rack that was mounted on a dark green Subaru Forester. They each slid into their respective vehicles and headed out of the parking lot, Tyler leading the way and the woman following. Jane hurried to her car and exited the parking lot less than a minute after them. Traffic was light and she caught up to them fairly easily. She followed until they parked in Tyler's driveway on Brava Street. Jane pulled over to the curb and watched as they walked through a side gate and into the backyard, still laughing and carrying their surfboards. Watching them, Jane felt the stab of anger and jealousy. If her birth parents had kept her she would have everything that Tyler had.

After they disappeared into the back yard Jane turned her Nissan towards Leisel's residence. This time she turned left on Skyline rather than driving past it. This section of Skyline was short, perhaps fifty feet or so, and dead ended into Sunburst Road. Sunburst Road was a thin oval. Jane picked up her phone and started to video the houses. She held the phone as if she was talking to someone and hoped it looked natural as there were a few people in their front yards. She made a quick loop, then exited the small street and drove back on Skyline toward Tamarack. She had not seen Leisel's Highlander but had been able to eliminate some of the houses, perhaps a dozen or so, that had multiple cars in the driveway or children's play equipment on the front lawn.

Jane turned right on Tamarack then left on El Camino Real. She merged onto Highway 78 and headed east towards Escondido. She stopped at the CVS drugstore before going to her house and printed the pictures she had taken of Tyler and the woman at the beach. When she got home she added the pictures to her information wall in her office. She printed a Google map of Sunburst Road and, after reviewing the video on her phone, drew X's through the houses she was sure weren't Leisel's. She wasn't sure how to research ownership of the other houses but she was confidant she could figure it out.

28

LOYAL TRUESDALE

L oyal arrived home just after 2:00 pm. He parked the buggy in the garage, then moved his truck back into the driveway. He had a smile on his face and he was feeling happier than he had in quite some time. He went into his house and spent a few minutes petting Boo. When he had moved into his house the previous October he had found the little guy in his garage. They had bonded over sandwich meat. Loyal was surprised by the depth of his affection for the small black cat. Having been a single father to his daughter, Stella, and simultaneously pursuing a demanding career, Loyal had never had time for a family pet. He was finding that he liked it very much.

Loyal took off his jacket and removed his phone from the pocket. He had turned it off for the buggy ride. The wind and engine noise made it impossible to use a phone. He turned it on now and saw that he had a text from Stella and missed call and voicemail from Maggie. He looked at the message from

Stella first. It was a picture of his grandson, Mason. He was asleep. The text message read

Hey Dad, Just checking in to let you know we are having a great time on vacation. Check out Mason's foot. I got him an Owlet Baby Sock. It monitors his vitals while he sleeps. Love you

Loyal zoomed in on his grandson's foot and looked at the Owlet device. He shook his head and thought for a moment how different Mason's childhood would be to Stella's. The boy would be constantly monitored.

Loyal zoomed in on his grandson's sleeping face and smiled. The kid was pretty damned cute. After looking at Mason for a moment Loyal turned his attention to Maggie's voicemail.

Hey Loyal, its Maggie. I was wondering if you found the information for Jane? About her sibling? I just got home from physical therapy and she has taken the entire week off. I tried to call but she didn't answer. Its not a big deal, just curious. Call if you have time.

Loyal hit the call back button and listened as Maggie's phone rang. She answered on the fourth ring.

"Hey Loyal," she said.

"Hey Maggie," said Loyal, "I got your message. I did give Jane her brother's name and address yesterday. You said she took the entire week off work? Hopefully that means they connected and its a good thing."

"So the sibling is a brother? That's exciting. I'm hoping they connected too," said Maggie. "Hey," she added, "I talked to Winnie this morning. She's going to continue Saturday breakfasts at Lake Wohlford Cafe."

"That's great," said Loyal, "I'll try to make it this week."

They spoke for a few minutes more then disconnected.

Loyal sat heavily on his couch, his phone still in his hand. Without really thinking about it he began scrolling through the pictures on his phone. He had taken a lot of his grandson, Mason, and scrolled slowly through those. He skipped quickly past the ones he had taken in Taos, his father's storage unit and mountain cabin reduced to ashes. As the images took him back in time he came upon many of Trinity; them together at Stone Brewery, watching the sun rise over Fonts Point in Borrego, Trinity strolling down the beach on Coronado Island. He paused when he came upon one of his favorites. It had been taken in his apartment on Roosevelt Street. Trinity, wearing soft gray pajamas, sat in his armchair sideways, her legs hanging over one of the arms. Her beautiful profile was visible and she held a mug of coffee in her right hand. The morning sun was streaming in through the kitchen windows and her body was illuminated by the rays, her ginger cinnamon colored hair looked like fire. Loyal used his fingers to zoom in on her face. The urge to call her was nearly overwhelming. He set his phone on the coffee table with a loud thunk and lay back against the couch cushions. Trinity had initiated this break. Trinity would have to be the one to end it.

29

TRINITY GLASS

T rinity walked into her house and sat in a kitchen chair to remove her running shoes. She was taking a few weeks off from the Office of Strategic Investigations. She had been part of a team of agents who had spent months in Houston uncovering a complex spy ring at the Chinese consulate there. Arrests had been made and the consulate had been closed indefinitely. Trinity had not been to the home she had inherited from her parents in Bellingham, Washington in over a year. Her parents had died in a terrorist attack in 1997 in Sri Lanka. Her brother had joined the military and died some years later, the victim of a sniper's bullet. Trinity's parents had been only children, so with the death of her brother she was, essentially, alone. She had been involved in various romantic relationships over the years, but her job as an OSI agent had always gotten in the way of anything permanent. Until Loyal, that is. To Trinity Loyal felt permanent.

She rose from the chair, walked to the bathroom, and faced the mirror. The wound from her accident in Taos was healed but an angry scar remained. It began about an inch above her right eyebrow and ended by her right temple. Trinity was fair and the scar stood out against her pale skin. She rolled her left shoulder and winced at the pain. Her collarbone had been broken in the accident as well and was still healing. Her doctor had told her collarbones typically take 10-12 weeks to heal and he had been right. The accident had happened thirteen weeks ago. Trinity had endured 8 weeks of physical therapy, but had taken no time off work to allow her body to rest. She supposed she was paying the price for that now.

With a final glance at her damaged face Trinity turned and walked back through the house to her parents' office. This was her favorite room in the house. Her parents had been an Architect/Interior Design team. They worked on luxury properties owned by the small percent of the population who could afford the services of Edwin and Eleanor Glass. Not wanting to be away from their children for extended periods, they took Trinity and her brother with them wherever they went. A tutor accompanied them as well.

Edwin and Eleanor had designed the entire Bellingham estate that belonged to Trinity now. Trinity felt their presence everywhere, but most deeply in their office. It was a huge room, nearly 700 square feet, with floor to ceiling windows making up two of the walls. The view was made up of a lake and many tall Douglas fir trees. The other two walls of the office contained bookshelves on one and a giant stone fireplace on the other. Two desks were located in the center of the room. One large couch faced the windows and its twin faced the fireplace. Trinity started a fire and settled on the couch. During the first year after her parents' death the room had somehow retained their scent. Now, however, so many years later, any remnants had dissipated. Trinity took a deep breath in through her nose and let it out through her mouth. She pulled her phone from the pocket of her leggings and navigated to photos. She spent some time scrolling through pictures of Loyal and herself and found that she was smiling. Perhaps, she thought, it was time to end the break.

JANE GRAY

It took Jane less than an hour to figure out which house was Leisel's. Anything was available online for a price. Jane charged $29.99 to her credit card and received access to property records across the entire United States. She ran the addresses that were printed on Google's map and got a hit on the eleventh property she entered. Leisel's house was owned by the Timmerman Family Trust. She entered Tyler's address on Brava and saw that it, too, was owned by the family trust. She printed these pages and added them to her wall of information.

TYLER TIMMERMAN

After rinsing and drying their surfboards, Tyler and Jolene hung them on the racks in Tyler's garage and headed into the house. Jolene wrapped her arms around Tyler's torso from the back and laid her head against his back. His skin was warm from the sun.

"How about a shower?" she asked.

Tyler swiveled so that they were facing each other. He kissed the top of her head. She raised her head to look at him. He kissed her lips, gave her a squeeze, and was just opening his mouth to say yes when his phone rang.

Jolene kept her arms around him. "Ignore it," she said.

Tyler pulled his arms back and very gently pushed her away. " I can't," he said, "I'm expecting a call."

He walked to the kitchen counter and picked up his phone. It was an unfamiliar number but he answered hoping it was the DNA company.

"Hello," he said as he turned to look at Jolene. She slid slowly out of her bikini and let it fall to the floor. "Your loss," she said as she turned and walked toward the bathroom leaving the swimsuit where it had fallen.

"Mr. Timmerman?"

Tyler pulled his eyes away from Jolene and turned his attention to the voice on the phone.

"Yes," he said.

"My name is Derrick Durbin," said the man on the phone. "I work for Genomcestry and had a message to call you."

"Yes," said Tyler, "I'd like to delete my account with you."

"I can see that your account has already been deactivated," said Derrick.

"Yes," said Tyler, "but I want it deleted. And my sample destroyed," he added.

"Accounts can't be deleted," said Derrick, "and samples belong to Genomcestry for 35 years. You agreed to that when you agreed to our terms of service and privacy policy."

"I read those last night," said Tyler, "I don't agree anymore."

"I'm afraid you should have read them before you agreed sir," Derrick said. "They are legal and binding contracts."

"I have excellent lawyers," said Tyler. He was getting frustrated and could hear the edge in his voice.

"We have excellent lawyers as well sir," said Derrick. "As I stated previously, you agreed to our terms of"

Tyler disconnected the call before Derick could finish his sentence. He wished he had an old fashioned rotary phone like he had seen in old movies. It would have been very satisfying to slam the receiver into the cradle when hanging up on Derrick rather than just tapping the red circle on his phone. He set the phone on the counter. He knew Derrick was correct. His father's lawyers wouldn't be able to undo what Tyler had done. Besides, he thought, they might tell Charles what Tyler had asked them to do. Then his father would know about the DNA test. "Dammit," he said. He turned and saw Jolene's bikini on the floor. He listened and heard that the shower was still running. Tyler slipped his own bathing suit off and dropped it on the floor next to Jolene's. Maybe a shower with her would ease some of his frustration.

32

JANE GRAY

Jane wasn't sure what her next move should be. She spent some time reviewing everything she had taped to the wall in her office. She couldn't understand why she was unable to locate a marriage certificate for Charles and Daisy or birth certificates for Leisel and Tyler. She had searched some free sites, then used her credit card to access a paid site. Even with the paid site she had found nothing. She checked the time. 3:16. She hadn't eaten anything since the bagel in the morning. She decided some food was in order. She opened a can of minestrone soup, poured it in a bowl, and heated it up in the microwave. As she ate she decided on her next move. She would drive to Carlsbad and see Leisel's house.

By 4:00 Jane was in her car and driving toward Sunburst Road. She took Tamarck to Skyline, crossed Hillside Drive, and drove past the *Not a through street* sign and turned left on Sunburst. As she made the turn she saw Leisel's white Highlander coming toward her. As the two cars passed by each other both drivers turned their heads toward each other. Their eyes met for the briefest of moments, then they were past each other. Jane drove to the end of the street and turned back toward Skyline. When she got there the Highlander was gone.

Jane turned right on Hillside, the right on Horizon. She pulled her car to the curb just below Leisel's back yard. Amazingly, there was no fencing around Leisel's house, just a small cement wall that Jane guessed to be about three feet in height. Jane looked around. Horizon was a quiet residential street. No one was in their front yards and no cars had driven past in the few minutes she had been parked here. Could she do it, she wondered. Could she simply climb the small bank that separated her from Leisel's back yard? She looked around again. No people on the street or in their yards, no cars driving past. Jane slid out of the Nissan and closed the door as quietly as possible. She walked to the sidewalk, took one more look around, then simply walked up the bank and stepped over the cement wall. Just like that, she was in Leisel's backyard.

33

LEISEL TIMMERMAN

L eisel and six of her closest friends had been meeting for wine and appetizers at Campfire restaurant in Carlsbad each Monday for several years. They called it the "Too bad it's Monday" wine group and all seven women lived within what they considered a safe driving range. The drive from Leisel's house on Sunburst Road took about ten minutes. She was still thinking about the woman she had passed on her street. Their eyes had locked for the briefest of seconds, but when Leisel mentally reviewed the moment she saw it as if in slow motion. Leisel was sure she did not know the woman, and yet there had been something so familiar about her. The moment had left Leisel feeling unsettled.

She sat in the parking lot behind the restaurant for several minutes thinking about it. Could it have something to do with Craig? She didn't think so. She had kicked her boyfriend of three years out of her house after she came home early one day and found him in bed with another woman. That had been four months ago. The image of them in bed, the woman on top and Craig beneath, was burned into her memory. It had taken her an hour to dump all his belongings into a pile on the driveway. Craig had followed her around the house, begging her to forgive him. Eventually the begging had turned to yelling and the yelling to threatening. Leisel had called the police and two officers had watched silently while Craig piled everything into his truck. Leisel had hired a locksmith to change the locks and had bought a new bed. She had slept on the couch until it arrived.

Leisel shook her head and slid out of the car. There was no way that woman could have had anything to do with Craig. She walked around to the front of the restaurant and entered. Her friends were all there, sitting at their usual table. The bartender walked up with a glass of cabernet for Leisel as soon as she sat down. She felt the tension ease with the first sip. These Monday night get togethers were her favorite part of her week. She took a second sip and joined the conversation with her friends.

34

PATRICK O'KEEFE

P at spent the rest of the afternoon finishing his examination of the suspected drug dealer's computer. He organized everything he had found into an electronic file and sent it to the vice detective working the case. Pat was hoping he had found enough evidence to ensure the guy did some solid time. Overdoses around the entire country were at an all time high and this guy was knowingly selling heroin and pills laced with fentanyl. He considered starting in on the box Hammond had left on the desk, but when he glanced at the clock he saw it was 4:45. He picked the box up off the desk and slid it underneath where his feet usually rested. He'd head home now, he decided, and start fresh tomorrow.

As he walked out to his car Pat's thoughts returned to a subject that had been bothering him all day. He couldn't get Jane Gray and Tyler Timmerman out of his mind. He was regretting giving Loyal Tyler's contact information and was wondering if Jane had acted on the information yet. The Timmerman family was rich and powerful and, judging by their lack of internet presence, extremely private. Pat had a wife and three small children to consider. Blowback from the Timmerman family would be swift and punishing if they were able to discern that Jane's information came from him. Pat slid into his car and called Olive. He voiced his concerns and asked if she minded if he stopped by Loyal's house before heading home. She said she didn't mind, but Pat knew her well enough to hear the hesitation behind her words.

The drive took less than fifteen minutes and Pat was relieved to see Loyal's truck in the driveway. He parked along the curb, slid out, walked to the door, and rang the bell. Loyal's face broke into a wide smile when he opened the door.

"Pat," he said as he motioned him inside, "this is a great surprise. Come on in."

Pat walked in and took a seat on the couch.

"You want a beer?" asked Loyal.

Pat shook his head. "I can't stay long," he said.

"Something wrong?" Loyal asked.

"It's this whole Jane Gray and Tyler Timmerman thing," said Pat. "I'm having second thoughts about giving Jane his information." He looked up at Loyal who had remained standing. "Did you give her his name and address yet?"

Loyal took a seat on the couch. "Yeah," he said, "yesterday. I don't know if she has acted on it though." Loyal paused then added, "Actually Maggie called today and told me that Jane took the whole week off work. Maggie tried to call Jane but she didn't answer."

"Do you still have her number?" asked Pat.

Loyal nodded and pulled his phone out of his pocket. "Want me to try and call her?"

Pat nodded. Loyal tapped Jane's number and held his phone to his ear then shook his head. "Two rings then it got sent to voicemail."

Pat frowned. "I'm getting a bad vibe about all this Loyal," he said. "I don't think we should have helped her."

35

JANE GRAY

Jane took a minute to look around Leisel's back yard. It was small but beautifully designed. A wooden deck stretched out about ten feet from the house and held four chairs and a small round table. Wooden french doors led to what Jane figured was the living room. Pavers extended the length of the deck another ten feet. A stone fire pit and more chairs were arranged on the pavers, along with a variety of potted plants. A hot tub, enclosed on three sides by a wooden wall, was located outside sliding glass doors that Jane assumed led to the master bedroom. Jane walked slowly to the french doors. She looked around for cameras or a security system but was unable to locate any. She thought it unusual for someone of Leisel's status to not have some form of home security, but at this point she didn't care. If any of the doors or windows were unlocked she was going in.

As Jane reached out to grasp the handle of the french doors her phone rang. She pulled it out of her pocket and sent the call to voicemail then slipped it back into her pocket. She took the handle in her hand and turned it slowly. She was met with resistance. The door was locked. Jane paused for a moment then reached up and felt above the door frame. Perhaps Leisel had a hidden key somewhere. She found nothing above the door. Jane turned and scanned the entire back yard. She thought about a book by Dean Koontz that she had read recently. The main character had hidden a key underneath the leg of a patio chair. Jane quickly turned all the chairs but found no key. She turned next to the potted plants, quickly turning each pot over. She moved as fast as possible; she didn't know how long Leisel would be gone. She found the key underneath a pot containing a gorgeous purple iris. The key was attached to the bottom of the pot with a tiny strip of velcro. Smiling, Jane peeled the key off the pot and walked back to the french doors. The key fit. Jane unlocked the door and gave the handle a twist. The handle turned easily in her grasp and the door opened out towards her. Jane hesitated, waiting for an alarm to sound. She could be down the bank and back in her car in less than a minute. Nothing happened. The house was silent.

Jane slipped the house key in her pocket, took a deep breath, and walked in to Leisel's home. Like the back yard, the house was beautifully designed. Jane was no expert, but the furnishings looked expensive. Jane wandered through the living room. Her hand trailed along the edge of a large white couch that faced a stone fire place. The design of the house was open and Jane could see into the dining room as well. She moved silently past the dining room table and turned into the kitchen. It was spotless with the exception of a half empty coffee cup and a lap top on the counter. Jane leaned down and smelled the contents of the cup, then raised the cup to her lips and took a small sip. Apparently Leisel liked cinnamon.

.   .   .

Jane made her way slowly through the house looking for some souvenir to take home with her. She used her phone to take pictures of each room as well. She wanted to remember everything. There was a home office and a guest bedroom which were both generic and didn't contain anything of a personal nature. The guest bathroom held nothing personal as well. The last room she entered was the master bedroom which was large and had a walk-in closet and a huge bathroom. There was a large piece of abstract art on the wall. Jane leaned in closely and saw that it was signed by someone named Dornberg, an artist who she had never heard of. When Jane looked at the end table next to the bed she saw the item she was taking home with her. She picked it up and carried it with her as she walked back through the house. She unlocked the front door and left it cracked open. She went back to the guest bedroom and opened the window. She closed the door to the guest bathroom which had been open when she had arrived. That done, Jane took her souvenir and stepped out the sliding glass door. She picked her way down the bank, slid into her car, and drove away.

36

LEISEL TIMMERMAN

Leisel drank three glasses of wine which was one more than she usually allowed herself. She wasn't drunk, but she definitely wasn't sober either. The time with her friends had been, as it always was, exactly what she had needed. She drove home carefully and breathed a sigh of relief when she pulled into her driveway. A DUI was the last thing she needed. She gathered her purse and slid out of her car. The night was quiet. A cool breeze caressed her skin. The stars twinkled in the clear sky. She took a long breath in and let it out slowly then walked towards her house.

The front door was ajar. Leisel stood still on the front porch and eyed the gap warily. She held her house keys in her right hand. She had been reaching out to insert the key in the door when she noticed it was slightly open. She stood still for a moment and thought back to when she had left the house. Had she closed and locked the door? She thought so. For a moment she considered the possibility that Craig had broken in. If he was in there would he hurt her? She slid her keys into her purse as silently as possible and removed her phone. She keyed the numbers 911 into the keypad. She let her thumb hover over the green button on the bottom of the screen as she slowly eased the door open and entered the house.

She paused in the entry way and listened. The house was silent and dark. She reached her hand to the right and slid it along the wall until she touched the light switches. She gathered her courage and flicked them on. The house brightened. The living room was visible to her left and the dining room to her right. Both were empty and looked exactly as she had left them. She moved slowly through the room flicking on light switches as she went. She peeked to her right. No one was in the kitchen. Her coffee mug, half full of cold coffee, was on the counter next to her lap top. Leisel remembered setting it there as she rushed out of the house earlier in the day. The door to the guest bathroom at the end of the hall was closed. She usually left it open. Leisel looked down at the phone in her hand. She refreshed the screen so that she could call for help with the tap of her thumb and eased the door open. The bathroom was empty.

She let out a breath she had not been aware she was holding and turned to the guest bedroom on her left. She turned the door handle, pushed the door open, and immediately drew back. The window was open. The curtains were moving and she felt the breeze. She checked the phone again, then entered the room. It appeared empty. She checked the closet and under the bed. There was no one there. She knew for a fact that the window had been closed when she had left. She crossed the room, closed the window, and returned to the hall. She stepped quietly into her home office which proved to be empty as well. The only room left to check was her bedroom.

The door was closed. Leisel knew that someone had definitely been in her house. She lived alone and never closed her bedroom door. Her hand trembled slightly as she reached for the door handle, images of Craig and the other woman flashing through her brain. She hesitated a moment, then threw the door open and stepped into the room. It was empty. She checked the closet, the bathroom, and under the bed. No one was in the room. Leisel sat on her bed and tried to calm her pounding heart. Someone had been in her house but nothing appeared to have been taken. Her computer was in the kitchen and she had seen her television as she passed by the living room. She looked around the bedroom slowly. Her Bob Dornberg abstract painting, which had cost over $10,000 remained on the wall. Leisel lay back on the bed and turned her head to the right. It was then that she realized what was missing. The framed family portrait she kept on her bedside table, taken just last year, was gone.

37

JANE GRAY

Jane pulled into her garage and sat in the car as the door slowly descended. The adrenaline coursing through her veins was causing a tiny tremor in her hands. She had actually done it! She closed her eyes and pictured herself walking through Leisel's house. Her *sister's* house. Jane opened her eyes and reached over to the passenger seat where the framed family portrait sat. She lifted it and her purse from the seat and slid out of the car. She walked into the house, set her purse on the kitchen counter, and carried her phone and the portrait into her office. She sat heavily in her chair and set the portrait and her phone on the desk. She stared at the family photo but in her mind she saw Tyler and the woman on the beach again. They were so comfortable with each other, so familiar. Jane felt a slow burn of anger deep within her. Why hadn't her parents wanted her? Why had they given her away? If they had kept her she would be like Tyler who was so clearly confidant and comfortable with himself. She wouldn't be alone.

· · ·

Jane had had one long term relationship in her life. She had met Rodney in college during her sophomore year, just months after her grandmother had died. They had been partnered together for a class project. They had quickly become friends and eventually became lovers. Rodney had been four inches shorter than Jane. She had known that they made a funny looking couple, but she hadn't cared. He had been shy and sweet and had treated her kindly. For the first time in a very long time Jane had felt loved. She had no longer been alone. They had stayed together until graduation after which Rodney had accepted a job in Silicon Valley and had moved to San Jose. They had kept in touch for a time, but it hadn't been the same. The relationship hadn't actually ended, it had just sort of faded away. Jane had gone on a handful of dates over the years since then, but nothing had ever come of them. Outside of work and her clients she had become, again, alone.

Jane blinked and brought herself out of her memories. She hadn't thought about Rodney in a very long time. She supposed he was probably married by now and had a family of his own. The thought of family brought Jane's attention back to the family portrait on her desk. She looked at it for a long moment. She stood, placed her phone on the bookshelf and activated the self timer. She took several steps back and smiled at the camera as it counted down from ten and took her picture. She connected her phone to her computer and imported the photo then printed it. She cut the picture from the page and inserted it into the framed photo of the Timmerman family. "There," she said quietly. "Now I have a family of my own too."

38

LEISEL TIMMERMAN

When Leisel realized that the family portrait had been taken she went through her house again looking for missing items of a personal nature, rather than expensive things, that might have been taken. While she moved through the house she made sure that every window and door was securely closed and locked. She didn't find anything else missing. She considered calling Tyler, but decided against it. He would just start his usual tirade about the lack of security in her home. After she had kicked Craig out Tyler had tried to convince her to install a ring doorbell and cameras. He had even offered to set the system up for her. Lieisel had declined his offer. In Liesel's opinion all technology could be reverse engineered. She didn't want a security system that could be used to spy on her.

Liesel poured herself a glass of water and sat down on the edge of her bed. Her eyes were drawn to the empty space where the family portrait used to sit. Who would want to take the picture, she wondered, and why? She finally settled on Craig. It had to have been him. Who else was there? A tiny wisp of a thought slid into Liesel's mind. She had convinced herself that Jane Gray was a scam, that someone was after her family's money. Now she found herself wondering if, perhaps, the woman might actually be real.

39

JANE GRAY

Jane lay in her bed, deep asleep and dreaming. In the dream she was in her car and approaching Tall T Ranch. As she neared the gates they slowly swung open for her. She pulled into the driveway and the gates reversed their direction and closed silently behind her. Jane parked next to Tyler's truck and Leisel's Highlander and slid out of her car. She approached the front door with caution, unsure what to expect. In her waking hours Jane had looked up the property on several real estate websites and had a general idea about the layout of the house. Her unconscious mind gladly filled in the blanks.

As Jane reached her right hand toward the doorbell the front doors swung open. All four family members stood there, arms open wide, smiles on their faces, welcoming her to the family home. Jane allowed herself to be drawn into a group hug. The hug lasted moments, but in those moments Jane felt as if she was truly home. The family released her and her father,

Charles, led her through the house and into the back yard. He pointed to a newly installed guest house on the other side of the pool.

"That is your new home," he said with a wide smile.

Leisel grabbed Jane's hand and led her toward the small home. "Come see," she said, "I designed the interior just for you."

"Yes Jane," said Tyler as he grabbed her other hand, "everything is tailored just for you."

As her brother and sister pulled her toward the guest house Jane turned and looked back at her mother and father. Daisy stood just to the left and slightly behind Charles. Jane couldn't be sure from this distance, but it looked as if tears were running down Daisy's cheeks.

Tyler and Leisel escorted Jane through the entire guest house. They pointed out all the special details; the supple leather couches, the stone fireplace, the state of the art stereo and television systems, and the gorgeous four poster bed. Jane took everything in, still amazed at the generosity and slightly dizzy from the waves of love flowing from her family.

"You get settled in," said Tyler as he and Leisel turned toward the front door, "we'll come get you when it's time to eat.

Jane wandered through the house, marveling at the opulence, touching this and examining that. It was only when she sat down on the bed that she realized she had no luggage.

As she sat on the bed pondering her situation she felt a tiny pin prick of heat on her right cheek. She raised her hand to the spot and saw a spot of what looked like ash on her fingertip.

She felt another pin prick on the tip of her nose, then another on the top of her head. Jane looked up and saw the ceiling was on fire. Embers were dropping down on her. As she watched the flames grew larger, defying the laws of gravity and stretching down toward her on the bed rather than reaching for the sky. Jane stood and raced through the house toward the front door. The entire ceiling was engulfed in flames. The roiling mass flashed and sparked as it reached its flaming tendrils towards the floor. Jane ran to the front door and grabbed the handle intending to throw the door open and run out. The handle did not turn. It was locked, apparently from the outside. Jane struggled with it for a moment, then gave up and headed to the windows.

Heavy curtains hung in front of the living room window. Embers had landed on them and they were just catching fire when Jane flung them aside and looked out the window. Tyler, and Leisel stood outside the window. When they saw Jane they started to laugh. As they laughed their faces began to distort and stretch, much the way an image will do in a fun house mirror. They pointed at Jane and, surprisingly, she could hear their cruel words despite the roaring flames and the locked window.

"You really thought we would accept you?" Tyler said.

"With your limp and scar you could never fit in," screeched Leisel. "We only allow perfection in our family. Your imperfections make you unacceptable."

Jane dropped to her knees and covered her ears with her hands. The flames roared above her, throwing themselves toward the floor. She began to scream.

. . .

Her screams brought Jane out of the nightmare and back into her house in Escondido. Sweat was pouring off her skin. Her hair was drenched. The covers were wrapped tightly around her like a cocoon. She struggled for a moment and finally freed herself from their embrace. She flung her body out of bed and raced to her office, the depth of her anger and humiliation from the dream was something she had never before experienced. She picked up the framed photograph and flung it against the information wall. The glass shattered and the frame cracked. As the pieces fell to the ground Jane felt the anger dissipate. It left her body in an instant and was replaced with deep regret. The dream had just been her subconscious dealing with her deep insecurities regarding her birth family. She gently picked up the pieces of broken glass and deposited them in the trash can. She taped together the broken frame and put the picture, including the image of herself, back together as best she could. She lay it on the desk and left the office.

40

LEISEL TIMMERMAN

Leisel did not have a good night's sleep. Every small sound brought her out of her shallow slumber. She finally gave up as the first rays of the sun were peeking over the horizon. She wrapped a thick green robe around her body, made a large mug of coffee, and sat in her back yard watching the sky change from dark blue to red then orange then back to a lighter shade of blue. She could tell already that it was going to be another spectacular spring day.

Once the sun was fully in the sky and beginning its slow march west Leisel stood and went back into her house. She set the empty mug on the kitchen counter and walked into her office to check her schedule for the day. Although she and Tyler were considered full time employees, and paid for forty hours each week, in actuality they both worked considerably fewer hours. According to her calendar she had a meeting at the foundation's offices in Encinitas at 11:30. Both Tyler and her father would be there as well. Daisy attended important events but didn't involve herself in the day to day inner workings of the foundation. Leisel was sure her mother would be spending the day working with her new Arabian. Daisy adored her horses and occasionally Leisel found herself wondering if her mother loved her horses a tiny bit more than she loved her children. With a small sigh, Leisel pushed that thought from her mind. She walked through her house and double checked that all doors and windows were locked, then headed to the bathroom for a quick shower.

41

JANE GRAY

Jane took a cold shower, keeping the temperature as low as she could bear. She scrubbed her skin with an intensity bordering on painful abuse as she attempted to erase completely the vestiges of the horrible dream. When she was able to close her eyes and the image of Tyler and Leisel laughing at her and taunting her no longer appeared in her mind she turned off the shower, dried her skin, and wrapped her hair in a towel. She dumped her drenched pajamas into the laundry hamper and dressed in loose sweatpants and a T-shirt. She heated water in the teapot and poured it over a bag of chamomile tea. She stood at the kitchen window, sipping tea and thinking.

Eventually Jane made her way back into her office and sat at the desk. She looked at the damaged picture frame and decided she would buy a new one to replace it. Her eyes ran over the information wall again. She was frustrated by her inability to locate birth certificates for any of the Timmerman's. She pulled up vitalsearch.com again and entered Tyler's name. She typed slowly and carefully, double and triple checking that everything was spelled correctly, yet still got no results. She did the same with Leisel's name and achieved the same results. None. She entered her own name and her birth certificate appeared on the screen. As she stared at it she recalled Loyal's question about how her father, a single man, had been able to adopt an infant, especially a girl. After her grandmother's death, Jane had gone through both her grandmother's and her father's rooms thoroughly. She had never found any adoption papers. She hadn't really thought much about it at the time, but she thought about it now. Both her father and her grandmother had kept all their important papers in a fireproof safe in her father's closet. She had found birth certificates, a death certificate for her grandfather whom she had never met, the deed to the house, and life insurance policies. If adoption papers existed surely they would have been in that safe.

42

LOYAL TRUESDALE

Tuesday morning at 10:00 am Loyal could be found sitting on his couch staring out the large window at the front of his house. His gaze was unfocused, the long stare typically used to describe people who had lost hope or were completely exhausted. Boo, who was getting a little large for this position, sat on his left shoulder. Loyal held a cup of very strong coffee in his hands. Sleep the previous night had been a complete disaster. Loyal had remained shaken by Pat's visit. The fact that Pat had been swayed by Olive's entreaties on Jane's behalf was clear. If Loyal had made the same inquiry Pat would have certainly refused the request.

Loyal had spent some time the previous evening on his computer. He had read about the Timmerman family trust, a few articles in which Charle's achievements were highlighted, and a website that listed the top 500 richest people in the world. Charles Timmerman was number 496. A man that rich and powerful would be a dangerous enemy to have. Jane didn't know about Pat's involvement in bringing the information regarding Tyler to light, but she definitely knew about Loyal's, and Maggie's as well.

Loyal also had spent several hours reading the privacy policy and terms of service on genomecestry.com. The more he had read the more concerned he had become. Once a person agreed to the privacy policy and terms of service, and submitted their DNA sample, the sample no longer legally belonged to the submitter. Genomecestry owned it for 35 years. The speed with which Pat had found Tyler's information suggested the site had major security problems. If Pat could uncover Tyler's personal details then surely someone else with strong computer skills could do so as well. Someone with malicious intent could surely make the connection between Jane and the Timmerman family. It had been well after midnight when Loyal had finally gone to bed. He had lain in bed, thoughts racing and heart pounding, until finally falling asleep just after 7:00 am. He had woken at 8:06.

Sitting on the couch now, jacked up by the caffeine and exhausted at the same time, he found himself agreeing with Pat's opinion that they ought not to have gotten involved in Jane's affairs. He carefully lifted Boo off his shoulder and set him gently on the couch. The cat looked up at Loyal with round green eyes that seemed to ask why he had been removed from his favorite spot. Loyal stood slowly. He swayed as a wave of dizziness washed over him, then regained his balance and walked to the kitchen counter where his phone was plugged in and charging. He picked it up and considered calling Trinity but somehow resisted the urge. Instead he pulled up Maggie's contact information and called her.

She answered with her trademark, "This is Maggie."

"Hey Maggie," said Loyal, "it's Loyal."

"Hey there," Maggie said, "you ok Loyal? You sound tired."

"Yeah I'm fine," said Loyal. He paused then asked, "You ever get a call back from Jane?"

"Nope."

"Yeah, me neither," said Loyal. "It's like she dropped off the face of the earth."

"Don't you think that's a bit dramatic?" said Maggie.

"Probably," said Loyal. "Will you let me know if you hear from her? Ask her to call me if she calls you?"

"Sure," said Maggie. She waited a breath then added, "Is something wrong Loyal?"

"I'm not sure," said Loyal, "but I'd sure like to talk with her."

Maggie promised to call if she heard from Jane and to ask Jane to give Loyal a call. She reminded him about Saturday breakfast with Winnie and some members of the buggy club. He told her he would do his best to be there and they disconnected the call.

43

JANE GRAY

The ringing of her doorbell brought Jane out of her memories and back to the present moment. Her hand still held the tea cup but the tea inside the cup was clearly cold. She was a bit concerned about the way she seemed to be drifting between the past and the present since she had found out who her birth family was. This wasn't the first instance where a chunk of time had seemingly vanished as she wandered through her memories. She set the cup down, stood, and walked through the house to the front door. When she opened it she saw that a deliveryman had left a cardboard box on the front step. He was already halfway down the driveway and back to his van. Jane leaned down and picked up the box. It was light. She carried it into her office and opened it. Inside were the two trackers she had ordered on Sunday evening. She smiled. She had forgotten about these.

She opened the packages and read the instructions. She needed to place the trackers directly on the vehicles then she could follow their movements on her phone. There was a disclaimer that listed the laws of all 50 states regarding the placement of trackers on vehicles. Jane skimmed down to the California laws. According to Ca penal code 637.7 individuals were prohibited from placing a tracker on a vehicle to determine the location and movement of a person. Exceptions to this rule were registered owners, lessors, or lessees who were tracking their own vehicles. In California, the literature continued, it was a misdemeanor to place a GPS inside a car you didn't own or to enter someone's garage to place the tracker. If a car was on a public street, however, placing the tracker was technically not illegal. Jane read all the paperwork but had already made the decision that she was going to place the trackers.

Jane set the trackers up and downloaded the app to her phone. Her concerns about drifting into the past forgotten, she dressed for the day in tan slacks, a light blue sweater, and tennis shoes. She wasn't sure how much time she would be spending on her feet so she wore the Hoka's she usually reserved for work. She could literally stand up all day in in these shoes. She grabbed her purse, the camera, and the backpack that still contained the snacks she had packed the day before. By 10:10 she was on the road and heading for her first destination which she had decided would be Tyler's house.

Jane reached Tyler's house just before 10:45. She was disappointed that his truck was not in the driveway. She drove past his house, turned right on Carlina and made the loop around until she was back to Brava. This time she crossed Brava and continued on Hataca. She was surprised, and pleased, to find a tiny community park that backed up to Tyler's house. There were only five parking spaces and none were occupied. Jane parked, grabbed her phone and keys, and slid out of the car. The park was very small and contained only a small cement walking trail that wound its way through the grass right behind Tyler's house and a few benches. Jane set out on the trail. She held her phone up in front of her face as if she was speaking to someone on speaker phone. In reality she was snapping pictures.

When she had traversed the entire path, which took less than ten minutes, she slid back in her Nissan and studied the pictures she had taken. Tyler's backyard was enclosed by a six foot wooden fence. When she zoomed in on the picture Jane could see he had a camera facing out from his back porch roof. She started the car and drove slowly by the front of his house again. There were no visible cameras, but she took a picture of the front of the house that she could study later. If he had a camera in the back of the house then it was very likely he had one or more in the front as well.

44

LOYAL TRUESDALE

After disconnecting with Maggie Loyal unplugged his phone and carried it back to the couch with him. He placed it on the coffee table, picked up Boo, then lay down on the couch with Boo tucked against his stomach. He closed his eyes, intending to try and nap, but just like the previous night thoughts and images kept flooding his mind. Loyal began taking slow even breaths in and out. He counted to five with each inhale and to five again with each exhale. Gradually he felt himself relaxing. He was just on that strange edge of awareness, that moment right before the mind took the plunge into sleep, when his phone pinged, indicating a text message.

Loyal sat up in a daze. For a moment he struggled to remember where he was. His phone pinged again and his trance faded away enough for him to slip back into reality. He picked up the device and became truly awake when he saw the caller ID. Trinity. Loyal clicked on the message and read the words.

. . .

I miss you Loyal. Do you have any time? You want to talk?

Loyal read the short message three times just to be sure he wasn't somehow still asleep and dreaming. This was exactly what he had been waiting for. Without bothering to text back he simply navigated to Trinity's contact information and tapped the home button. She answered on the first ring.

"Loyal," she said.

"Trinity."

There was an extended silence on the line as their ears absorbed each other's voices, drawing the tones in like a breath of fresh sea air, clean and invigorating. The silent moment was both awkward and not. Neither seemed to know exactly what to say, yet it was life affirming, silent acknowledgement of the emotional connection between them which appeared to have been strengthened rather than weakened by their separation.

Loyal broke the silence first by saying, "You were right, Trinity. I did have some stuff to work through."

"How's that going?" she asked.

Loyal thought for a brief moment then said, "I'm not angry anymore so I think that looks good in terms of us." He paused again, but very briefly, then added, "If you still want an us."

"I do."

"How are you healing from the accident?" Loyal asked.

"I'm okay," said Trinity, "the shoulder still gives me trouble." She paused then said, "And there's the scar on my forehead."

"I'm so sorry Trinity," said Loyal, "that's all my fault."

"Not completely," said Trinity, "I chose to be there. I just underestimated the danger.

"We both did," said Loyal. "Where are you now?"

"Bellingham," said Trinity. "Taking a few weeks off."

"Can we see each other?" Loyal asked.

"You want to come up here?"

"Yes," said Loyal, "yes I do."

45

PATRICK O'KEEFE

P at had arrived at the Sheriff's Department just after 7:00 am. He had spent nearly four hours looking through the phones, computers, and various social media accounts of Miles and Hope Bannon, the husband and wife Hammond had asked him to look into. Pat had also looked at photos from the scene and read the notes of both Hammond and the tech team. The photos were distressing and painful for Pat to look at. Hope had clearly been shot while she was asleep. She looked almost peaceful if Pat ignored the bullet wound in the side of her head and the blood and brain matter on the pillows. She lay on her right side with her hands placed gently under her right cheek. Her pose reminded Pat so much of how his daughter Piper slept that his eyes filled with tears when he first saw the photos.

Miles Bannon, on the other hand, did not look peaceful. He had stepped away from the bed before turning the gun on himself. Pat made the assumption that Miles had been left handed because he shot himself in the left temple. His body had crumpled to the ground and he lay on his right side. His head was bent at an unnatural angle and his left hand was flung outward, away from his body, the gun resting mere inches from his fingertips. When Pat zoomed in on Miles' face he could see the remnants of tear tracks still drying on the man's face. It was this detail that had stuck out to Pat and he had kept those tear tracks in his mind's eye as he had worked his way through the Bannon's electronic life.

By 11:00 Pat had researched a basic background on both Hope and Miles Bannon. They both preferred Instagram to Facebook and Pat had been able to follow their stories back in time. Hope had been online more frequently than Miles and it was through her story that Pat had been able to piece together the timeline of their relationship. In 2019 the Instagram app had begun saving stories to the archives rather that deleting them after 24 hours so Pat had been able to access several years worth of posts. He had gone back as far as he could and had started the review of Hope's stories in May of 2019. Pat preferred to create his own background before reading any background materials provided by detectives or transcripts of interviews with family, friends, and co-workers. He leaned back in his chair and held the notepad full of his hand written notes in front of him. Hope had been twenty four years of age at the time of her death. Miles had been twenty eight. Pat hadn't yet been able to pinpoint exactly how or where they had met, but some of Hope's posts alluded to a young adult Christian group at a local church. They had been married in June of 2019 and honeymooned in Hawaii. When they returned from their vacation they settled into a seemingly peaceful and uneventful life together. Hope worked as a dental hygienist in Poway and Miles was a youth pastor working with teenagers at a church in San Marcos. Pat recognized the name of the church. He drove past it twice each day; once on his way to work and again on his way home.

Pat leaned back in his chair and dropped the notepad on his desk. He closed his eyes and ran his hands over his cropped red hair. He let images of the church flow through his mind and stopped on one that he had seen only a week or so ago. The church had a large playing field to the west of the sanctuary. Pat had seen teenagers playing a game that resembled capture the flag on that field. The image was imprinted clearly in his mind because it had reminded Pat of his own youth and the games that he and his friends had played on fields in community parks. He had watched the scene for a moment then driven on with a smile on his face. He wondered now if it had been Miles Bannon's youth group that he had been watching. And if it had been, Pat wondered how all those teenagers, who likely looked up to Miles, were going to be dealing with the fallout from this tragedy.

46

JANE GRAY

Jane left Tyler's house and drove toward Sunburst Road. The fact that she and Leisel had previously made eye contact, however brief, made Jane hesitant to actually drive past Leisel's house. That concern dissipated when Leisel's Highlander appeared at the corner of Skyline and Hillside less than a football field in front of Jane. Leisel made the left turn onto Hillside and Jane simply fell in behind her, leaving a few car lengths between them. She followed the Highlander on Hillside until it reached Tamarack and made a left turn. Jane executed a left as well and soon both vehicles were on Interstate 5 heading south. Leisel exited the freeway at Encinitas Blvd, turning left. Jane did the same. At Saxony Road Leisel turned left again and Jane followed her to a parking lot behind some executive offices. Leisel parked in reserved parking, Jane parked at the far end of the lot. Just as Jane was turning off her car she saw Tyler's truck pull into the lot and park next to Leisel. The siblings exited their cars and entered a back door of the office building, Tyler opening the door and graciously allowing his sister to enter first.

. . .

The door swung closed behind Leisel and Tyler and Jane felt a slow smile spread across her face. Lady Luck was with her today. Placing the trackers would be simple. She slid out of her Nissan and, trackers in hand, walked between the Highlander and the truck. Pretending to drop something, Jane knelt down and placed the trackers, first on Tyler's truck and second on Leisel's Highlander. In case anyone was looking Jane stood and pretended to study the list of businesses located inside the office building. Only one stood out to her, The Timmerman Family Foundation.

Jane wasn't sure why she did it, but she took out her phone and took a picture of the Timmerman Family Foundation signage. She slipped her phone back in her sweater pocket and walked slowly back to her car. She slid in and leaned her head back against the headrest. She was at once exhausted and exhilarated. She felt, simultaneously, that she could sleep for days or never sleep again. She closed her eyes to contemplate her next move. She had researched the family online, found out where each one of them lived, and found her siblings place of employment. The trackers were activated and affixed to the two vehicles that were most available to her. She'd love to have one on Daisy's car but wasn't even sure the woman actually drove. She was at a crossroads, unsure what her next move should be. Eventually she decided to pick up some food and head home. The trackers would alert her to Leisel and Tyler's movements so there was no reason for her to stay in this parking lot. She pulled out her phone and googled take out restaurants near her.

. . .

Jane chose The Taco Stand on Highway 101. She called and ordered two tacos, one carne asada and one beer battered fish, along with rice and beans. She picked the food up fifteen minutes later and turned her Nissan towards Escondido. She chose to take Del Dios Highway instead of the freeway. Despite the fact that the water level in Lake Hodges was extremely low, she enjoyed the drive and the view. She turned right at Via Rancho Parkway and came into Escondido from the south passing the Westfield mall and San Pasqual high school on her way into town. When she reached her home on Highland Street Jane parked in the garage and took her food into her office. She returned to the kitchen for a glass of water then settled herself at her desk. She ate her food quickly, surprised by her hunger, then leaned back in her chair to study her information wall.

47

PATRICK O'KEEFE

When researching on a previous case Pat had started his in depth research in the present and worked his way into the suspect and his wife's past. The strategy had been successful because he had been able to chart Colleen Young's transformation - backwards - from a very unhappy woman to an incredibly enthusiastic life loving woman. He had watched the pounds and stress melt off the woman as he worked his way back in time. In the Bannon case he reversed his strategy. All the texts, posts, and emails from the current time were positive and upbeat. He decided to go as far back in the Bannon relationship as he could and work his way forward. Perhaps the trajectory of their relationship would reveal the cause of the horrific impact.

After several hours of research Pat had a fairly clear picture of a young couple, deeply in love, and trying to start a family. Hope had suffered a miscarriage in 2020 and two more in 2021. Despite the young couple's deep faith it was clear they were beginning to have doubts of their long held dream of parent-hood coming true. In all their communications that Pat was able to read, however, their love for each other never appeared to waver. If anything, it seemed to grow stronger with each disappointment. As he inched his way closer to the present day Pat found a text from Hope to Miles that he had either missed or misunderstood when he had read it before. It was short and to the point.

Two pinks!!

Pat leaned away from his computer, closed his eyes, and brought up the images of the home pregnancy tests Olive had taken over the years. Two pink lines for pregnant, one pink line for not. He opened his eyes and searched for a response from Miles. There wasn't one. Perhaps Miles had called her, Pat thought. He noted the date and time of the text then compared it to their phone call records. There it was. A phone call from Miles to Hope less than two minutes after he received the text. The phone call lasted six minutes and 22 seconds. It wasn't hard for Pat to imagine the content of the call. They would have been equal parts overjoyed and terrified. He looked again at the date then stood and walked to the calendar that hung on his office wall. Assuming Hope had missed a period, at the time of the test she would have been 4-5 weeks along. Pat counted the weeks that had passed since she took the test. Five. If she hadn't miscarried, at the time of her death Hope Bannon had been approximately 9-10 weeks along.

48

JANE GRAY

J ane studied the wall and watched the tracker app on her phone. She had overestimated her hunger and her stomach was distended and uncomfortable. She unbuttoned her slacks and leaned even farther back in her office chair. Her phone was tilted up against her computer so that she could see if Leisel or Tyler began moving. Jane remained prone in that position for a little more than ten minutes before the red tracker dots began moving, Leisel's a fraction of a second before Tyler's.

"Done with work already, huh?" Jane said out loud to no one in particular. "Gotta love the two hour workday of the über wealthy," she added. As she watched the trackers she made guesses about where each of the siblings was likely headed. She was correct in both cases. Tyler's destination had been fairly obvious because of the surfboard she had seen in the bed of his truck. He drove straight to Swami's beach and parked. Leisel drove straight back to her home on Sunburst Road.

·   ·   ·

Neither of these potential surveillance prospects interested Jane much. She was enjoying, she realized, the excitement of stalking (she was aware as she thought this that stalking was the correct word) and possibly getting caught. At the beach she'd probably just see the blond bimbo again, and at Leisel's nothing much seemed to happen. That thought about Leisel led Jane into a series of thoughts that led her to her next decision. She looked again at the picture of Leisel in the dressage contest. If Leisel liked horses then Daisy probably did too. The Timmerman family home was just down the street from an equestrian park. If Daisy liked horses perhaps that is where she would be. It wouldn't hurt to give it a try, thought Jane. If nothing came of it she would be closer to Tyler and Leisel if either of them decided to do something interesting.

Jane changed into black stretch pants and a loose green T shirt to accommodate her bulging belly. She threw her backpack with the camera and the binoculars on the passenger seat, along with a few water bottles and a black sweatshirt. As an afterthought she added a granola bar. At the moment she couldn't imagine ever being hungry again. But she knew, if the day stretched into night and the night into dawn, hunger would return. Planning for eventualities was difficult as Jane had no real hard and fast plans. The way things stood right now she was making decisions in the moment and on the fly.

49

PATRICK O'KEEFE

Pat was leaning back in his chair, eyes closed, considering the circumstances that could lead to a husband killing his pregnant wife when there was a sharp rap on his open office door. He opened his eyes, acknowledged Len Hammond and waved him in, then sat up straighter in his chair. Hammond tossed a stack of papers on Pat's desk.

"Autopsy report," he said as he sat in the visitor's chair. "I printed everything for you."

"Thanks," said Pat.

Hammond sat, rubbed his left hand across his forehead, then leaned forward in his chair.

"She was pregnant," he said, "eleven or twelve weeks."

Pat nodded then said, "I just figured that out. I'm trying to figure out a motive. Maybe Miles wasn't the father?"

Hammond nodded. "That thought crossed my mind. DNA should be available in a few days and we'll know for sure." Hammond paused then said, "You found anything I should know about?"

Pat shook his head. "Not really. They seemed totally

devoted to each other." He paused a moment then added, "They have suffered at least three miscarriages that I can document. I was thinking maybe she miscarried again and he lost it, killed her, then realizing what he had done killed himself. You're sure the pregnancy was viable?"

Hammond nodded, "Intact fetus. Died when Hope died."

The two men were silent for a beat then Pat asked, "What about the gun? Was it registered to Miles?"

Hammond shook his head. "Registered to a man named Andrew Van Grove. I saw him this morning. He and Miles have been friends since grade school. He kept the gun in a drawer by his bed. When I asked him about it he took me right to the drawer, no hesitation." Hammond paused. "He seemed genuinely surprised to find it missing."

"You think Miles just helped himself to the gun? Does this Andrew guy have any security cameras we can check?

"No cameras," said Hammond, "but Miles feeds Andrew's dog when he's out of town. He knew where the spare key was hidden."

Both men were silent for a moment then Pat said, "It wasn't spur of the moment then. Miles planned this."

Hammond let out a long slow breath. "Looks like it," he said as he stood. "Let me know if you find anything else I should know about."

Pat nodded his head. "I'll keep digging." He ran his hands through his cropped red hair. "Something's very wrong here, Hammond," he said, "and I think this," he pointed to his computer, "is where we are going to find it."

50

LOYAL TRUESDALE

T rinity and Loyal talked for a few more minutes then disconnected. Loyal went straight to his computer and checked flights to Bellingham International Airport. He found several and texted his potential itineraries to Trinity to see what would work for her. The first flight took off from San Diego at 7:30 that evening. The flight had a layover at SeaTac so his total travel time would be five hours and twelve minutes. This would put his arrival time at 12:42 am. If Trinity didn't want to pick him up at that hour he could book a flight that left the following morning at 9:45. Trinity texted back that she was fine picking him up at 12:42 so Loyal booked the flight.

When he turned from the computer Loyal saw Boo sitting on the cat post watching him. He walked over to the little cat and petted him.

"What am I going to do with you little guy?" he said.

Loyal mentally ran through a list of people he could ask to check on Boo and feed him while Loyal was away. He had booked a one-way ticket and had no idea when he would be returning to Carlsbad. He decided to call Maynard Lily, his lawyer and good friend. Maynard owed Loyal a favor and readily agreed to help. He promised to stop by before 4:30 to get a key and learn Boo's routine. That done, Loyal pulled his suitcase out of his closet and began to pack.

51

LEISEL TIMMERMAN

L eisel checked her entire house when she got home. She walked through every room checking behind and under furniture and in all closets. When she was convinced that no one was hiding in her house she sat down on the couch and reviewed her conversation with Tyler. She had pulled him to the side after their meeting at work and told him about the intruder and the missing family photo. She also told him about the light blue car she had seen when she was leaving to meet her friends for wine. Tyler had been on his way to Swamis to meet Jolene for surfing, but told her he would review all his security camera footage when he got home. If he saw the light blue car he would call her. He was concerned about how the intruder had gained access to Leisel's home. He had advised her to check under the potted plant to see if her spare key was there. Leisel had done this and been surprised to find the key was gone. She had contacted a locksmith and made an appointment to get the house re-keyed again. Tyler had also suggested she invest in some security cameras. Leisel was considering this.

. . .

Leisel closed her eyes and attempted to bring up the image of the woman in the blue car. The glimpse had lasted mere seconds. She recalled dark hair but facial features eluded her. She was sure she had never seen that car on Sunburst Road. Traffic on her street was extremely light and Leisel could recognize the cars of her neighbors. The light blue color was unusual and stood out. If Tyler found any footage of the car by his house she thought perhaps involving the police would be a smart idea.

Leisel stood and walked to her back yard. She loved this space and spent a lot of time outside. Looking at the yard now, with fresh eyes and from a security standpoint, she could see that her house was very vulnerable. The small cement wall certainly wouldn't stop someone from entering her yard. Leisel walked to the wall and looked down the slope. Horizon street was below her. She stood there for a full five minutes and saw no cars go by. Horizon was just as untraveled as Sunburst. Someone could park below her yard and walk up without anyone seeing them. She realized this is likely what her intruder had done. Leisel returned to her house and sat at the dining room table with a piece of paper in front of her. Starting with the back yard, she compiled a list of security issues that she needed to address.

52

JANE GRAY

Jane parked in the corner of the equestrian park and slid out of her car. She placed the backpack over her shoulders and picked up a water bottle. She walked to a small wooden frame that held a map of all the trails in the park. She studied the map for several minutes but failed to understand it or get her bearings. In the end she decided to simply set out on the nearest trail and see where she ended up. There were several trail heads to choose from. Jane chose the one that looked as if it headed in the direction of the Timmerman property. The trail was fairly wide and comprised of hard packed dry dirt. Trees lined both sides of the trail. Jane wasn't sure what type of tree they were. They were large and their leafy branches arched over the trail providing shade.

After about ten minutes Jane saw two horses approaching in the distance. As they got closer she could see that one of the riders was an adult and the other appeared to be a child. When they were about fifteen feet from her Jane could make out their faces. The adult was a man who appeared to be in his mid thirties. His hair color was covered by a riding helmet, but the thick brown mustache below his nose suggested he was a brunette. The child was a girl. Jane didn't think she could be older than seven or eight. As they drew nearer Jane stepped to the side of the trail to allow them to pass by easily and without spooking the horses. Both riders smiled and waved at Jane, then they were past her and she was alone again on the trail.

Seeing the man and the girl brought Jane's thoughts once again to her father, William. Sometimes she missed him with such an intensity that she felt physical pain. A realization slowly formed in her mind. Even if the Timmerman family acknowledged her they would never love her like William had. She would always be an outsider. She would never truly belong. On the heels of that realization came a sudden wave of anger. It hit Jane with force. Her birth parents had given her up. They hadn't wanted her then and they wouldn't want her now. They had brought two more children into the world after Jane and showered those replacement kids with all their love and affection. It was so damn unfair. Jane had started this process in search of family and love. The emotions she was finding were turning out to be jealousy and anger.

Jane stopped her forward motion and stood in the center of the trail. Tears had flooded her eyes. She blinked them back, refusing to allow one drop to spill down her cheek. This was crazy. Her life before the DNA test had been a bit lonely but certainly not unhappy. Her life since the DNA test had been a rollercoaster of emotions. She let out a deep breath and walked slowly towards a large stack of boulders on the left side of the trail. She worked her way to the top and turned a complete circle taking in the view. To the east she saw a long line of black wrought iron fencing. She slid down the other side of the boulders and made her way towards a large gate in the fence line. As she got closer she was able to make out the insignia in the center of the gate. It was a T. This was, she realized, the back side of the Timmerman property. Jane peered through the fencing but couldn't see much. She knew from her internet search that the Timmerman property was large. It was just over fifteen acres and from this side Jane couldn't see much more than the roofline of the house.

Jane stood at the gate for a few minutes then turned and walked back to the boulders. She climbed them again and sat down at the top. She took a long drink from the water bottle then closed her eyes and raised her face to the sun. The warmth felt nice on her skin. She brought an image of William up in her mind's eye and felt her lips curve in a small smile. She sat this way for several minutes then opened her eyes and prepared to stand. Movement to her right caught her attention. She turned her head and saw a figure on a horse in the distance. Jane pulled her camera out of the backpack and zoomed in on the rider. Judging by the slender build Jane assumed it was a female. The facial features were obscured by a riding helmet and sunglasses. The horse and rider moved gracefully along the fence line of the Timmerman property. As they approached the gate the rider held out her arm and the gate began to open. In that moment Jane realized that the rider must be Daisy. She shoved the camera back into the backpack, stood, and hurried down the boulders. In her haste she tripped and tumbled down the last few feet. By the time she stood Daisy was inside the gate and it was closing slowly behind her. Jane called out but she was too far away for Daisy to hear her.

53

TYLER TIMMERMAN

Tyler and Jolene spent over an hour in the ocean hoping for a decent set of waves which never did materialize. As they were drying off Jolene suggested that she follow Tyler to his house to spend some time with him. Tyler declined the offer, explaining that he had some things to do. They walked up the stairs to the parking lot, shared a long kiss, and went their separate ways.

Tyler drove home, cleaned his surfboard, and took a quick shower. He made himself a tuna sandwich and sat at the kitchen table to eat it. His lap top was open in front of him. The first thing he did was check his weekly activity that was recorded by his Whoop, a digital tracking device he wore on his wrist. The Whoop tracked all his vitals, recorded sleep performance data, and provided data regarding how his body was adapting to stressors and exercise. Once he had reviewed that Tyler began looking through video recorded by his security cameras. He had two on the back of his house and one on the front. He began with the front working his way back in time. It didn't take long for him to see a light blue car. It had driven slowly past his house at 10:58 that very morning, and again 17 minutes prior to that at 10:41. He froze the footage and attempted to zoom in on the driver. He could make out dark hair and sunglasses, but no facial features. He took a screenshot of the image then continued looking through the footage.

By the time he had finished with the front camera, scanning through seven days of footage, Tyler had seen the blue car on four different occasions in the past three days. The first appearance had been Sunday afternoon at 4:32 pm. The car had parked across the street and several houses down from his. When Tyler had pulled out of his driveway the car had followed. Monday morning at 8:15 the car had driven by again. Then there had been the two instances that morning. Tyler took screen shots of each instance. Next Tyler began looking through footage from the back cameras. The blue car appeared just one time. The driver had parked in the parking lot of the small park that butted up against Tyler's backyard fence. This time Tyler got a good look at the driver because they had actually exited the vehicle and walked around the park. It was a woman. She was wearing tan slacks, a light blue sweater, and tennis shoes. She held her phone in front of her face as if she was speaking to someone. This obscured most of her face. Still, she looked familiar. It took Tyler a minute or so to make the connection. When he did he felt a sinking feeling in his stomach. He wasn't positive, but he was fairly sure the woman was Jane Gray.

54

JANE GRAY

Jane reached the gate and grabbed ahold of it. She shook it with all her strength and continued to yell at Daisy, who had already disappeared from sight. Hot tears streamed down Jane's face as she rattled the gate and screamed. Eventually she slid down to her knees and remained there, giant sobs wracking her body. Some time later, she wasn't sure how long, she quieted. She used her shirt to wipe the tears and mucus from her face. They left smears on the front of her green shirt but she didn't care. Images were flowing through her mind. She saw Tyler and the blond woman surfing then kissing, Leisel's perfectly appointed home, Charles and Daisy's giant estate behind locked gates, Daisy riding a horse without a care in the world. These things should have been hers as well. As she mentally reviewed these images Jane felt something unclench inside of her. A feeling was released, something she had never felt before and took a moment for her to identify. Rage. It was pure unadulterated rage and it was flowing through her body like a river after a torrential downpour. This was more than anger. This was a feeling that Jane could not control. This rage had control of her and, rather than attempting to manage it, Jane gave herself into it. She had been wronged, gravely, and someone was going to pay.

TYLER TIMMERMAN

Once he had finished looking at the footage Tyler called Leisel. She answered on the second ring. Before she could ask him anything Tyler said, "The blue car has driven past my house four times since Sunday Leisel."

"What?" she said.

"Yep," said Tyler, and I think she may have followed me to Mom and Dad's on Sunday."

"No," said Leisel, "are you sure? Could you see her?"

"I'm not positive about Mom and Dad's," said Tyler, "but I saw footage of her. She walked around the park and I think, shoot, hang on" Tyler paused then said, "I need to call you back Leisel. There's someone knocking on my door. My Ring camera doesn't seem to be working."

Tyler disconnected the call and walked through the living room to the front door. He looked through the peephole and still didn't see anyone. He reached out his right hand and opened the door.

LOYAL TRUESDALE

Maynard Lily arrived just after 4:00 pm. When Loyal opened the door Maynard held up a six pack of Pacifico that he held in his right hand.

"You have time for a beer?" he asked Loyal.

Loyal opened the door wider and ushered his friend in.

"Sounds good," he said. "Want to sit in the back yard?"

Maynard set the six pack on the kitchen counter and grabbed two bottles out of it.

"Opener?" he asked.

Loyal picked one out of a kitchen drawer and handed it to Maynard. When the two bottles were open each man picked one up and Loyal led the way to the back yard. Two Adirondack chairs and a small table sat underneath a large magnolia tree. The tree was well over thirty feet tall and its large graceful branches and green leaves provided shade for the small back yard. Loyal and Maynard settled in the chairs and each took an appreciative sip of beer.

. . .

"How've you been?" asked Loyal. "We haven't really talked since I got back from New Mexico. The FBI find your man?"

Maynard shook his head. "They've connected multiple cases. The guy's a chameleon. Never looks the same. I'm the only one who ever got an actual picture of him. They found his house in New Mexico through the über he took from the hospital when he escaped but there's nothing there that leads to his actual identity."

"So he's in the wind, huh?" Loyal said. "And your money's gone with him I guess."

Maynard took a long drink of beer and nodded. "But we are doing ok." He tipped the bottle one more time, drained it, then stood. "You know Loyal, I never thought of you as a cat guy," he said with a smile. "You ready to walk me through the little guy's routine?"

It took Loyal less than ten minutes to show Maynard the food and the litter box. Boo stayed on the cat post and watched their every move with suspicious eyes. When Maynard attempted to pet him he leapt off the post and ran through the cat door into the garage.

"You might not see him when you are here," Loyal said as he walked Maynard to the door, "but I'm sure the food will be gone every time you come by."

57

PATRICK O'KEEFE

Since Pat worked with all the departments in the sheriff's office he kept a radio in his office so he could listen to emergency calls. He kept a notepad next to the radio and would jot down the time, location, and nature of the call. He felt that this habit enabled him to be ready to hit the ground running whenever any detectives asked for his help on a case. Just as he was packing up his things in preparation for going home for the day a call came in regarding a house fire. Pat picked up his pen and noted the date, time, nature of the call, and the address. This particular call involved a house on Brava Street. Pat stared at the address after he had written in down. It seemed so familiar. He opened his computer and pulled up information on the house. A chill crept over him when he saw the owner of the house. It was owned by the Timmerman family trust. Now he understood why the address seemed familiar to him. It was the address he had given to Loyal. Tyler Timmerman lived there.

. . .

Pat sat heavily in his desk chair and ran his hands over his cheeks. When he pulled his hands away from his face he noticed a slight tremor in them. He dropped them into his lap. What were the odds of Tyler Timmerman's house catching fire mere days after Pat had provided his contact information to a complete stranger. He was pulling his phone out of his pocket to call Loyal when the radio came to life. Again the call was about the house on Brava Street but this time the code was 11-44; a dead body had been found in the house.

Pat's hands were visibly shaking now as he picked up his phone and called Loyal.

"Hey Pat," said Loyal as he answered his phone.

"There's a fire at Tyler Timmerman's house," said Pat, "and they just radioed in a dead body in the house."

"What? Have they identified the body?"

"No, it's an active scene," said Pat. "Loyal, we have to tell the captain what we did."

There was a long pause as Loyal considered this. Finally he said, "I'll tell the captain what I did Pat. We leave you out of it."

"Loyal," Pat began, but Loyal cut him off.

"I did it Pat. On my own. If the body is identified as Tyler I'll come in and tell the captain everything."

"Ok," said Pat, "I'll let you know as soon as I do."

58

LOYAL TRUESDALE

Loyal disconnected the call and sat heavily on his couch. He should have never let Maggie talk him into getting involved with Jane. Perhaps he'd been swayed because he had been emotional following Bruce's memorial. Loyal knew that was just an excuse. The blame lay squarely on his shoulders if Jane had anything to do with this situation. His eyes fell on the suitcase sitting by the front door. Trinity. He couldn't leave now, not until he knew the identity of the body. If it was Tyler and foul play was involved he wouldn't be going to Bellingham for quite some time. Loyal lifted his phone and placed a call to Trinity.

They spoke for nearly half an hour. Loyal told her everything. Trinity listened carefully and asked a few pertinent questions.

"I'm pretty surprised that you offered to help this woman Loyal," she said, "it doesn't sound like something you would volunteer for."

"I'm regretting it more and more," said Loyal.

"If it is this young man's body you are going to have to speak with Captain Williams," she said.

"Yeah, I know," said Loyal, "but I want to keep Pat out of it."

He paused for a moment then said, "You could come down here."

"I'm still decompressing Loyal," she said, "I'm not up for travel."

Loyal tried to keep the disappointment out of his voice when he said, "I understand," but he heard it and was sure Trinity did as well.

"I'll only be a phone call or text away Loyal," said Trinity. "Will you keep me updated?"

"Of course," said Loyal, "and as soon as this is worked out I'll reschedule my flight.

They spoke for a few more minutes then disconnected the call. Loyal sent a quick text to Maynard letting him know that his travel plans had changed, then set his phone on the counter, picked up Boo, and sat down on the couch. The cat looked at Loyal for a moment with his bright green eyes, then yawned, turned a circle in Loyal's lap, and settled down for a nap. Loyal petted Boo's black fur absentmindedly and thought about everything he knew abut Jane. He realized after a brief moment that he knew very little. He had accepted everything that she had told him as the truth. Could it all have been lies, or an elaborate plot? Perhaps to steal money from the Timmerman family? He pictured Jane in the coffee shop. He had wondered briefly about her sincerity and state of mind. Something had seemed slightly off about her. He pictured her shaking hands. The movement had been slight but noticeable. She'd had the scar and the limp to match the story of the accident but those could have been manufactured and faked. He supposed it came down to the fact that Maggie had believed Jane. Loyal and Maggie had become good friends over the last year and a half. He trusted her and her judgement. He thought briefly about calling Maggie but decided in the end to wait for more information before contacting her.

59

TRINITY GLASS

Trinity stood in front of her refrigerator. The door was open and she was looking at the contents. The selection was small. She picked a Tupperware container off the middle shelf and opened it. It held leftover chicken thighs and roasted vegetables from three nights ago. She closed the refrigerator, dumped the contents of the Tupperware on a plate, and placed the food in the microwave. When it was heated she carried the food to the kitchen table and sat to eat. She considered opening a beer or a bottle of wine but rejected the idea. She ate the food quickly, rinsed the plate, and wandered aimlessly around the house. To get her mind off Loyal she settled on the couch in her parent's office and picked up the book she was currently reading. It was a giant novel by Anthony Doerr called Cloud Cockoo Land.

Trinity was 407 pages into the 640 page novel. She was enjoying it so much that she was actually trying to slow down when reading it. She wanted it to last.

. . .

Trinity's plan to make the novel last did not work out. She read the last word just after 2:00 in the morning. She set the book down beside her and immediately found her thoughts back with Loyal. She had been excited about seeing Loyal and was disappointed that he wouldn't be coming to Washington. She was worried abut him as well. Trinity had met Charles Timmerman once and knew he was a wealthy and powerful man who had lots of connections in the United States government. If the information Loyal had gotten for Jane had led to the death of his son, Charles Timmerman would move mountains and stop at nothing to bring Loyal down.

Trinity considered going to bed but knew that she would not sleep. She wandered around the house double checking that all the doors were locked then found herself back in the office, this time at her mother's desk. Trinity opened her laptop and looked at flights from Bellingham International to San Diego. She quickly figured out that if she drove to Seattle and flew from there to San Diego she could book a nonstop first class ticket for about $800. The drive to Seattle would take about an hour and a half. The flight left at 6:20 am and took less that three hours. She glanced at the clock. 2:37; she had the time. Trinity booked the flight and arranged for a rental car in San Diego. She took a quick shower, dried her long hair, and packed a bag. By 3:45 am she was on the road.

60

LOYAL TRUESDALE

L oyal slept fitfully, his dreams populated by burning houses and charred corpses. When he glanced again at the clock beside his bed and saw it was 3:58 he let out a long sigh and sat up in bed. He had not heard from Pat again the previous evening. He usually left his phone in the living room when he slept, but had kept it by his bedside so as not to miss a call. He picked it up now and carried it with him as he went into the kitchen and started a pot of coffee. Boo, who apparently was not having any difficulty sleeping, stayed in the bedroom.

Loyal brewed some coffee and stood at his large living room window looking out at the dark. Sunrise was still several hours away. The only light in in his house was the kitchen light. It provided enough glow that Loyal could se his reflection in the glass of the large window. He was angry and frustrated with himself. Not wanting to look at his reflection, Loyal turned off the kitchen light and returned to the window. All he could see now was blackness, which suited his mood just fine. Loyal consumed three cups of coffee and the gentle pre-dawn twilight was just becoming visible when his phone finally rang.

Loyal knew it would be Pat before he even glanced at the caller ID. It was 5:47 in the morning. There wasn't anyone else who would call so early. He took a deep breath in, let it out slowly, and accepted the call.

"Pat," he said.

"Body is pretty badly burned," said Pat, "going to have to do DNA analysis to confirm the identity." He paused a moment but when Loyal didn't respond he continued. "The ME says the body's size is consistent with Tyler Timmerman's height."

"Shit," said Loyal.

"Yep," said Pat. "We have to talk to Captain Williams Loyal."

"I have to talk to Captain Williams," Loyal said putting extra emphasis on the word I. "I told you before Pat, we need to keep you out of this."

Loyal paused then added, "Let me get Maynard on the phone. I'd like him to be with me when I speak with the captain."

"Call him soon," said Pat. "We," Pat paused, "I mean you can't wait too long on this."

61

PATRICK O'KEEFE

Pat disconnected the call with Loyal and set his phone on the kitchen table. He picked up his half full cup of coffee and drained it. He stood and set the cup quietly in the sink then returned to his bedroom. Olive was sleeping. She had lifted Ava out of the the bassinet and the two were curled up together. Pat watched them sleep for a moment. He felt bad about Loyal taking the heat on his own, but knew deep down that Loyal was right. Pat couldn't risk his career and family. With a quiet sigh he turned and went into the bathroom.

Pat showered, shaved, and dressed as quietly as he could. When he emerged from the bathroom he saw that Olive was awake. Her eyes tracked him as he crossed the room and sat down on the bed beside her.

"You hardly slept last night," she said.

"I'm sorry if I kept you up," said Pat.

"You want to talk about anything?"

Pat looked at Ava who was still sleeping peacefully.

"Do you have about fifteen minutes to spare?" he asked. "Can we talk in the kitchen?"

Olive nodded and slid quietly out of bed. She slipped on a robe, checked Ava one last time, and followed Pat to the kitchen. They each poured a cup of coffee and sat down at the kitchen table. It only took Pat a few minutes to tell Olive about the house fire, the body, and the tentative identification of the victim. He explained Jane's mysterious disappearance as well, and Loyal's insistence that Pat not reveal his involvement in locating Tyler for Jane.

Olive was quiet for several minutes as she processed everything Pat had just revealed. He waited patiently. He knew her habit of thinking things through thoroughly before expressing her thoughts. He deeply respected Olive's intelligence and opinions and never pressed her for a hurried response. Before she spoke Olive reached out and clasped Pat's hands in her own.

"I'm shocked," she said. "Do you think Jane could have done this? I can't imagine what her motivation would be to kill her brother."

Pat slowly shook his head. "I don't know Olive," he said, "I never actually met her. We ran a background check on her and she was clean."

"I think Loyal is correct about not revealing your involvement in locating her brother for her," said Olive. "It has the potential to destroy your career."

Pat nodded. "I've come to that realization as well. Loyal is going to speak to the captain today. He's bringing a lawyer with him."

"Well," Olive said, "I think that's a smart move on his part."

62

LOYAL TRUESDALE

oyal waited until 7:00 to call Maynard. To pass the time he took a long, very hot, shower and shaved. He dressed in tan slacks and a short sleeved light blue button-down shirt. Boo was awake by this point so Loyal fed him and gave him a few minutes of attention. Then he picked up his phone and placed the call. Maynard answered on the second ring saying, "Don't tell me you've changed your plans again Loyal."

"No," said Loyal, "I don't need your help feeding the cat Maynard, but I need your legal assistance."

Maynard listened while Loyal told him the entire story, starting with Bruce's memorial and ending with a burned body that was likely Tyler Timmerman.

Maynard Listened without interruption. When Loyal was finished talking Maynard said he would rearrange his morning appointments and be to Loyal's house within the hour.

"There is a lot for us to discuss Loyal," he said. "While you are waiting for me write down everything you just told me. Leave nothing out."

"I'm leaving Pat out of it Maynard," said Loyal, "there's no discussion on that."

Loyal did as Maynard had asked and wrote down everything that had happened since the memorial on Sunday. Today was Wednesday morning. Where had Jane been for the past two days, he wondered. He picked up his phone and called her number again. This time it went straight to voicemail. Loyal did not leave a message. He considered, again, calling Maggie but decided to wait until his meeting with the captain was finished. With nothing else to do Loyal picked up Boo and sat down on the couch to wait for Maynard.

Maynard arrived at 7:45. He sat down at the kitchen table and motioned for Loyal to sit next to him.

"I'm recommending against speaking with your captain Loyal," he said. "There are strong federal and state laws against hacking someone's information. The Computer Fraud and Abuse Act is Federal anti-hacking legislation. Accessing a computer and obtaining information without permission can get you 1-5 years in prison."

"I had permission," said Loyal.

"Yes," said Maynard, "from one party. You had Jane's permission, but not Tyler's." Maynard paused and looked directly in Loyal's eyes. "At the very least it's a civil violation that could lead to a civil lawsuit."

Loyal stood and walked to the large living room window. He was quiet for a moment while he thought this information through. Eventually he turned back to face Maynard.

·　·　·

"This information is important Maynard," he said. "The department needs to know."

"It's only illegal to withhold evidence if you are actively being questioned by the authorities Loyal, said Maynard. "You don't have to come forward with what you know."

"Pat knows too," said Loyal, "and I need to keep him far away from this. If I don't speak up he will."

Maynard stood, let out a long sigh, and joined Loyal at the window.

"This is going to be a very high profile case. You could lose everything in a civil lawsuit. And a criminal trial is a very real possibility. The Timmerman family is connected to the government at high levels. If this is murder they are going to push hard."

Loyal ran his hands through his hair.

"I need to talk to Pat," he said. "I'll see if I can buy myself 24 hours to try and find Jane on my own. After that I'm going in and I would sure appreciate it if you were there with me."

63

PATRICK O'KEEFE

Pat settled himself behind his desk and opened his computer. He read and answered a few emails, but his attention was elsewhere. He had two things on his mind. The first was, obviously, Tyler Timmerman. The second was Miles and Hope Bannon. He decided to focus on the thing that he could control. He pulled out the bankers box containing the Bannon's electronics and removed the computer that was labeled as belonging to Miles. The warrant covered email accounts and Miles' provider had supplied email addresses and passwords for both Hope and Miles. Pat logged in and was just starting to read when his phone pinged. The text, short and to the point, was from Loyal.

We need to talk in person

Pat responded in the affirmative and asked Loyal where he was at the moment.

. . .

Home

Pat replied that he would be there in twenty minutes. He closed Miles' computer and his own, grabbed his keys, and left his office.

Pat pulled into Loyal's driveway just past 8:30. Loyal had the door open before Pat was even out of his car. He and Maynard Lily approached the driver's side of the car as Pat slid out. There was an awkward silence as the three men stood in the driveway and then Maynard spoke.

"I've advised Loyal not to speak with Captain Williams," he said.

Pat looked at Loyal. "You have to tell him what you know Loyal," he said, "it's important to the investigation."

"I know Pat," said Loyal, "and I will talk with him but I need a day or two to see if I can find Jane."

"You are asking me to sit on this information?"

"Just for a day or two," said Loyal.

Pat was quiet as he digested Loyal's words.

"There are serious legal ramifications here," said Maynard. "If Loyal can bring Jane in it would be very helpful."

Pat felt anger boiling up inside him.

"Damn it Loyal," he said, "why do you keep involving me in your craziness?"

"Olive asked you to do it," said Loyal.

Pat put his face close to Loyal's. "Don't even suggest that this is her fault, Loyal," he said. His voice was tight and low. "You came to the house that day to ask me to do it. Don't try to pretend any different."

Loyal held his hands up in a placating manner.

"You're right Pat," he said, "I shouldn't have brought Olive into this. Or you. If you can just give me a few days to find Jane I think I can make everything right."

Pat looked at Loyal for a long minute.

"I used to really look up to you," he said. "You know that? But you've gotten me mixed up in so much bull shit these past two years."

Pat looked at the ground then back at Loyal.

"Two days," he said, "after that I'm going to the captain if you don't."

64

TRINITY GLASS

T rinity's plane touched down just after 9:00 am. Since she was flying in first class she was one of the first people to deplane. By 9:30 she had retrieved her checked bag, secured her rental car, a dark blue Toyota 4Runner, and was on interstate 5 heading north towards Carlsbad. She hadn't contacted Loyal. She had never been to his new home but he had sent her the address when he had purchased it. She plugged that into her phone now and navigated towards his home in Carlsbad.

During the flight Trinity had researched state and federal laws regarding Loyal's actions. The results were unnerving. The DA in San Diego County was aggressive in her prosecutions regarding privacy online. Civil suits were common as well and often resulted in large judgements. Trinity had also researched Charles Timmerman. Once she saw his photograph she recalled that she had met him quite a few years ago at an official event in Virginia. She remembered that he had been quite tall and stern looking. They had been introduced by Trinity's boss, Doug Caldwell. They had spoken for less than five minutes, but Trinity remembered thinking that his personality did not match his appearance. He had seemed almost gentle.

Trinity flinched when the computerized voice from Google maps interrupted her thoughts, reminding her to exit Interstate 5 in one mile. She pushed the thoughts of prosecutions, civil cases, and Charles Timmerman from her mind and followed the prompts until she was parked at the curb outside of Loyal's house. She sat quietly for a moment taking in the house, the small lawn and the large living room window. The house was small, but neatly kept and just two blocks from the beach. Loyal's truck was parked in the driveway.

Trinity slid out of her rental then reached in and pulled her bags out as well. She felt butterflies in her stomach as she approached the front door. Usually overflowing with confidence, she was surprised to find herself feeling oddly vulnerable and uncertain about her decision to arrive unannounced. She rang the bell and the twenty seconds it took for the door to be opened felt like minutes. Then the door was open and Loyal was standing there looking at her. She saw as his face registered first shock, then secondly pure joy. Neither of them said a word. When Loyal opened his arms Trinity dropped her bags and fell into them.

An hour later, freshly showered and holding hands, Trinity and Loyal walked the two blocks to the beach. They climbed an empty lifeguard tower and sat, side by side, with their backs against the wall and facing the ocean. The sky was free of clouds, the temperature in the low 70's, and a gentle breeze caressed their skin. Loyal reached out and clasped Trinity's hand in his again.

"I still can't believe you are here," he said.

Trinity turned so she was facing him.

"I've really missed you," she said. "When you called and said you couldn't come to see me I just decided to come see you." She paused then added, "Maybe I can help with your situation."

Loyal's hand gently traced the scar on Trinity's forehead.

"I'm so sorry about this," he said.

Trinity reached up and brought his hand down to her side.

"It will heal Loyal," she said, "it just takes time." She took a slow breath in and let it out. "We need to talk about this mess you are involved in Loyal," she said. "I did some research on the flight and you could be prosecuted and face a civil suit as well."

"I spoke with Maynard this morning," said Loyal. "He has advised me not to tell the captain what I know."

"Sound advice," said Trinity, "but something tells me you aren't going to take it."

"The most important thing to me is to keep Pat out of this," said Loyal. "I spoke to him this morning as well. He's willing to give me two days to find Jane before he goes to the captain."

"Ok," said Trinity, "then let's find Jane."

Loyal pulled his phone out of his pocket.

"We ran a background check on her before we moved

forward with locating Tyler." He tapped a few buttons on his phone. "It included her address. I know it's here somewhere."

While Loyal was searching his phone Trinity pulled her own phone out intending to conduct some searches herself. As she raised it the phone rang. Caller ID indicated Doug Caldwell.

"Glass," said Trinity as she accepted the call.

"Where are you Glass?" Caldwell said. "I'm at your house. How soon can you get back here?"

"My house in Bellingham?" Trinity asked.

"You have another one I don't know about? How soon can you be here?"

"Not soon at all," said Trinity, "I'm in Carlsbad."

"California?"

"I am on vacation Doug," said Trinity, "I have the right to travel if I choose to."

Caldwell let out a long sigh.

"I need to talk to you Glass," he said, "privately, with no chance someone can listen in."

He paused for a moment then said, "How soon can you get to the Carlsbad FBI office?"

"Forty minutes," said Trinity.

"I'll head to the Bellingham satellite office," said Caldwell. "We can use their SCIFs. I'll call in forty minutes. Be there."

He disconnected without saying goodbye.

65

TRINITY GLASS

Trinity returned her phone to her pocket and turned to see Loyal looking at her.

"Everything ok?" he asked.

"Caldwell wants to talk to me on an encrypted line," she said. I need to be to the Carlsbad FBI office in forty minutes to use their SCIF."

"SCIF?" said Loyal as they made their way down the ladder and across the sand.

"It's an acronym," said Trinity, "it stands for Sensitive Compartmented Information Facility. It's a special room that is very secure and is used to prevent intrusion or surveillance. We have them all over the country. Some are permanent and others are mobile and temporary."

Loyal nodded. "I know what they are," he said, "just wasn't aware of the acronym. What's up with Caldwell?"

"I have no idea," said Trinity, "he wants to speak on a secure line. He showed up at my house in Bellingham unannounced though, so it must be something big. He's never done that before."

. . .

They reached Loyal's house in less than ten minutes. Trinity took ten more minutes to change into a suit and put her long hair in a bun.

"You brought a suit on vacation?" Loyal said when she emerged from the bedroom.

"I always have one suit," said Trinity. "This isn't the first time Caldwell has interrupted a vacation."

"How about I drive you over there? asked Loyal. "I'll wait in the car. I can use the time to make some calls. See if I can get a line on Jane."

Trinity shook her head. "I'll drive myself. I have no idea how long I'll be. Why don't you head out to Jane's house? I'll call when I know what's going on with Caldwell."

Loyal nodded. "Sounds good."

He wrapped his arms around her and held her tightly for a long moment, then leaned down and kissed her. They each gathered up their phones and keys and headed out the door.

Trinity arrived at the FBI office with only three minutes to spare. They were expecting her and, after examining her ID, a female agent led her to the SCIF. The room was fairly large. Trinity counted 10 workstations with phone lines and electrical outlets. Each station was numbered. The agent led her to station number 7, plugged in a phone, and left the room. The door closed with a quiet but firm thud. Less than thirty seconds after the door closed the phone rang. Trinity picked it up and said "Glass."

66

LOYAL TRUESDALE

Loyal Google mapped Jane's address and headed east towards Escondido on Highway 78. He exited on Center City Parkway heading south and took Second Avenue east through Escondido until it intersected with Grand Avenue. He turned right on Ash, then left on Oak Hill. Jane's house was on Highland Street, a short residential street very near a local elementary school. He took a right on Linwood Street, a left on Kingston Drive, and a final right turn on to Highland Street. He located Jane's house about halfway down the street on the right. The absence of traffic made a u-turn possible. Loyal pulled in along the curb across the street from her house and parked. He turned off the engine and spent several minutes studying Jane's house and the surrounding neighborhood. There was no car in her driveway. The neighborhood was almost eerily quiet. Loyal glanced at his phone. It was one o'clock in the afternoon on a Wednesday and the street was deserted. Loyal was well aware that neighbors were likely inside their homes and potentially looking out their windows.

Additionally, technology like security cameras and Ring door-
bells nearly assured that he would, at the very least, be
captured on film approaching Jane's house.

Loyal checked his phone to make sure he hadn't missed a text
or call from Trinity then slid out of his truck and crossed the
street. Jane's house was tan with white trim. The blinds were
closed in all the windows that faced the street. There was a
small lawn in front of the house. A giant magnolia tree rose
from the center of the lawn. Loyal knew from his own magnolia
tree that the smell would be delightful when the massive tree
bloomed in early summer. Magnolias were his favorite tree
and, although he was not a superstitious man, he decided the
fact that Jane had such an amazing one in her front yard could
be taken as a good omen. He walked up the three steps to the
small front porch and rang the doorbell. He could hear the
chime sounding inside the house. Loyal waited a full minute
then rang the bell again. When Jane failed to appear he raised
his hand and knocked loudly. There was no response from
inside the house.

Loyal stepped off the porch and returned to the driveway. Jane's
garage doors were the type with windows along the top. He
approached, raised himself up on his tip toes, and peeked
inside. Although the interior was dark, Loyal could just make
out the shape of a light colored vehicle in the garage. When he
had met Jane for coffee she had parked around the corner from
the shop so Loyal didn't know what type of car she drove. Logic
suggested that the car inside the garage was indeed Jane's.

Loyal lowered himself back onto flat feet and turned around to find an elderly man standing about two feet away from him. He was about 5'6" and was wearing baggy jeans that were held up by bright red suspenders. His T-shirt was white and had stains from some type of food running down the front of it. The man's hair was pure white and fluffy. At first glance he reminded Loyal of a dandelion. He held a cane in one hand and a phone in the other.

"Do I need to call the cops?" he said.

Loyal held his hands up in front of himself.

"No," he said, "no need to do that. I'm just looking for Jane."

"What do you want with Jane?" the man asked.

"We were supposed to meet for lunch," said Loyal. "She didn't show up so I was just checking to make sure she was ok."

The man still held his phone out in front of him ready to make a call but Loyal saw his posture relax just slightly.

"We had coffee on Sunday," said Loyal, "and were supposed to have lunch today. Have you seen her?"

"Maybe she didn't have as much fun at coffee as you thought," said the man with a small smile.

Loyal smiled back and tried to arrange his facial features in a sheepish fashion.

"Maybe not," he said.

"Last I saw her was yesterday evening," said the man. "I think it's time for you to move along now," he added. "If I see her I'll tell her you were looking for her."

Loyal thanked the man and crossed the street to his truck. He slid in and drove away without turning his head to look back at the man. He could see him when he looked in the rear view mirror though, standing in Jane's driveway watching Loyal drive away. Loyal drove back across Escondido to the In-N-Out on East Valley Parkway. He hadn't eaten anything all day and realized he was starving. He drove through the drive through then parked in a parking lot just to the east of the restaurant and settled down to eat and wait for Trinity's call.

67

TRINITY GLASS

rinity exited the SCIF thirty-eight minutes after she entered it. She thanked the agent who had escorted her to the secure room and made her way out to her car. She slid in and closed the door but did not start the engine. Her mind was spinning. Caldwell had informed her that she was to investigate the fire at Tyler Timmerman's house and also his cause of death. He had requested an expedited autopsy but wasn't sure when it would actually happen. If the body was identified as Tyler, which Caldwell had no doubts about, and the cause of death was homicide it could be disastrous from a national security point of view. While Tyler's job was officially with the Timmerman Foundation, he had deep knowledge about his father's projects and contracts with the DHS. The possibility that he had been tortured for information was very real. Caldwell had informed Charles Timmerman that he was assigning Trinity to the case and he had instructed Trinity to proceed to the Timmerman family home in Olivenhain immediately upon completion of their call.

. . .

Trinity sat in the 4Runner for a full five minutes processing everything they had discussed. This was the first time in her career that Trinity had withheld pertinent information from her boss. She had said nothing about what Loyal had done for Jane. She had been grateful that it was a phone call with Caldwell rather than a face to face. He knew her so well he would have known something was off. She wanted Loyal to have the two days to find Jane. Thinking about the fact that Loyal's first day was almost half over spurred her into action. She finally started the ignition and drove out of the parking lot. She had already put the Timmerman address on Lone Jack Road into her phone and the automated voice began directing her to their house. When she was within a few miles of the house she began looking for a place to pull over and call Loyal. She noticed a small sign for an equestrian park and quickly pulled into the dirt parking lot. Leaving the engine running she placed a call to Loyal.

"Trinity," he said as he answered the call.

"I only have a minute," she said. "Caldwell has assigned me to investigate Tyler Timmerman's death. I'm representing the government and the family's interests now."

"We can still work together Trinity," said Loyal, "we are working toward the same goal."

"That's not necessarily true anymore Loyal," Trinity said. The words were painful for her to say. "There's a huge conflict of interest for me now. I'm in a bad position."

She paused and when Loyal didn't say anything she continued on saying, "I didn't tell Caldwell anything about your situation Loyal. I think you deserve the two days. I'm on my way to the Timmerman's house now. Did you find Jane?"

"No," said Loyal. "I need to get into her house but she has one hell of a nosy neighbor."

Trinity was quiet for a moment then she said, "Let's meet back at your house in two hours. We'll figure out a plan. I'd like to help clear Jane and get you as far away from all this as possible. I think there is something much bigger in play than Jane Gray."

68

LOYAL TRUESDALE

L oyal disconnected the call and set his phone on the passenger seat. He finished his burger and the last of his fries and washed them down with lemonade. He placed all the trash in the bag and set it down in the passenger footwell then picked up his phone and called Maggie.

"This is Maggie," she said when she answered.

"Hey Maggie," said Loyal. "How's the knee?"

"About the same," said Maggie. "How are you?"

"I'm good," said Loyal. "Hey, I was wondering if you have had any contact from Jane yet?"

"Nope," said Maggie. "I left a few messages for her but now her phone goes straight to voicemail. I guess that means you haven't found her yet either?"

"No, I haven't," said Loyal, "and frankly I'm getting a little concerned."

"Yeah, me too," said Maggie. "I'll call you immediately if I hear from her."

"Thanks Maggie," said Loyal. "I'll do the same."

· · ·

With the call to Maggie out of the way Loyal realized he really didn't have any other avenues to follow in his search for Jane. If he parked near her house the nosy old man would undoubtedly call the police. He had no idea who any of her friends were. He knew where she worked but also knew that she had taken the entire week off of work. He pulled up her background check on his phone again. Under the section for relatives and acquaintances their were only two names; her father and grandmother were listed. How could no one else be associated with Jane, Loyal wondered. It made no sense. She had to have some friends. He scrolled down to the employment section and found a copy of her application to work at the physical therapy office. Under the reference section there was only one name listed, Eden Jackson. Loyal dialed the number listed and the call went straight to voicemail. He left a brief message explaining who he was, his contact information, and that he was trying to get in touch with Jane Gray. Unable to think of anything else to try at the moment, Loyal started his truck and headed west towards his home.

69

CHARLES TIMMERMAN

C harles and Leisel were sitting silently in the living room of the Timmerman family home. Charles had just hung up from a phone call with Douglas Caldwell and he was waiting for the arrival of an OSI agent Caldwell had assigned to the case. Caldwell had assured Charles that Agent Glass was one of his best. While he waited Charles reviewed his conversation with their family doctor earlier in the day. Dr. Cole had been kind enough to make a house call. Daisy had become hysterical upon receiving the news about Tyler. Dr. Cole had injected her with a sedative and she was asleep in their bedroom at the moment. As they had walked to the front door Dr. Cole had turned to Charles and said, "This will help her in the short term Charles, but Daisy is going to need some serious help coming to terms with what has happened. I can't keep her sedated forever."

Charles stood and walked to the bedroom he shared with his wife. She was asleep in the middle of their king sized bed. She looked so small and childlike. Charles approached the bed and looked down at Daisy. Her face was drawn and pinched even while she was in the drug induced slumber. A wave of emotion swept over Charles as he gazed at her. He had spent the majority of his life protecting Daisy but even he, with his vast resources and connections, couldn't protect her from the aftermath of the death of their son.

The sound of the doorbell brought Charles out if his thoughts. He strode quickly through the house and opened the front door. Charles felt a brief moment of surprise that the agent was a woman. Caldwell hadn't specified on the phone and Charles had simply assumed the agent would be a man. Agent Glass looked competent and was surprisingly attractive. She held out her hand to him.

"Hello Mr. Timmerman," she said, "I'm Agent Glass. Agent Caldwell has assigned me to your son's case."

Charles shook her hand and stepped to the side.

"Please come in Agent Glass," he said.

He led her to the living room and introduced her to Leisel who stood and shook her hand as well. Charles motioned towards the couch and all three sat down.

"I'm terribly sorry for your loss," said Agent Glass, "and I'm sorry to intrude during this devastating time. I spoke with Agent Caldwell on a secure line and he filled me in on the basics. I came straight here after our conversation. He's messaging me all the official reports that have been generated so far. I'll have them tonight."

Charles nodded. "Have we met before Agent Glass?"

She nodded. "Yes Mr. Timmerman," she said, "some years ago at an event in Virginia. We spoke briefly."

"I remember you," he said. "You've risen in the ranks since then. And please," he added, "call me Charles."

"Yes sir, I have," said Agent Glass, "and feel free to call me Trinity."

"I'd like to ask you a few questions if I may," said Trinity.

Charles nodded his assent.

"Do you know of any enemies Tyler or your family may have? Any individual or group with a grudge?"

"My type of business has its inherent dangers," Charles said, "it comes with the territory." He paused a moment. "I just don't see how someone could get to Tyler though. He has every type of smart device available including security."

Leisel's hand went to her mouth and she let out a small gasp.

"I was on the phone with him Dad," she said. "Someone knocked on his door and he said he had to go see who it was because his Ring doorbell camera wasn't functioning properly."

"I'm going to need all that footage," said Trinity.

"I'll call the company right away," said Charles.

"Footage from any security cameras he had," said Trinity, "everything from the past ten days."

"Done," said Charles.

70

TRINITY GLASS

Trinity was opening her mouth to ask another question when the front door slammed open.

"Tyler? Tyler are you here?" a female voice called out.

"Jolene," said Leisel and a moment later a small athletic blond woman in a wetsuit ran into the living room. She stopped when she saw Charles, Leisel, and Trinity sitting on the couches. Her face was streaked with tears.

"Is Tyler here?" she said frantically. "We were supposed to surf today. He didn't show up so I went to his house. It's burned down and there's crime scene tape around it." She looked from face to face waiting for some sort of reassurance. Of course none came. Charles rose and walked to Jolene. He put his arm around her shoulders and guided her towards the couch he had been sitting on. He eased her down gently and sat beside her, then turned and took her hands in his. Jolene began crying silently as he explained what had happened.

"I hired a private investigator," he gestured towards Trinity, "to figure out what happened."

. . .

Trinity was surprised and impressed with the gentle way that Charles dealt with Jolene. His kindness was endearing and unexpected during this tragic time. She gave a small cough and everyone's eyes returned to her.

"I'd like to talk with each of you privately," she said. Her eyes returned to Charles. "Do you have a private space where I can conduct the interviews?"

Charles nodded.

"Good," said Trinity as she rose from the couch, "why don't you show me and we can start with you."

Trinity and Charles spent nearly half an hour in his study. When they emerged she had a good working knowledge about the nature of his business and he had a list of assignments to complete. She had asked about interviewing his wife and he had explained that she was under a doctor's care and would be unable to sit for an interview at this time. He added that Daisy was completely removed from his business with the exception of attending fundraisers and galas occasionally. He didn't think she would have anything to add.

Trinity returned to the living room to find Leisel alone.

"She left," Leisel said in response to the question in Trinity's eyes. "I can give you her contact information if you want to talk to her."

"I'd appreciate that," said Trinity.

"She's an idiot anyways," said Leisel, "I doubt she could tell you anything helpful."

Trinity shrugged, "You'd be surprised," she said. "Can I speak with you then Leisel?"

Leisel rose from the couch and followed Trinity to the study. They sat side by side on a large leather couch, knees angled toward each other.

Leisel walked Trinity through her and Tyler's duties at the foundation. She gave Trinity contact information for Jolene and several of Tyler's closest friends.

When the interview appeared to be wrapping up Leisel said, "I do have one more thing to tell you. I don't know if it has any relationship to my brother's death. It could just be a coincidence."

Trinity pulled out the pad of paper she had been taking notes on and looked at Leisel.

"Everything is important in an investigation," she said.

"My brother did a DNA test in January," said Leisel. "He was contacted by someone who said they were his full sibling. A sister supposedly."

Trinity felt a jolt of adrenaline flow through her but remained outwardly calm.

"Did he contact her?" she asked.

Leisel shook her head. "No. In fact we had two pretty big arguments about it. I thought it was a scam. Then he brought up DNA testing at Sunday dinner and my dad went ballistic. Told Tyler if he did a DNA test he'd be kicked out of the family. So Tyler cancelled his account and my dad never found out he actually took the test."

"Did he show you the messages from the person claiming to be the sister?"

Leisel nodded again. "He did. Her name is Jane Gray. She claims to live in Escondido. She sent a picture too. It looked so much like Tyler I thought it was photoshopped."

"You never know what's real anymore," said Trinity. "I'll definitely look into it."

Trinity stood and held out her hand. The women shook hands and Trinity thanked Leisel for her time and, once again, expressed her sorrow for Leisel's family's loss. Leisel walked Trinity to the door. Promising to be in touch soon, Trinity turned and walked to her car.

71

LOYAL TRUESDALE

Loyal pulled into his driveway just after 3:00 pm. He didn't exit his truck immediately after turning off the engine. Instead he sat and thought about what he had accomplished so far, or rather, what he had not accomplished. He was well into day number one of his two day reprieve from Pat and he knew as much now as he had when the day started. He thought about Trinity's news as well. Charles Timmerman was a big deal in the US government. It made sense that Trinity, an agent with the Office of Strategic Investigations, would be assigned to his son's apparent murder. Could the murder have happened because of something Tyler knew about his Dad's business dealings, he wondered. That actually made more sense than Jane killing her brother. He wondered if Trinity would even be able to tell him anything about what she learned at the Timmerman house that day.

Loyal slid out of the truck and entered his house. The sight of Trinity's luggage brought a welcome smile to his face. He said hello to Boo then walked into the kitchen. One look in the fridge and he knew he was going to be leaving again. Some grocery shopping was necessary if he was going to have a house guest. He didn't know how long Trinity was going to be staying. He hoped it would be for a good amount of time. He pulled a piece of paper and a pen out of a kitchen drawer and made a list. Not wanting to interrupt Trinity with a phone call he instead wrote a quick note in case she returned before him. Then he picked up his keys and headed back out to his truck.

72

PATRICK O'KEEFE

P at sat at his desk in the Sheriff's Station. His computer was open in front of him but his focus was elsewhere. All he could think about was the Tyler Timmerman situation and the role he himself had played in getting the information for Jane. This could be a career breaker for him if his involvement was exposed. At 3:30 Pat gave up trying and called it a day. When he walked in the front door Olive looked up from the living room floor where she was building blocks with the kids.

"You're home early," she said, "you okay?"

Pat tried for a genuine smile but from Olive's concerned expression he could tell he had missed the mark.

"Can you put a movie on for the kids?" he asked, "I need to talk to you."

Once Olive had the kids settled in front of the tv she joined Pat in the kitchen.

"What's going on Pat?"

"Loyal's lawyer has advised him not to go to the captain. It isn't illegal to keep information to yourself if you aren't actually being questioned about it officially."

"Okay," said Olive.

"Loyal asked me to give him two days to find Jane before he goes to the captain. There are some pretty serious state and federal privacy laws that prohibit what I did. Possible prosecution and civil lawsuits."

"I can understand him not wanting to go to the captain then," said Olive. "If he finds Jane maybe he can clear her involvement and then not have to say anything."

"I told him if he doesn't go to the captain after two days then I will," said Pat.

"No way Pat," said Olive. Her voice was loud and she lowered it when she continued speaking. "You don't say a word about finding that information. You want us to lose everything?"

"You are the one who suggested that I do it," said Pat.

"I didn't know it was illegal Pat," Olive said. "You're the police officer."

"Oh, so you're throwing it back on me then? I wasn't going to do it until you put pressure on me."

By the look on Olive's face Pat could see that his words had struck a nerve. Olive was angrier than he had ever seen her.

"Actually Pat," Olive said, "I'm throwing it back on Loyal. If he wouldn't have come here we wouldn't even be having this conversation."

"Yeah," said Pat, "I guess this time Loyal tricked you...not me."

Pat's last comment was the final straw. Olive turned and walked out of the kitchen without another word. Pat sank into a kitchen chair, exhaustion surrounding him like a heavy fog. He hated fighting with Olive and regretted saying much the same thing that Loyal had said that morning. Loyal had tried to shift the blame to Olive and Pat had been furious. And yet, just a few hours later Pat had tried to use the exact same argument. In his heart he knew none of this was really Olive's fault. The blame lay squarely on Loyal's shoulders and, if he was being totally honest, on his own shoulders as well.

73

LOYAL TRUESDALE

Loyal arrived home before Trinity. He had finished putting the groceries away and was in the process of putting a bottle of wine and some beers on ice when he heard the front door open. Trinity came into the kitchen and wrapped her arms around him. She gave him a long kiss then leaned back so she could look him in the eyes.

"I have very good news for you," she said.

"I'll take any good news I can get," said Loyal.

"Tyler told his sister Leisel about Jane Gray. I interviewed her today and she told me the whole story. You are off the hook Loyal. I have the information now, from a different source. You and Pat don't have to admit your involvement."

"Thank God," said Loyal.

"I tracked her phone. Its in the house Loyal. I went to Captain Williams and requested a warrant to search her home. He'll call as soon as he has it signed."

"I can't believe this," said Loyal, "I need to call Pat right away."

"I looked for him when I was at the station but he wasn't there."

Loyal picked up his phone and tapped Pat's name. It rang four times before Pat answered.

"What now?" he said. His voice was heavy and cold. Loyal could hear the anger in it.

"I have good news Pat," he said. "Tyler told his sister about Jane. The captain has the information now. We are in the clear."

"I could have used that news about an hour ago," said Pat.

"I just found out," said Loyal. "Trinity got assigned to the case and she just got back from interviewing the family. The captain is working on a warrant for Jane's house."

Pat let out a long sigh.

"I told Olive I was going to the captain if you didn't," he said. "We had a huge fight. She's madder than I've ever seen her."

"I'm sorry Pat," said Loyal, "you want me to talk to her?"

"I think that's the worst idea you've ever had," said Pat, "and you've had plenty in the last few years. I don't know if you will ever be welcomed into our house again Loyal." He paused then added, "Hell, I'm barely welcome here right now."

Loyal apologized again and they ended the call. He told Trinity what Pat had said.

"I can't blame them for being angry Loyal," she said, "it wasn't one of your best ideas."

Trinity was smiling while she said the words and Loyal knew she didn't mean them unkindly. He knew his judgement had been poor and he felt awful about the situation Pat was facing at his house.

"Will you keep looking for Jane?" Trinity asked.

"Would it help you?"

Trinity nodded. "Then I could concentrate on other aspects of the case." She paused as she approached him. "I'll read you in on what I can but some things are going to be confidential."

Loyal nodded.

"Are you ok with me getting a temporary mobile SCIF for your backyard?" she asked. "Or I can stay somewhere else?"

"Stay here," said Loyal, "get whatever you need."

74

TRINITY GLASS

T rinity nodded, picked up her phone, and placed a call to Caldwell.

"I need a mobile SCIF delivered. She recited Loyal's address on Los Robles Street."

"That's a house," said Caldwell. "AirBnB?"

"I'm staying with Loyal."

"No way," said Caldwell, "I'll arrange something else for you."

"You and I both know another agent could have handled this for you," said Trinity, anger creeping into her voice. "You brought me in because of my connections in the Carlsbad Sheriff's Department. I'm staying where I please and that's with Loyal." Trinity's voice was tight and cracking. "So get me the damn SCIF so I can do my job."

There was silence on the line and Trinity wondered if perhaps she had pushed too far. When Caldwell finally spoke his voice was as hard and angry as Trinity's.

"He's not to be read into anything Glass," he said.

"I'm a better agent than that."

"The SCIF will be there by the morning," said Caldwell. He disconnected without so much as a goodbye.

Trinity set her phone on the kitchen counter and turned to face Loyal.

"The SCIF will be here in the morning," she said.

Loyal nodded.

"Do you have a side gate to the back yard?" asked Trinity.

Loyal nodded again.

"From your side of that conversation it sounded like Caldwell doesn't want you staying with me," he said.

Trinity let out a long breath.

"I don't really care what he wants Loyal," she said.

"Yeah, I got that. I've never heard you speak to him that way."

"I never really have," said Trinity. She paused then added, "I'm not apologizing."

Loyal held his hands up in front of his body. "I wasn't suggesting that you should," he said. He walked toward Trinity and opened his arms. She closed the distance between them and leaned up against his chest. He closed his arms around her and lay his chin on her head.

"You guys will work it out," he said. "I did some grocery shopping today. Let's have some food and wait for the warrant for Jane's house to come through."

Trinity pulled away and looked up at him. "That sounds good," she said. "I stressed the urgency to Captain Williams. It should be signed soon."

Loyal scrambled some eggs and toasted two slices of sourdough bread. The opted to drink sparkling water rather than the beer or wine. They were just clearing the dishes when Trinity's phone pinged indicating a text message. She read the message and turned to Loyal.

"The SCIF is a 7' by 10' portable unit. It will be here between 7:00 and 9:00 tomorrow. They'll use a tractor to get it into the backyard. Is your gate wide enough for that?"

"I think so," said Loyal. "I have a tape measure in the garage. I'll measure the space."

As he turned toward the door leading to the garage Trinity's phone rang.

"Hold up Loyal," she said, "it's the Sheriff's Department."

"Glass," said Trinity as she answered the phone.

"Agent Glass it's Detective Hammond. We have the signed search warrant for Jane Gray's residence. You ready to go?"

"Absolutely," said Trinity.

"I've got a team at the station," said Hammond, "how soon can you get here?"

"Twenty minutes," said Trinity.

She disconnected the call and turned to Loyal.

"Warrant's ready," she said, "let's go."

75

LOYAL TRUESDALE

Loyal and Trinity walked into the Sheriff's Department eighteen minutes later. Both were dressed in blue jeans and dark jackets. Trinity's jacket had OSI emblazoned on the right side of her chest in bright yellow and the agency's symbol on the left side. Hammond and three other officers were waiting in the lobby. Hammond's eyes widened when he saw Loyal walk in with Trinity.

"What's he doing here?" said Hammond pointing a finger at Loyal.

"He's on my team," Trinity responded, "he's coming."

Hammond looked directly at Loyal.

"Don't touch anything," he said. "Anything needs to be moved or removed from the house it's done by Agent Glass or myself."

Loyal shrugged his shoulders and said, "It's your guy's show. Did you contact Escondido PD?"

Hammond turned away without answering. Loyal was positive Hammond had contacted the Escondido department. He didn't have to. He could execute a warrant anywhere in California. Contacting the department was more of a practical matter in case any neighbors called 911.

Loyal and Trinity rode together in her car. Hammond and the other officers took a cruiser. Trinity followed Hammond to Escondido. Hammond pulled into Jane's driveway and Trinity pulled to the curb in front of the house. It was 6:45 and the sun had long since gone down. Street lights illuminated portions of the street; the neighborhood was quiet and still. Jane's house was dark. Hammond and the three officers approached the door. Hammond rang the bell then knocked loudly. He identified himself as a police officer then knocked again. When no one answered Hammond waved one of the officers forward. He held a kinetic breaching tool in his hands. This tool was new to the department. Loyal had heard of them but had never seen one in action. The breaching tool looked to be about three feet long and, judging by the ease with which the officer handled it, wasn't very heavy. The officer placed the front end of the tool against the door next to the lock. When he pulled the trigger a .45 caliber blank was fired in the chamber. This released 850 ft/lb of pressure which forced a hardened steel ram out the front of the tool. It destroyed the lock without breaking the door completely. The officer fired a second blank at the deadbolt then pushed the door open.

Just as they were about to enter the house a voice came from behind Loyal and Trinity. They turned and Loyal saw the same old man he had seen earlier in the day.

"What's going on here?" the man said.

"Search warrant," said Trinity, "back off."

The old man pointed a shaky finger at Loyal.

"You're the guy who was here earlier looking for Jane," he said.

"I'm not going to tell you again," said Trinity, "back off."

The old man stared at Loyal for a long moment then turned and headed back toward his house. Loyal and Trinity turned back to Jane's house and saw Hammond standing on the front porch looking at them. The three officers had entered the house to clear it.

"You were here earlier?" Hammond said. "Why?"

Loyal shrugged. "I was seeing if she was home."

"You aren't active duty anymore Truesdale," said Hammond.

They could hear calls of "clear" coming from inside the house.

"He's working with me," said Trinity.

"He's not an agent," said Hammond. "You can be sure I'm bringing it up with Captain Williams tomorrow."

"Feel free," said Trinity as she pushed past Hammond and, gun raised, entered Jane's house.

Loyal moved to push past the detective as well but Hammond grabbed his upper arm and pulled Loyal close.

"This is bull shit Truesdale," he said. "Something's up with you. This is my homicide. I might be forced to work with Glass but you can be damned sure I'm not working with you."

Loyal smiled. "You gonna tase me again Hammond? Break a few ribs so I'm out of commission?" Loyal laughed as he pulled his arm from Hammond's grip. "We both know you're going to leave me alone."

76

LOYAL TRUESDALE

oyal entered Jane's house and paused for a moment. His thoughts went back to the previous spring. Loyal's personal trainer had been brutally murdered and Loyal had been working the case privately. Hammond hadn't liked his involvement and had tasered him as he was exiting his car one night. While Loyal was down Hammond had delivered some hard kicks that had broken several of Loyal's ribs. Loyal had motion detecting security cameras and the entire event was captured on film. Loyal had given a copy of the video to Hammond. If the video ever made its way to Captain William's computer Hammond would be in deep trouble.

Loyal blinked and brought himself back to the present. He looked around the interior of Jane's house. It was was neat and tidy. There was a small living room, a dining room and a kitchen to the right. A door opened from the kitchen into what Loyal assumed was the garage. To the left was a hallway with doors opening to the left and right and a bathroom at the end of the hall. Trinity emerged from one of the doors on the right side of the hallway. She had a strange look on her face that Loyal wasn't sure how to read.

"You need to see this," she said.

Loyal followed her into the room and stopped. It was clear the room was an office. An L shaped desk sat in front of the one window in the room. A bookcase occupied the space to the left of the desk. It was the wall to the right of the desk that stopped Loyal in his tracks. It was covered with printed papers, a picture of the Timmerman family, and several pictures of both Leisel and Tyler Timmerman that had been printed from the computer. As he moved closer he saw pictures taken with an actual camera and printed as well. They had been taken at the beach and were of Tyler and a blond woman.

"His girlfriend," Trinity said quietly, "Jolene. I met her today. Look at this Loyal." She pointed at the desk. A family portrait of the Timmerman family sat on the desk. The frame had been broken and then taped back together. Tucked into the frame was a picture of Jane.

"Your girl is losing her shit Loyal," said Trinity. "She might have actually done it."

It was nearly 10:00 by the time the team wrapped up and left Jane's house. The old man had, indeed, called 911. Police officers from Escondido drove out and spoke with him then stopped and let Hammond know what had happened. Hammond and Trinity took pictures and video of the office wall then had the officers carefully take everything down and bag it up. They took the damaged portrait and frame as well. Jane's cell phone had been sitting on the kitchen counter. This was bagged and removed to give to O'Keefe. They failed to locate a computer, a purse, or any keys to the house or the car, which remained in the garage. Receipts and a copy of the search warrant were left for Jane should she return. A door kick form was left for the damaged door. Jane could file a claim if she chose to. Hammond had not spoken to Loyal the entire time. Loyal had seen his eyes widen when he saw the office wall, but that was the only interaction the two men had. Trinity and Loyal were the first to leave.

Driving back to Loyal's Trinity had asked him if he thought Jane capable of murdering Tyler and setting fire to his house in an attempt to cover up the crime. Despite the damning evidence in Jane's office Loyal still replied in the negative.

"I just don't see her killing him," he said.

"She's definitely unraveling though," said Trinity. "Breaking the picture frame then repairing it shows she's emotionally up and down. And inserting her picture into the frame?" Trinity paused. "I don't know Loyal. I would have put the murder on competitors or enemies, even foreign interests. I'm not sure now though. I'm leaning toward Jane on this." Trinity looked at Loyal and when he didn't respond she added, "And where the hell is she?"

77

PATRICK O'KEEFE

P at woke early Thursday morning. He and Olive had barely spoken the previous evening after their argument in the kitchen. Pat was grateful that Olive hadn't suggested that he sleep on the couch. Despite the fact that she was very angry with him and had slept as close to the edge of the bed as she could, he had been comforted by her presence in their bed. He slipped out of bed quietly, brewed some coffee, and sat at the kitchen table running the past few days through his mind. He was certainly relieved that Tyler's sister had known about Jane Gray. That fact removed a lot of the pressure he was feeling. He hadn't told Olive yet. He'd mention it when she decided to speak to him again.

By 6:00 Pat had downed three cups of coffee. He rinsed the mug, took a quick shower, and dressed for the day. Olive was either still asleep or pretending to be. Pat couldn't tell. He didn't disturb her to say goodbye opting instead to leave her a note next to the coffee pot. He apologized, professed his love, and promised to steer clear of Loyal. Pat knew Olive loved him and that they would work through this, he just hated the feeling in his stomach when they weren't getting along. By 7:00 he was in his car and headed toward Carlsbad.

78

TRINITY GLASS

Sun streaming through the slats in the bedroom blinds woke Trinity at 6:07 am. She slid out of bed without waking Loyal and stepped into the shower. She had forgotten to grab her soap, shampoo and conditioner out of her bag so she used Loyal's again. Everything he had was coconut scented. Trinity stepped from the shower smiling. She enjoyed smelling like him. She wrapped one towel around her hair and another around her body and stepped back into the bedroom. Loyal wasn't in bed and when she inhaled through her nose she smelled not only coconut but also coffee. She smiled again and headed to the kitchen to say good morning and grab a cup. As she rounded the corner she paused. Loyal had his little black cat Boo on his left shoulder. The pair stood at the large window in the living room, their backs to her, looking out at the morning. She couldn't hear what he was saying but she could tell that Loyal was talking to the cat. Trinity couldn't help but smile again at the sight.

. . .

As if he felt her eyes on him, Loyal turned to face her.

"Morning," he said.

"Morning," said Trinity, "I hope I didn't wake you."

Loyal shook his head. "Need to get ready for your SCIF," he said.

He pointed toward the kitchen.

"Grab a cup of coffee," he said. "I'm going to take a quick shower."

Trinity was just finishing her second cup of coffee when she heard the SCIF arriving. It was being delivered by a large oversized equipment hauler which, when Trinity looked out the window, barely fit on Loyal's small street. The giant vehicle had pulled just past Loyal's driveway and was effectively blocking the driveways of the neighbors to his north. Trinity grimaced, wondering what those neighbors were thinking about their peaceful morning being disturbed. The truck came to a stop. The driver turned off the engine and quiet returned to Loyal's neighborhood. By the time Trinity was out the door several neighbors had stepped out of their homes to see what was happening.

Trinity walked to the driver's side of the equipment hauler and watched the driver ease out of the seat. He stood about 5'11" and was powerfully built. His black hair was cut short and slicked away from his forehead. Tattoos covered both of his forearms. He consulted some paperwork he held in his left hand then looked up at Trinity. His eyes were brown.

"Agent Glass?" he asked.

Trinity nodded and held out her ID for him to see. He

looked, made a notation on the paperwork with a pen he held in his right hand, then handed Trinity both the papers and the pen.

"I'm Wes," he said. "Please sign on the highlighted lines."

Trinity took several minutes to read the paperwork. It was standard legal phrasing. She was taking responsibility for the SCIF and was the only authorized user of the compartment. She signed and handed the paperwork back. He set the paperwork on the driver's seat and turned back to Trinity.

"Where do you want it?"

"Backyard," said Trinity.

Wes and two other similarly built and tattooed men who had emerged from the passenger side of the equipment hauler walked with Trinity to the gate that led to Loyal's back yard. Loyal, hair wet from the shower and carrying another cup of coffee joined them there.

"How long is this going to take?" Loyal asked Wes. "It looks like I've got some pissed off neighbors."

"We are going to have to take down some of your fence to fit the tractor and SCIF through," said Wes. He gestured at some shrubs near the north side of Loyal's garage. "Those might be a problem too." Wes paused a moment then said, "Forty minutes."

Loyal nodded. "Let's get going then," he said, "some of the neighbors are already making phone calls. I don't care about the fence or the shrubs," he added, "just don't hurt the magnolia tree in the back yard."

79

LOYAL TRUESDALE

Wes's estimate of forty minutes and shrub damage proved to be true. When Loyal asked if the SCIF needed to be plugged into the house for power Trinity explained that, per stringent government guidelines, SCIFs were self powered and equipped with specialized power line filters. While Trinity had supervised the fence and shrub destruction and the placement of the SCIF Loyal had walked across the street to apologize to the neighbors. Having only been in his house six short months, Loyal did not really know his neighbors beyond a friendly wave now and then. Loyal had been fairly certain a few of the most disapproving had called the city to complain. The neighborhood did not have a home-owner's association. The only things Loyal had suspected he might get a warning about were blocking the road and the early morning noise.

By 8:10 the road was clear, the neighbors had dispersed, and the neighborhood was quiet again. Loyal and Trinity decided to make a quick breakfast before they began their days. Over scrambled egg breakfast burritos they discussed their plans. Trinity needed to spend some time in the SCIF. She needed to make contact with Caldwell and fill him in on the search the previous evening. She also planned to interview Jolene and meet with both Leisel and her parents. She was hoping they had some security footage for her to review. Loyal's plan was to continue the search for Jane.

"I really didn't think she was a viable suspect until we saw her office," said Trinity, "now I'm not so sure."

Loyal shook his head as he swallowed a bite of burrito. "I don't like her for it Trinity," he said.

"But that wall," said Trinity, "and the picture frame." She paused for a moment then added, "Where do you suppose she got that picture anyway?"

Loyal shrugged. "I'll ask her when I find her," he said.

80

PATRICK O'KEEFE

P at was not surprised to find that Hope and Miles Bannon had both submitted DNA samples to genomecestry.com. He found emails from the company in both of their personal email inboxes. He knew that direct to consumer DNA testing companies aggressively fought subpoenas from law enforcement and that the companies routinely won those fights. It was very rare for law enforcement to actually obtain what they were requesting. He knew it might be different in this case because Hope and Myles were both deceased. Before taking the time to author a warrant he decided to try to get into their accounts on his own.

Pat knew that, despite being warned of the danger, many people used the same password for multiple accounts. He started with Hope. Her email password did not work for her genomecestry.com account. He tried her birthday, the date of her wedding to Miles, Miles' birthdate, and the date of the final positive pregnancy test. None worked and after the fifth try he was locked out of attempting any more passwords. Armed with the knowledge that he would only get five tries Pat moved on to Miles' account. It only took one try. Miles used the same password for his genomecestry account as he did for his email.

Pat began with the results from Miles' sample. The information was divided into four sections: *Disease and health risks, Ancestry and Genealogy, Lifestyle,* and *Kinship.* Pat started at the top and soon learned that Miles appeared to be at risk for Alzheimer's Disease. He supposed that could have led to suicide, but certainly didn't explain Miles' killing of Hope as well. The second section listed Miles' ancestry and the percentage of each his DNA contained. Pat saw no red flags there. The lifestyle section listed nutritional tips, exercise suggestions, weight loss strategies, skincare tips, and strategies to try for a better night's sleep. This section even included what type of wine Miles would most likely enjoy based on his DNA sample. Pat couldn't help but chuckle at that. The last section, *Kinship,* indicated that Miles had a half sibling somewhere who had also submitted a DNA sample to genomecestry.com. A link was included that took Pat to the message board section of the website. It was here that Pat found the smoking gun.

81

TRINITY GLASS

Trinity punched the code into the SCIF alarm and unlocked the door. She stepped inside and pulled the door closed behind her. The SCIF was small and windowless. A claustrophobic sensation enveloped Trinity immediately. She crossed the small space quickly and picked up the encrypted phone. She dialed Caldwell's office line. His entire office was a permanent SCIF; his phone line was encrypted as well. He answered on the second ring.

"Caldwell," he said.

"It's Glass," said Trinity, "I'm in the SCIF."

"You have anything for me?"

Trinity spent a few minutes filling Caldwell in on her interviews with Charles and Leisel Timmerman, the DNA test, and the search of Jane's house.

"You have a line on this Jane Gray?" Caldwell asked.

"I'm working on it," said Trinity. "I need to interview Tyler's girlfriend this morning and I have some follow up questions for Leisel. I'm hoping for security camera footage from Tyler's house and the Timmerman family home as well."

"Keep me informed," said Caldwell and he ended the call.

Trinity exited the SCIF and stood for a moment beneath Loyal's massive magnolia tree. She supposed when it was in full bloom the air around it would be filled with the fragrance of the blossoms. She pulled her cell phone out of her pocket and dialed Jolene's number. She didn't answer. Rather than leave a voicemail Trinity sent a text, the standard form of communication for Jolene's generation. Sure enough, a response came within five minutes. Jolene gave her address and invited Trinity to come by at any time. Trinity responded that she was on her way.

Jolene lived a short fifteen minute drive from Loyal's house. Trinity arrived at the condo on S. El Camino Real at 9:45. She parked in a visitor's space and walked quickly to Jolene's unit. Trinity had googled the address and knew that the condos had been built in 1998 and were 650 square feet with one bedroom and one bath. Jolene's unit was on the first floor. Trinity rang the bell and waited. It took several minutes for Jolene to open the door and when she finally did Trinity barely recognized her. The young woman was dressed in baggy faded sweats and a stained T-shirt. Her blond hair lay flat against her head, lank and slightly greasy. It was her face that caused Trinity to take a quick breath in and ask, "Are you okay?" Jolene's skin was pale. Her eyes were red and puffy and there were black circles beneath them. The odor of stale booze emanated from the pores of her skin.

Jolene shook her head. "Not really," she said as she stepped aside and motioned Trinity into the condo.

. . .

"I don't really drink," said Jolene, "but I did last night." She led Trinity through a tiny living room that contained a single couch, a coffee table, and a large television mounted on the wall.

"Let's sit in here," Jolene said as she waved an arm toward a microscopic dining area. Trinity chose a chair and sat at the small kitchen table. Jolene sat across from her. When she raised her eyes to look at Trinity tears welled up then spilled silently down her cheeks.

"I don't know what to do," said Jolene, her voice barely a whisper. "I'm lost without him."

"I'm so sorry," said Trinity. She paused then added, "Are you up to speaking with me?"

Jolene nodded.

"How long have you been with Tyler?" asked Trinity.

"Four years," said Jolene. "I work for a high end catering company. We catered a gala the Timmermans attended. I never give my number out, but I did with Tyler. I wrote it on a napkin and slipped it in his pocket." Jolene smiled sadly. "I couldn't believe he actually called. We've been together ever since."

Jolene seemed to want to talk about her history with Tyler so Trinity let her go on for a little while. She learned that they were very active in the outdoors and that Tyler was extremely health conscious. He drank alcohol only once a week at his parent's house on Sundays. He exercised frequently by surfing and running, and also at home with his Peloton bike and Tonal interactive home gym.

"He was so into monitoring his body," said Jolene. "He always wore his Whoop."

"What's a Whoop?" Trinity asked.

"You wear it on your wrist," said Jolene. "It monitors your vital functions. It even tells you how good your sleep experience was." Jolene smiled that sad sort of half smile again. "I used to tease him that he was addicted to the internet of things. He loves," she paused, "he loved interactive devices."

"Did he have home security?" Trinity asked even though she already knew the answer.

"Oh sure," said Jolene, "a Ring doorbell and security cameras in the front and in the back."

"Did he store the footage?"

"Yeah," Jolene said, "in the cloud. I bet there's tons of footage."

"Has he mentioned anyone bothering him recently?" Trinity asked. "Has he had any issues at work?"

Jolene shook her head. Her eyes were downcast looking at the table "He never said anything," she said, "but now that I think about it he has been preoccupied by something for about a month or so. I asked him about it a few times but he always said everything was fine."

Jolene raised her head and looked at Trinity. "Do you really think it wasn't an accident Agent Glass? Do you really think someone killed Tyler?"

82

LOYAL TRUESDALE

L oyal drove by Jane's house again on the off chance that she had returned home. She hadn't. The kick notice was still on the door where Hammond had left it. Loyal didn't bother getting out of his truck. He could tell at a glance that Jane wasn't there and he didn't want to chance running into her nosy neighbor again. Instead he drove one street east, pulled over, and called Maggie. Maggie answered in her trademark way saying, "This is Maggie."

Hey Maggie," said Loyal, "it's Loyal."

"Hi Loyal," said Maggie, "what's up?"

Loyal spent about five minutes explaining the circumstances surrounding Tyler's death and Jane's disappearance. Maggie listened in stunned silence. When he stopped talking she said, "I'm shocked Loyal. I don't even know what to say."

"I need to find Jane, Maggie," he said, "if only to help prove her innocence."

"You don't think she did it?"

"Do you?" asked Loyal.

There was silence on the line while Maggie pondered his question. Finally she let out a long deep sigh and said, "Probably not. But the truth is I don't really know her all that well. I'm so sorry Loyal. I should've never gotten you involved in Jane's life. I'll keep reaching out to her."

"Don't bother," said Loyal, "the police have her phone."

Loyal and Maggie spoke for a few more minutes and both agreed to keep each other informed if they learned anything regarding Jane's whereabouts. When the call was disconnected Loyal sat in his truck thinking about places Jane could possibly have gone. Public transportation came to mind. He picked his phone back up and googled Escondido's transit website. According to the website the city was peppered with bus stops. All one had to do was look for the blue and white North County Transit District bus stop signs. Loyal decided to do exactly that.

A quick review of NCTD route maps gave Loyal all the information he needed. Each route had 18-22 stops and all ended at the Transit Center on West Valley Parkway. Jane could potentially have walked east to a stop on Oak Hill and Bear Valley, southeast to a stop on Glenridge and Mountain View, or northeast to a stop on Valley Parkway and Midway. From the Transit Center she could have gone virtually any direction. There were buses to the casinos on the reservations and there was the Sprinter that went west. Loyal didn't know if there were cameras on the buses, but he suspected that there were. He was confidant there were cameras at the transit station. He pulled up Pat's contact information and was about to place a call when he stopped. Pat was unhappy with him. He'd have to get Trinity to ask for warrants for the footage from the cameras. He placed a call to her instead. It went straight to voicemail. Loyal left a quick message then disconnected.

83

TRINITY GLASS

Trinity closed Jolene's front door and walked quickly to her car. She sat down in the driver's seat and pulled Leisel's contact information up on her phone. Without starting her car she placed the call. Leisel answered after several rings. Trinity identified herself and asked if they could meet up. Leisel gave Trinity her home address and invited her to come by any time. Trinity explained that she was just leaving Jolene's and would drive straight to Leisel's house.

Trinity parked along the curb in front of Leisel's house twenty minutes later. She exited her vehicle, walked to the front door, and rang the bell. Leisel opened the door quickly. She didn't look as downtrodden as Jolene had but she didn't look very good either. Her hair was clean but her eyes were puffy and red. Leisel gave Trinity a tired half smile and motioned for her to come into the house.

"Can I offer you something to drink?" asked Leisel. "I'm happy to brew up some coffee or tea."

"A glass of water would be fine," said Trinity.

Leisel pulled two glasses from a cupboard and filled them with ice and water. She motioned toward the kitchen table and the two women sat down across from each other.

"How's Jolene?" asked Leisel.

Trinity shrugged her shoulders. "Not great." She paused then asked, "How are you holding up?"

Leisel sighed. "Not great," she said, "I still can't believe he's gone." A single tear tracked down Leisel's left cheek. She brushed it away impatiently. "You have any leads?"

"I'd like to talk to you a bit more about Jane Gray," said Trinity, "and I thought you might be more comfortable here than at your parents' house."

Leisel nodded, "Definitely," she said, "my Dad would be so angry to know Tyler had taken the DNA test."

"Can you start from the beginning and walk me through everything again?"

Leisel told Trinity about her two arguments with Tyler and her father's ultimatum when Tyler expressed an interest in submitting a DNA sample.

"Do you know why your father is so against the test?"

"He and my Mom are both estranged from their families." Leisel ran a hand through her hair. "Estranged isn't really a strong enough word. They cut their entire families out of their lives a long time ago. I don't know why."

"You think your dad is concerned a DNA test might lead them back to you?"

"Maybe," said Leisel. "Listen, when you come from a family with as much money as ours you have to be very careful. My dad values his privacy for many reasons."

. . .

Leisel drained her glass. "At first I thought Jane Gray was a scam, but now I'm wondering if she might be real."

"Why the change of opinion?" asked Trinity.

"I think she's been driving by my house and Tyler's too."

Leisel told Trinity about the woman in the blue car and the intruder in her house.

"I know someone was in here because the front door was ajar and my hidden key from the back yard and a family portrait are missing. Also I asked Tyler to check his security footage for a blue car and he told me he saw it four times since Sunday." Leisel paused and leaned toward Trinity. "He also said he saw a woman walking around in the small park behind his house."

Trinity was taking notes on a pad of paper. She stopped writing and looked up at Leisel.

"When did he tell you that?"

"We were on the phone. Someone knocked on his door." Leisel paused then added, "I think he said his Ring doorbell system wasn't working." Leisel's eyes filled with tears. They spilled down her cheeks as she added, "He said he'd call me back Agent Glass, but he never did."

84

LOYAL TRUESDALE

L oyal drove by the Escondido Transit Center on his way back to Carlsbad. It was a hive of activity with buses and the Sprinter coming and going. He didn't park and look for cameras but he was confident that they were there. He drove through In-n-Out on his way back to his house, purchasing burgers and fries for both himself and Trinity. He wasn't sure when she would be back but it was likely that she would be hungry.

Loyal did not receive any friendly waves as he drove down Los Robles Street towards his house. The neighbor who lived directly across from his house was working in her front yard. She actually turned away as he pulled into his driveway. Loyal parked and thought about what he could do to appease everyone he had inconvenienced that morning. He thought a personal apology to each might be nice but as he thought about it he wondered what he could possibly say. *I'm sorry, but my top secret agent girlfriend needs a temporary SCIF.* He almost laughed as the phrase went through his mind. There was nothing, he realized, that he could say to his neighbors. He decided he would make sure everyone had ample warning when it was time to have the SCIF removed.

Loyal slid out of his truck and went to examine the damage to his fence. It was comprised of wooden slats. A large portion had been taken down in order to get the SCIF into the backyard. Wes and his guys had put it back up but it definitely would need to be professionally repaired after the SCIF removal. Looking at it now Loyal thought he might just have a brand new fence installed when this craziness was over. He stood there for several minutes, In-N-Out bag in his left hand, thinking about the last two years of his life. Life before retirement had been less eventful than life post retirement. Loyal had not actively sought out any of the "adventures" that had come his way. Two good things had come out of everything that had happened; he had met Trinity and he had come into some money.

Loyal turned and looked across the street at his neighbor. It was obvious by the way she abruptly knelt down in her flower bed that she had been watching him. Loyal smiled in case she still had him in her peripheral vision then turned and walked to his front door. When Loyal walked into the house Boo, who was sleeping on the cat post, sat up and stretched then jumped down and ran over to Loyal. Loyal scooped him up and set him on his left shoulder. He set the bag of food on the kitchen counter. When Boo jumped off his shoulder onto the counter Loyal opened the bag and gave the cat a bite of hamburger. He took a bite of the burger himself and petted the cat while he chewed.

"I guess we wait for Trinity now," he said. Boo just looked at him. Loyal was pinching off another bite for Boo when his phone rang. He pulled it out of his pocket and looked at the caller ID. Olive was calling him. Loyal hesitated for two more rings then, with a sigh, answered the call.

"Hi Olive," he said, "is everything ok?"

"Loyal," she said, "you know how grateful Pat and I are for your generosity."

"Yes," he said, "I'm sensing a *but* here."

Olive sighed. "Pat doesn't know I'm calling you Loyal," she said, "and I don't want him to know."

"Okay," said Loyal.

"I need you to give our family some space," said Olive.

There was a long silence on the line.

"I'm sorry Loyal," Olive finally said. "I know I'm the one who suggested Pat find the information for Jane, but you and I both know that you came over that day to ask Pat for help."

"Yeah, I did," said Loyal.

"Pat can't be involved in any more of your craziness Loyal," she said, "he almost died in New Mexico. He has a family and responsibilities." Olive paused then added, "We need him."

Her voice cracked as she said those last words and Loyal could tell she was close to tears.

"You're right Olive," he finally said, "I'll keep my distance."

"Thank you," said Olive. She hung up without another word.

85

TRINITY GLASS

Trinity slid into her car and sat still for a few moments. Her attempts to comfort Leisel had been fruitless. Tyler's sister had been sitting on the couch crying when Trinity said goodbye. Trinity pulled out her phone and placed a call to Captain Williams' direct line.

"Captain Williams," he said.

"It's Agent Glass," said Trinity.

"I was just getting ready to call you," said the Captain, "we've got a positive ID on Tyler Timmerman from dental records."

"Not much of a surprise," said Trinity.

"No, but it's good to be sure."

"Right," said Trinity. She could hear the annoyance in his voice at her comment. "I appreciate the information Captain. Any word on the autopsy?"

"The ME knows it's a top priority but she's backlogged. It might be a day or two."

"Okay," said Trinity. "Any luck on the warrant for Tyler's security footage?"

"Yes," said Captain Williams, "I should have that this afternoon."

Trinity told him her secure email address and asked him to forward everything to her. He agreed.

"I was wondering if you could spare a few uniforms to canvas the area around Leisel Timmerman's house?" Trinity asked. "I'm looking for any security camera footage from Monday between 4:00 and 9:00 pm."

"What are we looking for?" asked the Captain.

"She says someone broke into her house while she was out with friends. Her backyard isn't fenced so I think there's a strong possibility they came in that way. I'm looking for footage from her street, Sunburst Road, and also Horizon Street if they can find any."

"I'll put someone on it," said Captain Williams.

Trinity thanked him and disconnected then started her car and backed out of Leisel's driveway.

The drive to the Timmerman family home took nearly forty-five minutes. Road construction on El Camino Real constricted traffic into a single lane in each direction. Trinity was more than frustrated when she finally turned onto Lone Jack Road. She called Charles as she drove to let him know she was almost there and he assured her that the gate would be open. Trinity pulled into their driveway and parked in the same spot she had parked the previous day. She slid out of the car, approached the front door, and rang the bell. Charles Timmerman opened the door moments after she rang the bell. It was almost as if he had been standing at the door awaiting her arrival.

. . .

"Any developments?" he asked as he directed her towards the living room.

Trinity turned to face him. "Positive ID from dental records," she said, "I'm very sorry."

Charles closed his eyes for a brief moment then opened them again.

"I figured it was him," he said, "still a small part of me held out hope."

"Were you able to get the footage from your security company?" Trinity asked.

Charles nodded. "If you give me your email they will forward everything to you," he said. "We have multiple cameras around the house and fence line," he added, "it's going to be a lot to go through."

Trinity recited her secure email address and Charles used his phone to email it to the company.

"I'd like to speak with your wife today," said Trinity.

Charles shook his head. "My wife is very frail Agent Glass. She's not up to being interviewed. There isn't anything she can add to what Leisel and I have told you."

"You'd be surprised," said Trinity. "I'm going to have to speak with her at some point. When might she be available?"

Charles' eyes bored into Trinity's. His stare was hard and when he spoke his voice was harsh.

"She's under a doctor's care," he said. "He'll decide when, and if, she's available to speak with you. My wife is my first priority Agent Glass, and she always will be."

Trinity opened her mouth to argue and then closed it again without saying anything. She'd go through all the security footage first then try for an interview with Daisy again. She nodded at Charles and thanked him again then turned and walked back to her car.

P at picked up his office phone and dialed Hammond's extension. He answered right away.

"Detective Hammond," he said.

"It's O'Keefe," said Pat, "I have something you need to see. Captain Williams too. Can you meet me in his office?"

"Five minutes," said Hammond. He disconnected without another word. Pat waited four minutes then picked up Miles' laptop and walked down the corridor to Captain Williams' office. He saw Hammond stepping out of his office on the opposite side of Captain Williams' office and paused to wait for him. They entered the Captain's office together.

Captain Williams was sitting behind his desk staring intently at his computer screen. He looked up as they entered.

"I have something you both need to see," said Pat as he took a seat in one of the visitor chairs. Hammond sat in the other chair. Pat set the laptop on the table.

"Miles and Hope Bannon both sent DNA samples to a

direct to consumer DNA testing company called Genomecestry. I wasn't able to get into Hope's account, but Miles used the same password for his email and his Genomecestry account. What I'm about to show you is a message he received two days before the murder/suicide."

Pat opened the laptop and turned it so that both the Captain and Hammond could read the message. He watched their eyes move back and forth as they read and saw the absolute shock register on their faces as they reached the end of the message. Neither said a word; they simply raised their eyes and looked at Pat. Pat turned the laptop back toward himself and read the brief message again.

Hello,

I'm reaching out to you because genomecestry.com has indicated that we are related...half siblings. I was wondering if we could talk? I don't think the match is correct because my parents met as teenagers and have been together ever since. I suppose perhaps we could be cousins? It would mean a lot to me if you would reply to this message, email me, or even call. I live in Carlsbad Ca and my name is Hope Bannon.

Hope had included her email address and her phone number at the end of the email.

"They were related," said Hammond.

"It looks that way," said Pat, "and she was pregnant."

"You need to go talk to both families again," said the Captain, "find out if this is a possibility."

Hammond looked at Pat. "You have time to go for a ride?"

Pat nodded.

"I'll drive," said Hammond.

Pat nodded again.

Miles was originally from Bandon, Oregon, a small seaside town on the Pacific coast. His parents had driven down to Carlsbad after learning of his passing. They were staying at the Cape Rey Carlsbad Beach Hotel which was about a fifteen minute drive from the Sheriff's station. Hammond called them while he drove to make sure they were at the hotel. They assured him they were. Hammond had been to the hotel several times to speak with Miles' parents. Pat hadn't met them yet.

Eric and Joanne Bannon were polar opposites in the looks department. Eric was tall and thin. He had a large nose that reminded Pat of a beak. His hair was gray and thinning. Joanne Bannon reminded Pat of the grandmother from Little Red Riding Hood; she was short and stout with thick gray hair. They were both much older than he had expected. The only thing they had in common looks-wise was the deep grief in their eyes. Hammond introduced Pat and they all took a seat in the hotel suite's small living room.

"I'm very sorry for your loss," said Pat.

"We just don't understand," said Joanne, "Miles adored Hope. She meant everything to him and they were hoping to start a family soon."

"He was our only child," said Eric. Tears slid silently down the man's cheeks. Joanne reached out for her husband's hand.

.   .   .

On the drive over the two detectives had decided that Pat would be the one to lead the conversation.

"Mr. and Mrs. Bannon," he said as gently as he could, "was Miles your biological child?"

Both parents' eyes widened. They looked at each other for a long moment then back at Pat.

"How did you know that he wasn't?" Joanne asked. "We never told anyone."

"Not even Miles?" Pat asked.

Joanne shook her head. "It was a private adoption arranged through our pastor. Even the birth certificate says we are his parents."

"How did you figure out he was adopted?" Eric asked.

Pat opened his mouth to answer but Hammond interrupted him.

"This is still an ongoing investigation," he said, "we will share information with you when we can."

He stood up and signaled for Pat to do the same. Hammond thanked the Bannon's for their time and promised to be in touch soon. The detectives turned and walked out the door leaving the stunned parents behind them.

87

LOYAL TRUESDALE

L oyal was still reeling from his conversation with Olive when Trinity walked in the door.

"Any luck finding Jane?" she asked.

"I think she might have taken a bus," said Loyal. "I left you a voicemail. Any chance you can get your hands on security footage from the transit station in Escondido?"

Trinity looked at her phone. "Sorry I missed that," she said. "Why didn't you call Pat for help with the cameras?" Trinity asked.

Loyal sighed. "Olive called. She wants me to stay away from them."

Trinity crossed the room and put her arms around Loyal. "Oh Loyal," she said, "I'm so sorry."

Loyal wrapped his arms around her. "I understand it actual-ly," he said, "I'm always getting him in some kind of trouble. I thought life would be easier when I retired," he said with half a laugh. "You hungry? I picked up In-n-Out."

"Yes," said Trinity leaning away from him so she could look up at his face, "very."

. . .

When the burgers and fries were gone Trinity suggested going into the SCIF to look at security footage.

"You're going to let me in that thing?" Loyal asked in a surprised voice.

"I need another set of eyes," said Trinity, "but if you ever have the occasion to speak with Caldwell you were never inside of it. Leave your cell phone in the house," she added, "everyone we might need to talk to has the secure number."

Loyal followed Trinity across the yard. She entered a code, opened the door, and stepped in. Loyal stepped in as well. It was a small space. Loyal saw the encrypted phone and two computer workstations. There was a door in the north west corner of the SCIF. Trinity saw Loyal looking at it. "Bathroom," she said. "This SCIF is really small Loyal, very bare-bones. I've been in portable ones that have kitchens and sleeping areas too."

Trinity sat down in front of one of the computer stations. She motioned to the chair in front of the other station.

"Drag that over here," she said, "we have tons of footage to go through. I want to start with Tyler's."

Loyal pulled the chair next to Trinity and sat down. She located the email containing Tyler's security footage and opened it up.

"Let's start with the front cameras," she said. She pulled a pad of paper and a pen from the drawer beneath the computer station then started the footage. Trinity had requested everything from the previous ten days. The footage began on a Monday morning. The first six days they watched were nearly identical. Tyler surfed every day. Some days Jolene came home with him and some days he returned alone. Trinity and Loyal watched as he left the house apparently dressed for work, had friends stop by, and went for runs. It wasn't until the seventh day, the previous Sunday, that Trinity and Loyal saw what they were looking for. At 4:32 a light blue Nissan drove down Brava and parked across the street and a few houses down from Tyler's house. No one exited the vehicle. Trinity paused the footage and tried to zoom in on the driver's face but the picture was too grainy. Loyal recognized the car as Jane's and was sure Trinity did as well. Trinity tapped a key and the action resumed. After a few minutes Tyler's truck backed out of the driveway. The blue car followed him.

Trinity paused the footage and made a note of the time, the date, and a brief description on the note pad. They watched more footage and saw Jane three more times. She had driven by once on Monday at 8:15 am, then again on Tuesday at 10:41 and 10:58 am. The footage ended abruptly at 3:37 on Tuesday afternoon. The street was visible at 3:36 and Tyler's truck was clearly in the driveway. At 3:37 everything went blank.

"That's strange," said Loyal, "that's easily an hour before the fire was reported."

Trinity nodded. She turned to face Loyal.

"Jane drove by his house four times in three days Loyal. Our girl is looking a bit obsessed."

"That doesn't mean she killed him and torched the place Trinity," said Loyal.

A ping signaling an email interrupted their conversation.

"Captain Williams," said Trinity.

She opened the email and read it out loud to Loyal.

· · ·

Initial tests indicate use of accelerant. Type not yet identified.

"So where would "our girl"," Loyal used his finger to make quotation marks around the phrase, "get that?"

"Maybe she's more technologically sophisticated than we realized," said Trinity.

"Then why did she need me to help find Tyler?"

They sat in silence for a long moment then Loyal said, "I'm pretty good at reading people Trinity. I just don't like Jane for this."

"I've got good instincts too Loyal," said Trinity.

They sat in silence again. The tension was palpable. Finally Trinity spoke.

"Listen Loyal," she said, "let's not try to force any one scenario. We'll follow the evidence, okay?"

"Agreed," said Loyal.

88

PATRICK O'KEEFE

P at and Hammond slid into Hammond's car. They sat in silence for a moment.

"Should't we have told them about the DNA test?" Pat asked. "It would have been the kind thing to do."

"Not yet," said Hammond. "Let's go talk to Hope's parents first."

Hammond pulled out his phone and called Alan Stroud, Hope's father. Permission to stop by was granted. Hammond started the engine and shifted into drive.

"They live in La Jolla," he said, "you are going to shit when you see their house."

The drive took just under forty minutes. Hammond didn't seem to be in the mood for conversation which was just fine with Pat. Their occupations aside, the two men had very little in common. Pat knew that Hammond had been married for a short time and was divorced now. He didn't know for sure, but he didn't think Hammond had any children. He never talked about his personal life and Pat had never seen any pictures on Hammond's desk to indicate children or a significant other. Hammond exited Interstate 5 at La Jolla Village Drive then headed southwest on Torrey Pines Road. Traffic was heavy and their forward progress slowed. Hammond turned right on Ivanhoe Avenue E then executed a series of left and right turns. Eventually they pulled into the driveway of a large wood and stone house on S Coast Blvd.

They slid out of the car and approached the house.

"You weren't kidding," said Pat, "an ocean front house in La Jolla. What does something like this sell for?"

"Probably ten to twelve million at least," said Hammond. "Wait until you see the inside and the view."

They rang the bell and the door opened about a minute later. A woman with startling blue eyes and expensively styled honey blond hair opened the door. She had make up on but it was understated and applied perfectly. She wore white capri pants and a loosely fitting sea-foam colored silk blouse. Her feet were bare. She smiled and greeted Hammond, but the smile didn't reach her beautiful eyes. She led the detectives into the living room. The western wall was made completely of glass; the majestic Pacific Ocean was less than thirty yards from the back of their home. Hammond introduced her to Pat as Penny Stroud, Hope's mother. As she was motioning for them to sit on the couch her husband, Alan, walked into the room.

Alan was about 5'11" and solidly built. He had dark green eyes and black hair generously streaked with gray. He wore faded jeans and a short sleeved linen button down shirt. His feet were bare. He shook Pat's hand when Hammond introduced them, then he and his wife sat on the other couch. Pat found himself wondering what the two sets of parents had ever talked about when Hope and Miles were alive. They lived on the same coast but might as well have been from different planets. He took a deep breath in then said, "I've come across some information and I need to verify a few things."

Alan and Penny nodded.

"I know this is personal," Pat said, "and I'm sorry to ask, but I was wondering if either of you had ever given a child up for adoption?"

"Absolutely not," said Alan, "what kind of question is that? What does that have to do with my daughter's murder?"

Pat turned his eyes toward Penny. She sat so still she could have been a statue. Pat knew it before she said it. He could see it in her eyes.

"Yes," she said, "many years ago."

Alan turned to look at her.

"What?" he said.

She turned to her husband and took his hands in hers.

"It was before we met," she said.

Slowly the story slipped out of her lips. A stepfather who sexually abused her, a mother who wouldn't believe her, a pregnancy at fifteen, being sent to live with her aunt, giving the baby away.

"I met you about six months after he was born. I was afraid I'd lose you if I told you and then so much time went by. We had our children. It almost felt as if it never happened."

Alan and Penny spoke only to each other. It was as if they had forgotten the detectives were in the room.

"I don't understand how you could have gone all these years without telling me," said Alan.

"How could I Alan?" asked Penny. Her eyes were pleading for understanding. "There was a window of time to tell you," she said. "Once it had closed I didn't know how to open it again."

Alan ran his hands through his hair.

"This is going top take me some time to process Penny," he said.

Silent tears ran down Penny's face as she nodded her head. The despair on her face was hard for Pat to look at. Alan turned to Pat and said, "I still don't understand what this has to do with Hope's death detective."

"Hope and Miles submitted DNA samples to genomecestry.com," said Pat. He paused for a moment and let his words sink in. Understanding appeared on Penny's face first. Her eyes widened and her mouth dropped open. A muffled oomph, like she had been punched in the stomach, escaped her lips. A moment later realization dawned on Alan's face as well.

"Miles was Penny's son," he said, more to himself than to anyone else in the room.

"No," said Penny.

"My God,"said Alan

Hope's parents turned toward Pat and Hammond.

"Was Miles my son?" Penny asked.

"We think so," said Pat. "When Hope and Miles sent DNA samples to genomecestry.com the sibling relationship was revealed through the DNA testing."

89

LOYAL TRUESDALE

L oyal left Trinity in the SCIF and went into the house for something for them to drink. She told him she would open the door for him in exactly four minuites, which she did. He walked in with two bottles of Perrier and a set of coasters to set them on.

"I've emailed Captain Williams the address of a lab in Virginia," Trinity said, "they can complete a more sophisticated analysis of the accelerant used at Tyler's house."

She stood and stretched then walked to the A/C unit and switched it on.

"It gets stuffy in here," she said. "Ready to watch the footage from the cameras on the back of Tyler's house?"

Loyal nodded and sat down. Trinity returned to her seat as well. She tapped some keys on the computer and the park behind Tyler's house appeared on the screen. They didn't see anything of any significance until the previous Tuesday, just two days ago, at 10:43. The light blue Nissan pulled into the small parking lot. A few moments later a woman emerged from the driver's side door.

"Jane," said Loyal.

Trinity paused the footage and leaned in close to the screen to study Jane's image. After a moment, and without commenting, she started the motion again. Jane walked around the small park paying close attention to the back of Tyler's house. She held her phone up in front of her face as if she were speaking to someone.

"She's filming," said Trinity.

"I think so," said Loyal.

They continued watching until, at 3:37, everything went blank.

"Same time the front cameras cut out," said Loyal.

"I don't like it," said Trinity, "we need to canvas the neighborhood and see if any of Tyler's neighbors have cameras."

"You could ask Captain Williams for a few uniforms to do that," said Loyal.

"He's already done that for Leisel's neighborhood," said Trinity, "I doubt he'll give me more. We can do it ourselves after we finish watching the footage."

Trinity glanced at her notes on the pad of paper.

"Jane drove by Tyler's house four times in three days, Loyal," she said.

"Maybe she was working up the courage to knock on the door?"

Trinity shook her head. "I don't buy that," she said, "it looks to me like she was doing surveillance."

Trinity turned back to the computer and opened the email from Charles Timmerman's security company.

"Let's start with the Timmerman Foundation footage and then watch everything from the family home."

Loyal nodded and Trinity hit play.

90

PATRICK O'KEEFE

The drive back to the Sheriff's Department was quiet. Once the DNA information was revealed Alan Stroud had quietly asked the detectives to leave. Penny Stroud had not said a word. She remained on the couch, her gaze distant and unfocused, silent tears coursing down her cheeks. Pat felt absolutely sick inside. He hated being the bearer of bad news and the news he had delivered was horrifying. Penny Stroud's son had married her daughter then killed her and turned the gun on himself when the relationship was revealed through DNA testing. He couldn't imagine the depth of her despair or how she would possibly be able to process this discovery. Moving past it seemed impossible in Pat's mind.

As they drove Pat thought about Tyler Timmerman and Jane. Their relationship had been revealed through DNA testing as well. Pat hoped with every fiber of his being that Jane had not been the person responsible for Tyler's death. When

Hammond turned into the department's parking lot Pat asked him if there had been any progress on the Timmerman case.

"Positive ID through dental records," said Hammond, "and accelerant was detected. Still waiting on the autopsy. I have security camera footage from Tyler's house. Once I'm done with the paperwork from today I'll start on that."

Hammond parked and turned off the ignition. He turned to Pat and said, "You have time to look at Jane Gray's phone yet?"

Pat was reaching for the door handle. He stopped and turned toward Hammond.

"I wouldn't hold out any hope on that," he said, "if Apple wouldn't give the FBI the passwords for the San Bernadino terrorists they probably aren't going to give them to us. I'll definitely try though."

"Damn phone providers," said Hammond.

Both men opened their doors and slid out of the car. They walked into the Sheriff's department and returned to their offices without saying another word.

91

TRINITY GLASS

The Timmerman Family Foundation was housed in a business complex with several other businesses. Charles Timmerman owned the entire complex and had hired a state of the art security company to install the cameras. Trinity had received footage from a camera on the front of his offices facing Saxony and from a camera on the rear of his offices facing the parking lot. Trinity had requested ten days worth of footage. She and Loyal began with the camera on the front of the building. Nothing stood out to them until, just before 11:00 am the previous Tuesday, Leisel had driven past the front. Jane had been several car lengths behind her. Both women had turned into the driveway that led to the parking lot behind the building.

"Here we go," said Trinity. Loyal remained silent. Trinity quickly switched to the footage from the rear of the building. She fast forwarded to 10:50 am on the previous Tuesday. At this point she slowed the footage to half speed. When Leisel's car appeared Trinity adjusted the speed to normal. They both watched as Leisel pulled into the lot and parked near the back door. Jane pulled in 30 seconds later and parked in the very back of the lot. Moments later Tyler's truck pulled into the lot and parked next to Leisel. The siblings each slid out of their vehicles. Tyler opened the door to the office and allowed Leisel to step inside first then he followed her in. Less than a minute later Jane exited her vehicle and approached Tyler and Leisel's vehicles. When she was between the car and the truck she abruptly knelt down. Trinity froze the footage.

"What's she doing?" she asked.

Loyal leaned in toward the screen.

"Can you zoom in?" he asked.

Trinity zoomed in on Jane and started the motion again. Onscreen, a blurry Jane quickly placed something on the underside of each vehicle then stood up again. Jane stood still for a long moment, apparently looking at what appeared to be some type of signage. Eventually she held up her phone and took a picture of whatever she was looking at. She then returned to her car, sat in the driver's seat for four minutes, then drove away.

"It looks like she placed trackers on their vehicles," Loyal said in a very quiet voice.

"We'll need to check that," said Trinity. They were quiet for a moment.

"You still think she didn't do it?" Trinity asked.

Loyal sighed and ran his hands through his hair.

"I know it looks bad Trinity," he said, "but no, I don't think she killed Tyler."

92

LEISEL TIMMERMAN

Leisel and her father sat side by side at the kitchen
table in the Timmerman family home. Their backs
were to the kitchen entryway; untouched sandwiches
sat on the table in front of them.

"Tyler and I never resolved our argument from last
Sunday," said Charles quietly. His voice was rough and full of
grief. "We saw each other Tuesday at the foundation meeting
but didn't speak."

Leisel nodded but remained quiet. The secret she was keeping
from her father, Tyler's DNA test and Jane Gray, was a malig-
nancy inside of her that was growing larger as each moment
passed. It threatened to destroy her if she didn't get it out. She
desperately wanted to tell her father but was terrified of his
anger if she did. Just this morning she had woken to find a mass
of tiny black ants on her kitchen counter. This happened occasionally and normally Leisel calmly wiped them up. This

morning she had completely broken down. She had to tell him before she went crazy.

"Dad," she said, "I need to tell you something." Leisel felt Charles' gaze on her but kept her focus on her sandwich. The words came out in a rush. She started with Jolene's Christmas gift of DNA tests. She told him about the message Tyler received from Jane Gray and her own belief that it was a scam. She explained that after the argument at dinner Tyler had promised to delete his genomecestry account. Charles remained quiet and completely still the entire time.

"I think she found us Dad," Leisel said. She explained about the blue car driving past Tyler's house multiple times and about the intruder in her own home who took the family portrait. The relief Leisel felt as she let the words tumble out of her mouth was so intense it brought tears to her eyes. She turned her gaze to her father. His focus was back on his sandwich.

"Dad," Leisel said, "could it possibly be true? Is Jane Gray my sister?"

93

LOYAL TRUESDALE

L oyal and Trinity were just starting the footage from the front of the Timmerman family home when the secure phone rang. She looked at caller ID. "It's Williams," she said to Loyal before she answered.

"Glass," she said.

Loyal could hear the Captain's voice but could not understand the content of the conversation. Trinity listened intently for about 90 seconds then thanked the captain and ended the call. She turned to Loyal and said, "The officers canvasing the area around Leisel Timmerman's home found one bit of footage from the time of the break in. It was from a house on Horizon which is a street that is below and south of Leisel's. They didn't see Jane but the camera captured the front of her car as she parked below Leisel's back yard. They were able to zoom in on the license plate. Jane was definitely there."

Loyal nodded but remained quiet. He had nothing to say. He still didn't like Jane for Tyler's murder but the circumstantial evidence was mounting. Each new discovery was a nail that was being pounded into Jane's coffin. Loyal and Trinity exchanged a long look. They knew each other well enough that they didn't have to say anything to know what the other was thinking. Finally Trinity gave a small shrug and turned back to the monitor. They saw nothing of any importance until the previous Sunday when Leisel and Tyler arrived for dinner. Jane arrived as well, moments after Tyler, and parked across the street from the gate. Before too long an Encinitas sheriff's car pulled up behind Jane and parked. The officer stepped out of his vehicle and approached Jane's car. He tapped on the driver's side window, they exchanged some words, then Jane handed him what Loyal assumed was driver's license, registration, and proof of insurance. The officer returned to his vehicle for several minutes, then walked back to Jane. He handed her items back to her and returned to his car. Jane drove away and the sheriff followed moments later.

"It didn't look like he cited her for anything," said Loyal, "but he probably filed a field report. We can ask Captain Williams to request it."

Trinity moved to the other computer station.

"Let's just look for ourselves," she said as she began tapping keys.

"Are you hacking the Encinitas Sheriff's Department?" Loyal asked.

"Just taking a peek," said Trinity. She tapped some more. "Here it is. A resident of Lone Jack road complained because she was parked on a horse trail. Jane told the officer she was taking a phone call. He ran her through the system and she was clean so he let her go with a warning."

"You can't hack sheriff departments Trinity," said Loyal, "I'm going to need to let them know that they are vulnerable."

Trinity gave Loyal a long look. "You aren't even supposed to be in here Loyal," she said. "You never saw me do that." A slow smile spread across her face. "Besides," she said, "what happens in the SCIF stays in the SCIF."

Loyal looked at her for a long moment.

"You hacked Carlsbad too, didn't you? he asked. "Last spring when we first met. That's why you knew so much about Lacey's murder."

The smile remained on Trinity's face. "I can neither confirm nor deny," she said.

94

CHARLES TIMMERMAN

C harles was opening his mouth to answer Leisel's question when he heard a thump behind him. He and Leisel turned at the same time. Daisy was on the floor in the kitchen entryway. Charles leapt from his seat and raced to Daisy. He lifted her into his arms.

"Call Dr. Cole," he said to Leisel as he lifted his wife and carried her to the living room. He laid her on the couch. She was pale but breathing steadily. Charles wondered how much of Leisel's story Daisy had heard. Clearly enough to cause her to faint. He rubbed his fingers gently on her cheeks and murmured reassuring words into her ear. Gradually she opened her eyes.

"I can't live like this," she said, her voice barely audible. A tear slipped sideways down her cheek. Charles gently wiped it away.

"We don't have a choice," he said.

Daisy's eyes met his. Her gaze was unwavering.

"There's always a choice Charles," she said.

Leisel stepped into the living room. "Dr. Cole is on his way," she said.

"Thank you Leisel," said Charles. He paused then added, "Can we have a few minutes alone?"

Leisel nodded and backed out of the room. When Charles looked back at Daisy she had her eyes closed. Tears still leaked slowly out of the corners of her eyes. Charles wiped her cheeks with the corner of his shirt. He picked up her left hand and held it with both of his hands. He turned her hand so he could see the inside of her wrist. The scar was faded but visible. He traced it with his thumb. Charles had spent his entire adult life protecting Daisy. He had created a cocoon for her, building barriers that kept her safe from the real world. There was no way to keep the fact of Tyler's death from her. Daisy was going to have to deal with it. All Charles could do was be there to try to keep her safe.

95

TRINITY GLASS

T rinity ran the footage from the rear of the Timmerman family home on double speed. A woman who they assumed was Daisy went riding every day, but other than that there was no unusual activity until Tuesday afternoon. Loyal saw it first.

"Stop the footage," he said. "Rewind a bit then go forward more slowly. I think I saw something moving in the background."

Trinity did as he asked and they both stared intently at the screen.

"There," said Loyal pointing at the screen, "something is climbing up those large rocks in the background."

"I see it," said Trinity. She attempted to zoom in on the figure but the image blurred. "Animal or human?" she asked.

"Hard to say," said Loyal, "go forward at half speed. We saw Daisy go out on her ride," he added. "She should be returning soon."

. . .

Trinity inched the footage forward. The figure remained on the rock.

"It's sitting so still," said Loyal, "makes me lean toward it being an animal."

Trinity nodded then pointed at the left corner of the screen.

"Here comes Daisy," she said.

Loyal pointed to the figure on the rock.

"Look," he said, "they stood up. Definitely human."

Loyal and Trinity watched as the person raced down the rock, then tripped and fell. By the time they were up and running toward the fence line Daisy had entered the gate and closed it behind her. She didn't appear to notice the person running toward her. As the figure neared and came into focus Loyal said, "It's Jane."

"And she's losing her shit," said Trinity as they watched Jane fling herself at the gate screaming and crying. She shook the gate with all her strength then sank down to the ground crying hysterically. Eventually she quieted and used her shirt to wipe the tears and mucus from her face. She was only a few feet from the security camera and Trinity and Loyal were able to see the entire scene in perfect clarity.

After watching Jane walk away and disappear from view Trinity turned the monitor off and turned to face Loyal.

"The timing works Loyal," she said. "Jane could have driven to Tyler's and confronted him. Perhaps they argued and it got out of hand?"

"We need to canvas the neighborhood," said Loyal. "Someone on that street has to have footage."

"Agreed," said Trinity. "I could just hack everyone's internet based security systems," she added, "but signals intelligence will only get us so far. I want the human intelligence on this too."

She pushed her chair back and stood up.

"Let's get something to eat and head out," she said.

Loyal stood as well and together they exited the SCIF.

96

PATRICK O'KEEFE

P at was sitting in his office but his mind was back on S Coast Blvd with Penny Stroud. The pain on her face haunted him. He couldn't concentrate on his work and he found, surprisingly, that it was Loyal he wanted to talk to. Olive hadn't explicitly told him not to contact Loyal but he knew she would disapprove of any communication between the two men. Pat knew he needed to talk to someone about what he had discovered about Hope and Miles. He didn't want to bring this news home to Olive. He shared some things from work with her but felt that this would be too much. In the end he picked up his phone, walked out to the parking lot, and called Loyal.

Loyal answered on the third ring. Despite the fact that he sounded like he had food in his mouth, Pat could hear the surprise and concern in Loyal's voice when he said, "Pat. Everything ok?"

"Do you have a minute?" Pat asked.

"Sure," said Loyal.

Pat spent the next five minutes telling Loyal about Hope and Miles Bannon, the DNA tests, and the adoption. When he finished talking Loyal was quiet for a moment then he said, "That's a tough one Pat."

"I don't know if I want to do this anymore Loyal," Pat said, "or if I even can."

"Look Pat," said Loyal, "if you want people to like you, you want to be a hero, you should have been a firefighter. People only call cops when everything has gone to shit. They don't want the police around in good times. You're going to have to figure out how to deal with that."

"How did you?" asked Pat.

"Find somewhere to put the bad stuff," said Loyal, "don't give it any space in your head."

"That's easier said than done," said Pat.

"You have to do it," said Loyal. "Think about work at work. Leave it there when you go home. Concentrate on your family."

When Pat didn't respond Loyal added, "You are a good detective Pat. Don't give it up."

"Thanks Loyal," said Pat. He disconnected the call before Loyal could respond. Pat stood in the parking lot for a full five minutes before he gave a deep sigh and returned to his office.

97

LOYAL TRUESDALE

L oyal looked at his phone for a long moment then slipped it into his pocket with a small sigh.

"Sounds like Pat is having a tough time," said Trinity.

"Yeah," said Loyal, "it must be pretty bad if he called me. He's had a few rough cases over the last few months. Not handling it very well."

"He's sensitive," said Trinity, "he lets things get to him."

"Good at his job though," said Loyal.

"Yes," said Trinity, "true. He'll work it out."

Loyal let out a long breath. "You ready to canvas Tyler's street?"

Trinity stood up. "Let's go," she said.

They began with the house directly across the street from Tyler's. It had a ring doorbell which Loyal took as a good sign. A woman in her mid fifties answered the door. She had black hair that was cut in a short bob and dark brown eyes. The scent of garlic and onions wafted out the door when she opened it. Trinity spoke first. Holding out her badge she said, "I'm Agent Glass with the Federal Office of Strategic Investigations and this is my colleague. I was wondering if we might have a few minutes of your time Ms..." The woman looked at the badge for a moment then nodded and opened the door completely to allow them to enter her home.

"I'm Gloria Navarro," she said. "Is this about the fire across the street?" she asked. "I'm the one who called 911."

"We'd like to access your ring doorbell footage from that afternoon Gloria," said Trinity. "Starting at 3:00 pm."

Gloria led them into her kitchen. She walked to the stove and lifted a lid off a pot releasing a plume of steam.

"I'm just making some chicken stock," she said. "Have a seat at the table and I'll grab my laptop."

Gloria replaced the lid and walked out of the room. Loyal and Trinity sat at the table. Gloria returned with a silver Mac Book and sat down as well. She tapped some keys then turned the computer so that the screen was visible to all of them.

"Okay," said Gloria, "here's Tuesday at 3:00."

Loyal and Trinity looked at the screen. The camera showed Tyler's house clearly. His truck was parked in the driveway.

"Let's fast forward," said Trinity.

Gloria tapped some keys. The scene remained the same. There was no activity on the street.

"It's a quiet neighborhood," said Gloria.

Loyal nodded but said nothing in response. His focus was on the time stamp. At 3:36 the scene was crystal clear. At 3:37 the screen went blank.

98

TRINITY GLASS

Trinity and Loyal spent the next several hours knocking on doors. They went to every house on Brava Street. Nearly every home had some type of security camera. Without exception every screen went blank at 3:37. At the third house Trinity asked the homeowner to continue fast forwarding. The camera became active at 6:15 pm. At each successive house she asked the homeowners to fast forward until the footage resumed. Each camera resumed recording at 6:15. Trinity and Loyal asked, without success, about any cell phone footage people might have of the fire as well as any pictures or video they may have taken at all that day. Perhaps a picture of their dog in the back yard or their child playing outside? They finished with all the houses on Bravo Street and canvased four houses on Verde Avenue that had cameras on the rear of their homes with a view of the back of Tyler's property. The cameras on these houses had cut out at 3:37 as well.

. . .

Trinity and Loyal exited the final house on Verde Avenue. As they walked down the driveway Loyal said, "It's not a coincidence and I don't think Jane could have orchestrated this. There's something bigger in play here."

Trinity had her phone in her hand and was looking at the screen.

"I agree," she said. She showed Loyal the screen of her phone. It displayed a map of Tyler's neighborhood. Trinity pointed to a house on Hataca Road which was southwest of Tyler's house.

"Let's try this house," she said. "If they have a rear facing camera it might show a corner of Tyler's house."

Loyal nodded his agreement. They walked down Brava Street and turned right onto Hataca Road. The house Trinity had pointed out had an old Ford F150 in the driveway.

"Old truck," said Loyal, "doesn't bode well for high tech security system."

"Low tech is acceptable," said Trinity as she reached out and knocked on the door.

The door opened after about a minute. An older man looked out at them. He was about six feet tall but a bit stooped in the shoulders. He was rail thin with pale blue eyes and white blonde hair.

"Whatever you're selling I'm not buying," he said.

Trinity held out her identification.

"I'm Agent Glass with the Office of Strategic Investigations," she said. She waved a hand at Loyal. "This is my colleague."

"What do you want with me?" the man said.

"Do you have security cameras Mr...?" Trinity let her sentence trail off.

"Dale," said the man, "Richard Dale. And yes, yes I do."

Trinity looked at Loyal and gave a small smile then turned back to Mr. Dale.

"Would you be willing to show us your footage from Tuesday afternoon?"

"Can I see that ID again?" Mr. Dale asked.

Trinity held out her ID again. Mr. Dale took it and studied it for a moment then handed it back.

"Looks real enough," he said. "Come on in." He led them down a hallway and into a small home office that held a neat desk, an office chair, and a lamp.

"Are you military?" Loyal asked.

"Marine," said Mr. Dale, "Pacific theater in World War Two." He turned to look at Loyal. "SBD tail gunner; I flew 34 missions. How did you know?"

Loyal pointed to the brass plaque on the door to the office. Trinity turned to look at it. It read

Office of the Sergeant Major

Mr Dale opened a closet door and pointed to the equipment inside. There was an old TV, Trinity guessed at least twenty years old, and what looked like a VCR player.

"Designed the system myself," said Mr. Dale, "none of that newfangled internet crap for me."

Trinity turned again to glance at Loyal. She raised her left eyebrow slightly and smiled again.

"We're interested in any footage from the back of your house," said Trinity, "do you have a camera in back?"

"You bet," said Mr. Dale, "my property backs up to the park. Gotta keep an eye on that area. If someone is going to try to get in my house they are going to come from the back."

It took Mr. Dale a few minutes to locate the date and time they were interested in. The camera had a view of the small parking lot and some of the grassy area of the park. Tyler's back gate was not visible. Once he had everything set he began fast forwarding the footage. Trinity kept an eye on the time stamp. At 3:37 the view did not change. Mr. Dale's outdated equipment had not been affected. Just after 4:00 two figures appeared on the left side of the screen.

"Can you back up and slow to real time?" Trinity asked.

Mr. Dale did so. Trinity watched as two figures, both with dark hair and carrying what looked like three full size Yeti coolers crossed the screen and exited on the right.

"They are heading in the direction of Tyler's back gate," said Loyal.

Trinity asked Mr. Dale to fast forward again. He complied. At 4:52, just minutes before the 911 call regarding the fire, those two figures and a third person they hadn't seen before all crossed the screen heading in the opposite direction. From this perspective Trinity could see that all three people were of Asian descent and all three of them were carrying coolers.

99

TRINITY GLASS

Trinity asked Mr. Dale to rewind the tape to the scene when the people first appeared and freeze the frame. She leaned in and studied the people. One person carried a cooler in each hand, the other carried a single cooler in their left hand.

"The way that person is carrying the two coolers they look empty," said Trinity pointing at the screen.

"Agreed," said Loyal, "and the one the other person is carrying looks heavier."

"Fast forward to the footage where there are three people please," said Trinity.

Mr. Dale did as requested.

Trinity pointed at the screen again.

"Now all three look heavy," she said.

"I'm going to need a copy of that tape Mr. Dale," said Trinity.

The old man reached up and ejected the VHS cartridge. He handed it to Trinity.

"You can have this one," he said, "I have more blank tapes I can use."

Trinity accepted the cartridge and thanked Mr. Dale for his time. She and Loyal walked out the front door and down the driveway to the sidewalk. Trinity turned toward Loyal.

"You know anyone with a VCR?" she asked.

Loyal nodded.

"Actually I do," he said. There's a guy who has a tiny office on El Camino Real, just north of the 78, who transfers old tapes onto discs or zip drives." He pulled his phone out of his pocket. "I had some movies transferred a few years ago. I can't remember his name but I'm sure I can find his number."

"Good," said Trinity, "Let's see if he can do it today."

Loyal placed the call.

He'll meet us there in an hour," he said as he slipped the phone back in his pocket.

"Let's walk the park," said Trinity, "see if we can figure out where those three people were heading.

Trinity and Loyal positioned themselves in front of Tyler's back gate facing west. They followed the same trajectory the three people with coolers had been walking and discovered a narrow dirt trail which they followed. It led to some fenced in tennis courts and a set of steep stairs. They walked down the stairs and found that they were in another, much larger, park. There was a basketball court to their left, a large sandbox to their right, and a children's play area and a parking lot directly in front of them. They followed the cement walkway to the parking lot and found a sign which identified the area as La Costa Canyon Park.

· · ·

"They probably parked somewhere around here," said Loyal.

"Yep," said Trinity. "and it wouldn't surprise me if all the security cameras in this area stopped working at 3:37 on Tuesday." She let out a long sigh. "I don't think we will be lucky enough to find another person with a VCR."

"You think those three people had something to do with Tyler?" Loyal asked.

"It's doubtful," said Trinity, "but we need to follow every lead to its final conclusion."

"Absolutely," said Loyal.

"I have an idea," said Trinity. "Let's go get this thing," she held up the VHS tape she was still holding, "transferred. Then we can head back to the SCIF."

100

LOYAL TRUESDALE

Trinity and Loyal exited PME Audio/Video at 7:00 pm. The owner had been kind enough to meet them after regular business hours and transfer the footage to a zip drive. The drive back to Loyal's house took about fifteen minutes. Trinity headed straight into the SCIF telling Loyal as she walked out of the house that she would open the door for him in exactly ten minutes. Loyal stayed in the house to feed Boo and make ham sandwiches which he carried out to the SCIF. He had to wait just over a minute for Trinity to open the SCIF door. She let him in without saying a word then sat down in front of one of the computer stations and began pecking at the keys. Her fingers tapped the keys in short, almost violent, bursts. Loyal set the plate holding the sandwiches next to the computer and sat down beside Trinity. The image on the computer screen showed an intersection.

"Traffic cameras," said Trinity by way of explanation.

"Is there anything you can't hack?" Loyal asked.

"I'm an agent with the OSI Loyal," said Trinity, "I'm going to have some questionable skills." She stopped typing and turned to him. "If you have a problem with this you should probably step out."

Loyal shook his head. "I'm in," he said.

Trinity pointed at the screen.

"This is the intersection of La Costa Avenue and Rancho Santa Fe Road," she said. "The only way out of that neighborhood is La Costa Avenue. So they either went east or west. I started with east." Trinity pointed at the screen. "These cameras have excellent resolution. Look at the detail. I'm confident we can identify them."

Loyal shook his head. "I'm shocked by the detail. You can see right into the cars."

"Yeah," said Trinity, "privacy is just an illusion."

They turned back to the screen and watched the cars going through the intersection in silence. When the time stamp reached 5:30 pm Trinity decided they had watched the eastern route long enough. She exited the screen and tapped at keys for several minutes. Eventually a new intersection appeared on the computer.

"El Camino Real," said Trinity. Again, they studied the cars in silence. When the time stamp read 5:16 Loyal pointed at the screen.

"Stop the action," he said. "Go back a few minutes."

Trinity did as he asked.

"Can you go forward slowly?" Loyal asked.

Trinity slowed the footage to a crawl.

"There," said Loyal placing his finger on a dark blue sedan that was turning north on El Camino Real.

Trinity zoomed in so close it was as if the were standing on the hood of the car. The driver and front passenger were clearly visible. A passenger in the back seat was also able to be seen. It was definitely the three Asians from the park. The top of a Yeti cooler sitting on the seat beside the rear passenger was visible as well.

"Gotcha," said Trinity with a smile. "It's easy now," she said turning to face Loyal, "we'll just follow them through intersection cameras and see where they go."

The blue car stayed on El Camino Real for several miles then made a left on Palomar Airport Road. Loyal and Trinity watched as the car turned into Palomar Airport and parked in front of Western Flight, one of three jet centers located on the airport. The three people exited the vehicle. Each retrieved a cooler from the car. As Trinity and Loyal watched in stunned silence all three entered Western Flight.

101

CHARLES TIMMERMAN

Dr. Cole arrived within half an hour. Charles lifted Daisy in his arms and carried her into the bedroom. She lay quietly while Dr. Cole checked her vitals. Charles stood off to the side; Leisel remained in the living room. When he was finished examining her Dr. Cole removed the stethoscope from his ears and turned to face Charles.

"Let's talk in the living room," Dr. Cole said.

Charles nodded. He moved to the bed and leaned down to give Daisy a tender kiss on her cheek. Her eyes were open, her gaze seemingly focused on the ceiling. The despair in her eyes was visible to Charles. He had seen this look on Daisy's face before and it frightened him. He stood up straight and followed Dr. Cole into the living room.

"She needs round the clock care," Dr. Cole said. "She's clearly despondent. Her vitals are good but she's extremely dehydrated."

"I'm not putting her in a facility," said Charles.

"I'm not suggesting that," said Dr. Cole, "I'd like to put someone here with her. A nurse, round the clock, for at least a week."

Charles sighed. "Whatever she needs," he said, "anything."

Leisel stood up from where she was sitting on the couch.

"I can stay with her," she said.

Dr. Cole smiled. "You're a wonderful daughter Leisel, but I'm afraid your mother needs more care than you can provide."

Dr. Cole made a call and the nurse arrived within the hour. Dr. Cole introduced her as Phyllis. She appeared to be in her mid-fifties. She was small and slender with short blonde hair and sparkling green eyes. She arrived with a small suitcase, a large medical bag, and an IV stand which Charles looked at with questions in his eyes.

"Fluids," said Phyllis, "we need to hydrate your wife."

Dr. Cole and Phyllis went into the bedroom. Charles could hear the murmur of their voices but not the content of their conversation. After about ten minutes Dr. Cole came out of the room.

"They are all set," he said to Charles, "call me if you need anything."

Charles shook the doctor's hand and walked him to the door. When he returned to the living room Leisel was standing in the doorway, her arms crossed tightly across her chest. She looked Charles directly in the eyes and said, "We need to talk."

102

TRINITY GLASS

Trinity pushed away from the computer desk and turned toward Loyal.

"That's curious," she said, "straight from the park to the airport. I wasn't expecting that."

"Can you hack the airport security cameras?" asked Loyal.

Trinity smiled. "You on board with that now?"

Loyal smiled back. "I guess I have to be," he said. "I want to know where those folks are going."

Trinity turned back to the computer.

"This will be a little harder than the traffic cameras," she said. "Might take a bit but I'll get it."

Less than ten minutes later Trinity pointed at the screen.

"This is footage from the rear of the jet center," she said. "You can see our people walking out to that jet."

Loyal leaned in closer. "Yep," he said, "that's them."

They watched as the three people walked up the stairs and into a plane.

"That's a pretty big plane," Loyal said.

Trinity nodded. "It's a Global Express Bombardier," she said, "big, fast, and very expensive." She leaned closer to the screen. "Can you make out the N number?"

"Looks like N264T to me," said Loyal.

"Yeah, to me too," said Trinity. She picked up a pen and jotted the N number down on a pad of paper. She returned her fingers to the computer keyboard and began tapping again.

"Let's see if we can find the flight plan for the plane," she said. A few minutes later she leaned away from the screen and looked at Loyal.

"Shanghai," was all she said.

103

CHARLES TIMMERMAN

C harles and Leisel walked out into the back yard and sat in some deck chairs near the pool. They were side by side not facing each other. Both were silent for a time and when Leisel finally spoke her voice was firm but not unkind.

"Dad," she said quietly, her gaze still focused on the blue water of the swimming pool, "is Jane Gray my sister?"

Charles kept his focus on the cool water as well. He'd kept this secret so long and buried it so deep. It lived inside him, a dark ball tucked away in the corner of his soul. Only on a handful of occasions had he gingerly pulled the ball out into the light to briefly examine it then tucked it away again just as quickly. Acknowledging it caused him more pain that he would ever admit. Sharing it with Leisel would be tremendously painful, but, he realized as he stared at the quiet waters of the pool, she deserved to know the truth.

. . .

Charles drew in a slow deep breath and held it for a moment then let it out.

"Probably," he said, "DNA doesn't lie."

He turned to face Leisel. She stared straight ahead.

"You and mom gave a baby away?"

"We had no choice," said Charles.

Leisel turned to face him. Her eyes were filled with tears and Charles felt his own eyes fill.

"We never even got to hold her," he said.

Leisel reached out her left hand and took her father's right hand in hers.

"Will you tell me?" she asked.

Charles did.

104

TRINITY GLASS

Trinity was working on finding the owner of the Bombardier. It was listed as being owned by a company called Aegis in Singapore but she could find no names attached to the company.

"It looks like a shell company," she said. "I can't find any business activity associated with the business name."

"Anonymity," said Loyal, "but why?"

"Illegal activity," said Trinity, "tax liability avoidance, asset protection, or like you said to remain anonymous."

"Ok," said Loyal, "so what do we have? Security camera failures across the neighborhood, three people with coolers crossing the park and heading straight to the airport, and a flight directly to Shanghai in a jet owned by a shell company. I'm not seeing the connection to Tyler."

Trinity ran her hands over her face.

"I need to report in to Caldwell," she said.

"You want me to step out?" Loyal asked.

Trinity shook her head.

"You can stay," she said, "just keep quiet."

. . .

Caldwell answered on the second ring. Trinity had the phone on speaker so Loyal could hear both sides of the conversation.

"Doug," she said, "I have a few things to report to you."

It took Trinity about ten minutes to relay everything that she and Loyal had discovered. Of course she kept Loyal's involvement out. She described all the security footage they had reviewed, the neighborhood footage that had been compromised, the old man's VCR footage, the Asian's with the coolers, and the flight from Palomar to Shanghai. Caldwell listened without interrupting. When Trinity stopped speaking he was silent a moment longer then he said, "You are alone right now, correct?"

Trinity glanced at Loyal then said, "Yes."

"I mean this Glass," said Caldwell, "what I'm about to tell you goes no further. Truesdale is not to be read in on this."

"Understood," said Trinity.

"I have the autopsy results," said Caldwell. "They are sealed from everyone but you and me. Captain Williams isn't seeing this."

"Understood," said Trinity with a glance at Loyal. He nodded, indicating that he understood what he was about to hear could go no further.

"Timmerman's organs were missing," said Caldwell, "everything. Heart, lungs, liver, kidneys."

"He was badly burned," said Trinity.

"Yes," said Caldwell, "he was. But not so badly that the ME couldn't see that the organs were missing."

Caldwell paused for a brief moment then added, "Surgically removed."

Trinity thought about this for a moment.

"We aren't looking at Jane anymore then," she said.

"Nope," said Caldwell, "I'd say those people in the park with coolers just got a hell of a lot more interesting."

105

LOYAL TRUESDALE

Trinity disconnected the connection with Caldwell and turned to Loyal.

"I need to process this," she said. "I've been sitting too long. I need to move."

"Let's walk to the beach," said Loyal.

They both stood and walked out of the SCIF. The moon was full and hung low in the sky. The air was cool and a slight breeze was blowing. Trinity took in a long deep breath. She held it for a moment then let it out slowly. Loyal watched her without saying a word. He knew she was struggling to process everything they had learned today. He was as well. In a very short time everything had shifted. Jane had gone from suspect to something he couldn't yet articulate.

They walked into the house without speaking. Within five minutes they had both changed into T-shirts and sweat pants. Loyal was lacing his shoes when his phone rang.

"Hello," he said.

He listened for a moment then said, "Thank you for getting back to me Eden. I was wondering if you have had any contact with Jane Gray recently."

Loyal listened again then said, "Thank you again for calling. If Jane reaches out to you please let me know right away."

He disconnected the call and turned to Trinity.

"Jane's former PT," he said. "She listed her as a reference on a job application quite some time ago. She says she hasn't heard from Jane in years."

"Do you believe her?" Trinity asked.

"I think so," said Loyal, "she sounded genuinely confused. I can't think of a reason for her to lie." Trinity nodded and stood.

"Ready?" she asked.

Loyal nodded and they headed out the door.

The walk to the beach took about ten minutes. The moon was inching its way upward, the bright light reflecting on the water and sand. Loyal took Trinity's hand in his as they stepped on to the sand. She felt some of the stress of the day leach out of her body at his touch. She turned and looked at Loyal. Even in profile she could see that he was concentrating. She loved the way his brain worked and, surprisingly, didn't feel guilty about her deception with Caldwell. Loyal was smart and good at working out puzzles. She needed him to be read in on everything whether Caldwell approved or not. Loyal turned and looked at her.

"North or South?" he asked.

Trinity leaned up and gave him a slow kiss.

"South," she said.

106

TRINITY GLASS

They walked south for about ten minutes without speaking. Trinity was closest to the water and after the first few minutes she had paused to remove her shoes and socks and to cuff her sweatpants. She was walking with her feet in the ocean. The cool water flowed over her feet each time a wave rolled in. She still held Loyal's hand in hers but their arms were stretched out as his feet were not in the water. When Trinity saw a lifeguard station about thirty feet in front of them she pointed to it and said, "Let's sit for a few minutes." Loyal nodded and began moving toward the tower. He stepped to the side when they reached it and allowed Trinity to climb the ladder first. He followed closely behind her and they settled themselves on the platform with their backs against the wall.

The moon was higher in the sky now and its reflection was bright against the dancing waves. Trinity watched the movement of the ocean for a moment then turned to look at Loyal.

"What are your thoughts?" she asked.

"It's looking like stolen organs but I'm having a hard time wrapping my brain around that," said Loyal. "I mean just the logistics alone are mind boggling."

"Yeah, I'm feeling that too,"said Trinity. She paused and rearranged her body so that she was facing Loyal.

"Let's look at what we know for sure," she said. She held up her pointer finger. "The accelerant and the surgically removed organs take Jane out of the picture." She added her middle finger to the pointer. "The malfunctioning of all neighborhood surveillance cameras suggests strong technological skills." Her ring finger joined the other two fingers. "The Asians with the coolers were not having a picnic," she smiled, "I mean who comes here from Shanghai for a picnic?" She dropped her hand back to her lap and looked at Loyal expectantly.

Loyal smiled back at Trinity.

"Okay," he said, "let's assume for the moment that Tyler's organs were stolen and flown back to Shanghai." Loyal raised his own pointer finger in the air. "How was he chosen as a match," he added his middle finger, "and for whom?" His ring finger joined the other two. "How were the organs preserved for that long of a flight? Even in the Bombardier it has to be twelve to fourteen hours from Carlsbad to Shanghai." He let his hand fall back to his lap. Trinity pulled out her phone and started tapping keys.

"I read an article a few weeks ago," she said, "let me find it." She tapped a bit more then said, "Here it is. San Diego Union Tribune. Title is *New Tool May Reset Transplant Clock.*"

She handed the phone to Loyal and watched as he read. She remembered the content well. Researchers in Switzerland had developed a machine that could keep livers viable for transplant for days rather than hours.

Loyal handed the phone back to Trinity.

"Interesting," he said, "but it's years away from clinical use."

"Right," said Trinity, "but if Switzerland has developed it then China has it too. They steal intellectual property all the time. And if they have it they'll use it." She paused as she considered this then added, "China has more transplant tourism than any other country in the world Loyal. And those stats are just what they report. The true number could actually be much higher. They were removing organs from prisoners for God's sake."

"So now you think they are branching out and getting organs from America?" Loyal asked. "Prisoner organs weren't good enough?"

Trinity thought about that for a moment.

"Maybe not Loyal," she finally said. "It could be that prisoner's organs are for millionaires. Perhaps American organs are for billionaires."

107

LOYAL TRUESDALE

Loyal considered Trinity's statement for a full thirty seconds before letting out a sharp laugh, it sounded almost like a bark, and saying, "Now you are venturing into science fiction. There's no way."

Trinity stood abruptly.

"We need to get back to the SCIF," she said. "I want to focus on the N number of the Bombardier and look for similar cases. Burned bodies are found in houses all the time. Maybe I can find some more that were missing a few organs."

Loyal stood as well.

"I still want to find Jane," he said. "Can you hack into the North County Transit District cameras? I can search that while you chase ghosts."

Trinity nodded and climbed down the ladder to the sand. Loyal followed her. They took each other's hand and headed north.

It was just past 9:30 when they walked in the front door of

Loyal's house. As they were heading to the back yard Loyal's phone rang. He glanced at it then turned to Trinity.

"It's Stella," he said, "I need to take this. I'll make some snacks and meet you out there."

Trinity nodded. "Call me on the secure phone when you are heading out and I'll let you in," she said as she walked out the back door. Loyal nodded and accepted Stella's call.

They talked for about ten minutes. Stella and Mitch had decided to finish their vacation up by driving down the coast of California. They were currently in a small motel in Bodega Bay and hoped to be home on Sunday afternoon. Loyal sat down on the couch as they talked. He was used to seeing Stella and Mason almost every day and found that he really missed them. He was being truthful when he told Stella he couldn't wait to see them again. After they disconnected Loyal leaned back on the couch and closed his eyes. A smile formed on his lips as he brought up a mental image of little Mason. Loyal had never really pictured himself as a grandfather. He was finding, through Mason, that the role was a perfect fit. With the smile on his face and the mental image of Mason in his mind Loyal slipped easily into sleep.

108

TRINITY GLASS

Trinity pushed away from the computer and ran her hands through her hair. She glanced at the time on the monitor. 1:53 am. She looked down at the pages of handwritten notes. Her mind was spinning and she was feeling a sense of disbelief because of the things she had uncovered. She looked around the SCIF and realized Loyal wasn't there. She had been so focused on her research that she hadn't realized that he never showed up with the promised snack. She stretched her arms into the air then dropped at the waist and reached down to the floor. She returned to an upright position and exited the SCIF. She could see through the sliding glass doors that the kitchen light was still on in the house. She entered quietly and found Loyal asleep on the couch. She stood still and watched him for a moment. There was a small smile on his face. He looked so peaceful that she hesitated before walking over and laying a gentle hand on his shoulder. His eyes fluttered open and took a few seconds to focus on her.

"You fell asleep," she said.

"I'm sorry," said Loyal as he sat up straighter, "I guess I did. What time is it?"

"Two o'clock," said Trinity. "I'm sorry to wake you Loyal," she added, "but I really need to talk to you. Are you awake enough to come to the SCIF with me?"

Loyal stood and stretched. "Of course," he said.

They walked out to the SCIF and sat in the same position, both chairs in front of the computer Trinity had been using. Trinity spent a minute organizing her papers full of her notes.

"I've found 11 flight plans for our Bombardier over the last three years. The first was in May of 2019. It landed at Walla Walla Regional airport in Washington state. The town is located just north of the border with Oregon. The plane was there one full day. The day it left there was a single car accident outside of town in an agricultural area. Apparently the car veered off the road into a ditch and burst into flames. There were no witnesses to the accident and the driver, identified through dental records, was a 33 year old resident of the town."

"Okay," said Loyal.

"There were two more instances in 2019," said Trinity, one in August and one in November. The landings were at Hillsboro Airport just outside Portland, Oregon and Bellingham International in Washington respectively. A house fire occurred in Portland the day the plane flew away. One person died, burned beyond recognition. Identified through dental records. In Bellingham a missing person report was filed one day after the plane flew away. A nineteen year old young man. He's never been found."

Loyal kept his gaze on Trinity but said nothing.

"There were four instances in 2020 and three more in 2021," said Trinity. "The plane lands and the next day there is a single car accident or a house fire with one fatality. All the bodies were completely burned with the exception of one car accident in June of 2020 near Kenmore Air Harbor in Washington. A passerby had a fire extinguisher in their car and they were able to get the fire out." She looked directly into Loyal's eyes. "The driver of the car was a 35 year old man, Loyal, and the ME determined that his kidneys had been surgically removed."

Loyal ran his hands over his face.

"Car accidents and house fires happen all the time, Trinity," he said. "And it isn't uncommon for a nineteen year old man to go missing."

"I agree," said Trinity, "but the plane is the key. Every time it lands in the United States someone dies." She shuffled through the papers for a moment then said, "When the Bombardier leaves the US it always lands in Shanghai. Ruijin Hospital, one of the most highly rated in China, is located in Sahnghai."

"You think they are harvesting organs?" Loyal asked. "I'm finding this extremely hard to believe. Who are the organs for? And how would they even find a perfect match?"

Trinity leaned back in her chair. She closed her eyes for a moment then opened them and locked her gaze onto Loyal.

"I've got more to show you Loyal," she said, "and by the time I'm done I think you are going to agree with me on this."

109

LOYAL TRUESDALE

L oyal took a deep breath in and let it out slowly.

"You are one of the most brilliant investigators I've ever met," he said. "I trust your instincts implicitly. But I have to tell you I feel like you are way out in left field on this one."

"Just hear me out," said Trinity, "if you aren't on board once you have all the evidence I'll consider the possibility that I'm wrong on this."

Loyal nodded. "I'm listening," he said.

Trinity shuffled through her notes again.

"I was able to access the medical files of nine of the eleven deceased or missing people." She paused and looked up at Loyal as if expecting him to protest her invasion into their privacy. He remained quiet.

"I've got all their blood types and vital stats. The only common thread is that they were all very healthy individuals. All maintained a healthy weight and reported healthy diets and little or no alcohol use. None of them were on any prescription meds and all reported no recreational drug use."

Trinity turned to the computer and tapped a few keys. Seven pictures appeared on the screen.

"I found these through Facebook and Instagram accounts," she said. "You notice anything interesting?"

Loyal leaned forward and examined the photos. He could see immediately that Trinity was correct in her assessment of the health of each individual.

"They are all outdoors," said Loyal.

Trinity nodded. "Look at their wrists," she said.

Loyal looked. "They are all wearing watches."

"Yes," said Trinity, "and they are all watches that monitor the user's vital statistics and connect to the internet."

Trinity turned toward Loyal again.

"One in five Americans has submitted DNA to a direct to consumer testing company Loyal. We know Tyler did and the odds are strong that a few of these people did too."

"You think their information has been compromised?" Loyal asked.

Trinity shuffled papers again. "This is from a news article I found," she said. She read aloud from the article.

At a recent Aspen Security Summit, Army veteran and Democrat Rep. Jason Crow (D-Colo.) warned America's enemies, including Russia and China, are developing biochemical weapons that could target specific people. Crow added, researchers are using DNA data provided to private companies to tailor the weapons to that genetic

information. However, he lamented adversaries can get this informa-
tion easily and without much of a fight.

Additionally, Republican Sen. Joni Ernst (R-Iowa) said the threat
of a biochemical attack won't just hit humans specifically, but also
the food supply. She stressed, America's adversaries could weaponize
diseases that have already plagued the agriculture sector to kill off
animals and plants used for food.

She stopped reading and looked at Loyal. He was watching her intently. "None of this information is secure Loyal," she said. "If I could find all this so easily then so could anyone else."

Loyal nodded. "I'm thinking about where most of these fitness trackers and other internet based exercise equipment is made."

"China," said Trinity, "it's possible they've back doored everything."

"Reporting right back to the mother ship," said Loyal with a slight laugh. "Not that I think any of this is funny," he added. "I'm starting to come around to your way of thinking. It is entirely possible that these people were targeted for their organ compatibility. The bodies were burned to conceal the fact that the organs were missing."

Trinity nodded then ran her hands through her hair. "It's pretty hard to comprehend," she said, "but I think it might be true."

110

TRINITY GLASS

Trinity pushed back from the computer desk and stood. She paced around the small space a few times then leaned back down to look at the time on the computer.

"It's 4:15 am," she said, "7:15 in Virginia. Caldwell is probably in his office by now." She looked at Loyal. "I'll put the call on speaker if you want to be here to listen," she said, "same as before. I think you have a right to hear what he has to say."

Loyal nodded. "Thanks," he said, "I'll stay silent."

Trinity nodded, picked up the secure phone, and dialed.

Caldwell answered on the first ring.

"Glass," he said, "you have something?"

"Yes," said Trinity, "and it's big." She paused. "Hear me out before you say anything, okay Doug? My theory has a lot of moving parts but it all comes together at the end."

"Go," said Caldwell. Trinity did.

She started with the flight plans of the Bombardier,

outlined the eleven cases of burned or missing people, detailed the medical histories of the nine she had been able to access, explained about the health monitoring watches, gave the stats about one in five Americans submitting DNA, and read from the article about the senators and their concerns about the lack of security regarding the DNA data. Caldwell listened without interruption. When Trinity stopped talking there was silence on the phone line for a long enough time that she was concerned the connection had been broken.

"You still there Doug?" she asked.

"Yes," said Caldwell, "just processing."

"You ever find Jane Gray?" he asked after another moment of silence.

Trinity was taken aback for a moment by the shift in conversation.

"No," she said, "but I think she might have taken a transit bus somewhere. There are multiple stops near her home. That's my next avenue of investigation."

After another moment of quiet he said, "Open the drawer beneath the computer desk. There should be an external hard drive in there."

Trinity opened the drawer and looked in. There were three external drives in the drawer.

"There is," she said.

"I want you to put everything you just told me on the drive," said Caldwell, "all your documentation. Take it to the Carlsbad FBI office and have them messenger it to me."

"Okay," said Trinity.

"Then I want you to scrub that computer and destroy any

notes you have taken by hand. Anything that ties to what you just told me needs to be gone."

"I'm still working the case," said Trinity.

"No," said Caldwell, "you are off this immediately. If this is even a possibility it needs to go up the chain of command, higher that you or me."

"What about the senators I mentioned?" asked Trinity, "shouldn't they be made aware of this?"

"This is a direct order Glass." Caldwell's voice was firm. "Messenger me the external hard drive, wipe the computer, and destroy any notes. Am I clear?"

Trinity let out a sigh. "Clear," she said.

111

LOYAL TRUESDALE

Loyal kept his gaze on Trinity during her entire conversation with Caldwell. There was an intensity coming off of her and he felt it increase when Caldwell instructed her to send him the external hard drive and to destroy all her work. He had so much respect for her as an investigator and so much love for her as a person. Sometimes the magnitude of his feelings for her caught him off guard. When she disconnected the call she turned to look at him. He could read the question in her eyes.

"Are you going to do it?" Loyal asked.

Trinity reached into the desk drawer and pulled out two of the external hard drives.

"I'm going to messenger him his copy," she said, "but I'm going to keep one for myself as well."

"That's smart," said Loyal.

"Do you have a safety deposit box?" Trinity asked.

"Yeah," said Loyal, "and I have a safe in my house too." He paused then pointed into the desk drawer and added, "You might consider using all three of those hard drives."

· · ·

Trinity made three copies of all the information. Loyal put one copy in the safe located in the floor of his bedroom closet. She gave him the second one to take to his bank when it opened at 9:00 and placed the third in her purse to take to the FBI office and messenger to Caldwell. They took a shower together, which led to some time in the bedroom, then drank coffee under the magnolia tree while the sun rose in the east. Loyal burned Trinity's handwritten notes, which she had scanned and included on the hard drives, in his free standing outdoor fireplace. They both watched as the papers caught fire, curled, then disintegrated.

"I have a concern," said Trinity.

Loyal turned his head toward her.

"Jane Gray," said Trinity. "I don't like that she was the first thing Caldwell asked about."

"Why?" Loyal asked

"Because Tyler Timmerman is a high profile case," said Trinity. "His family will not accept an unsolved case. There has to be closure and Caldwell knows that. He certainly isn't going to tell Charles Timmerman our theory about organ harvesting."

"He said he was passing your information up the chain of command," said Loyal.

"Right," said Trinity, "and whoever gets this mess is going to have that same concern. The case needs to be solved and they aren't going to solve it by telling the truth."

"You are thinking Jane is the perfect fall guy for this," said

Loyal. He thought for a moment then added, "I don't think the case would hold up in court."

"That's just it," said Trinity, "this is a case that they would never let get to court. We need to find Jane, Loyal. And we need to find her before they do."

112

LOYAL TRUESDALE

Loyal waited in the passenger seat of Trinity's rental while she went into the Carlsbad FBI office to messenger the external hard drive to Caldwell. His mind was on Jane. Trinity hadn't said it explicitly, but she sure as hell had intimated, that whatever entity of the US government Caldwell handed this mess off to they wouldn't be adverse to using Jane in order to wrap up Tyler Timmerman's death in a neat little package. As he thought about that fact now he realized that when Trinity said "using Jane" she meant killing Jane. He could see it now. Charles Timmerman would be shown the footage from the back fence of his property. It was clear that Jane was coming apart at the seams. It would be easy to imagine that she had driven to Tyler's and confronted him. Perhaps they struggled and he fell and hit his head. In a panic Jane set the fire and ran away. The story would sell.

He turned his head as the driver side door opened and Trinity slid in.

"All set," she said.

"Good," said Loyal, "let's hit the bank and get back to the SCIF. We definitely need to find Jane."

Trinity nodded. "Agreed," she said.

The bank took just over ten minutes. Loyal added Trinity as an authorized user on his safety deposit box and left the third external hard drive safely at the bank. Trinity drove them straight back to Loyal's house. As they turned the corner onto Robles Trinity was forced to stop the car. The giant truck and trailer were back and completely blocking the road. Loyal jumped out of the car and ran toward his house. The side fence was dismantled again and the tractor was in the process of removing the SCIF. Loyal approached the man who was directing the tractor driver through the damaged fencing.

"What the hell?" Loyal yelled loudly to make sure he was heard over the noise of the tractor's engine.

"We have orders to remove this SCIF immediately," said the man. He gestured toward the truck blocking the street. "Paperwork is in the truck."

"You can't just come on my property when I'm not home," said Loyal.

"Orders from the federal government," said the man, "I'm to take the SCIF whether you are here or not."

Loyal was opening his mouth to protest when Trinity walked up beside him. She put her hand on his arm.

"Let them take it Loyal," she said, "We have no use for it now anyway."

She turned to the man.

"Do I need to sign something?"

He shook his head. She turned back to Loyal.

"Forget about this," she said waving her hand at the damaged fence and the tractor, "we have more important things to worry about. We can search on my personal laptop."

"You going to fix this fence?" Loyal asked the man.

He shook his head. "I'll leave a receipt," he said, "you can file a claim."

Loyal bit back the response that popped into his head. He simply turned and followed Trinity into the house.

113

TRINITY GLASS

Trinity set her laptop up on Loyal's dining room table. She plugged the charger into an outlet near the floor and started researching North County Transit bus routes in Escondido. Loyal pulled up a chair next to her and watched the screen.

"Okay," Trinity said as she pointed at the screen, "here's a map of bus stops near Jane's house. It looks like there are four likely options."

Loyal nodded, "I thought the same thing when I looked at the map."

Trinity's fingers flew over the keyboard for a few moments then an image of some bus doors appeared on the screen.

"This is the camera above the driver's seat that records everyone who gets on and off," said Trinity. "I'm starting the footage at 3:00 pm on Tuesday. I'll run it on double speed. Tell me if you see anyone who looks like Jane and I'll slow things down."

Loyal nodded and they began watching.

. . .

They found Jane at the stop on Glenridge Road and Mountain View Drive. At 4:02 the bus doors opened and Jane stepped on. She kept her head down and wore a baseball cap but both Loyal and Trinity recognized her. Trinity took the footage back a few moments and slowed it down so that they could get a better look.

"Definitely her," said Loyal.

"Yep,"said Trinity, "she's still wearing the same clothes she had on when we saw her at the Timmerman's back gate. I'll speed things up again and we'll watch for when she gets off."

Jane stayed on the bus until it reached the transit center on Valley Parkway just west of Quince Street. The transit center was packed with cameras that Trinity had no problem hacking. They were able to watch as Jane studied a listing of bus routes then shouldered her backpack and walked east on Valley Parkway. Trinity accessed stoplight cameras and they tracked Jane to a bus stop at 2nd Avenue and Center City Parkway. They watched through a stoplight camera and less than ten minutes later bus 371 pulled up to the stop. Jane stood up from the bench she had been sitting on and boarded the bus.

Trinity pulled up bus 371's schedule.

"Escondido to Borrego Springs," she said."It takes three hours and ten minutes to make the trip so there must be stops on the route that aren't listed here."

"Speed up the footage and let's watch," said Loyal.

"I feel like we should start driving now," said Trinity. "I can use my phone as a hot spot so I can keep watching while you drive."

Loyal stood."That's smart," he said, "let's move."

114

LOYAL TRUESDALE

I gnoring his ruined fence and the blatantly angry look on one of his neighbor's faces, Loyal backed out of the driveway and headed toward Highway 76. Trinity kept up a running commentary regarding the stops the bus made on the way through Ramona and Julian. Jane remained on the bus until Santa Ysabel. She got off right where the 79 met the 76.

"She got off near Lake Henshaw," said Trinity. She looked up from the computer screen and out the window. "Where are we?"

"Just crossed Interstate 15," said Loyal. "I'd estimate about 40 minutes to Lake Henshaw."

Trinity tapped some keys on her computer.

"There are cabins there," she said, "possibly willing to take cash."

She raised her head and turned to look at Loyal.

"Do you think you could get us there any faster Loyal?" she asked. "If we could track Jane this easily so can anyone else."

. . .

Loyal accelerated. Highway 76 was a windy two lane road. Loyal was aware that there were many accidents on this particular stretch of the 76, and most of them were fatalities. He made every attempt to keep his speed steady and his steering even and smooth through the many curves.

"Tell me more about China and," he paused and thought for a moment, "transplant tourism I think you called it."

"Yeah," said Trinity, "it's a real thing. China does the most transplants, but Pakistan, Columbia, Egypt, and the Philippines aren't far behind."

"How does it work?" asked Loyal.

"Well think about what you know about organ donation," said Trinity.

"Not a lot beyond the DMV wanting us to put stickers on our licenses saying we will donate."

"Okay, so not much. Lots of people are on transplant lists, Loyal. Many wait for years for an acceptable organ, and some even die while waiting." She paused and thought for a moment.

"It's just like anything in the world Loyal," she said, "people with the means always find a way to jump the line."

"So they travel to other countries for organs?" Loyal asked.

"Exactly," said Trinity, "and those organs are often forcibly removed. China has the worst history. They've used prisoner organs since the 1970's. In the last five years or so they have imprisoned many people from the Falun Gong Buddhist sect and also Muslim Uyghur minorities. They are known as prisoners of conscience."

Loyal remained quiet as he thought about what she was telling him. When he didn't say anything she continued.

"It all really came to light in 2006 and 2007. Two human

rights lawyers exposed the forced organ harvesting program in China. I can't remember their names right now but they were nominated for a Pulitzer Peace Prize. Then in 2019 an independent tribunal was established to investigate forced organ harvesting in China. Their report concluded that forced organ harvesting has been committed throughout China for years on a significant scale."

"Do you have any idea how much an organ costs?" asked Loyal.

Trinity tapped at the computer that was still tethered to her phone. "This report says a kidney goes for $50,000 to $120,000 and a pancreas goes for $110,000 to $140,000."

"Jesus," said Loyal, "I can't believe I never heard anything about this. It's unbelievable."

He took his eyes off the road for a brief moment to glance at her then looked back out the windshield again.

"You think the forced organ donating has reached another level in China then?" he asked. "You think really wealthy people are willing to pay much more for perfect organs and that China can track Americans through the Internet?

"Absolutely," said Trinity, "it makes perfect sense. If a prisoner's organ is worth over $100,000 imagine what a physically fit American's would go for."

Trinity paused again then added, "There are almost 3,000 billionaires in the world Loyal. Lots of them are old men. What are the odds that some of them need a transplant?"

TRINITY GLASS

L oyal and Trinity didn't talk much after their conversation about forced organ harvesting. Loyal seemed lost in his own thoughts. Trinity imagined that he was having to rearrange some of his preconceived notions about the world and humanity. She had researched this topic extensively on her own time several years previously. She had appealed to Caldwell to research it officially for OSI but he had been unwilling to authorize it and refused to send it up the chain of command. Loyal navigated a roundabout at the base of Palomar Mountain and they began climbing in elevation. They passed a sign for the La Jolla Indian Reservation and began descending.

"Not long now," said Loyal. "Let's hope she's there and that we get to her first."

JANE GRAY

Jane sat on the couch in the small living room of the cabin she had rented at Lake Henshaw. Her shoulders were hunched and her head was bowed. She was mentally reviewing everything that she had done since she had driven away from the equestrian park near the Timmerman family home. The drive to Tyler's house was a blur. She didn't remember any of it. She did remember turning onto his street and seeing the fire trucks blocking access to his house which had been fully engulfed in flames. Jane's rage had dissipated and panic had filled the space left behind. She had turned her car around and driven straight home. She hadn't felt safe there either. Why, she couldn't explain. Something compelled her to pack a small backpack, grab all the cash she had in the house, and walk to the bus stop on Glenridge Road. She had ridden the bus to the transit station, checked the schedules and destinations of the buses, and decided on Borrego Springs. She had walked quickly to the bus stop on 2nd and Center City and boarded the last bus to Borrego.

. . .

As the bus left Escondido and drove towards Ramona Jane had felt some of the panic ease. She was just another anonymous bus rider. None of the other passengers had even glanced her way. Most were concentrating on their phones. Jane had left her phone at her home so she just rode and stared out the window. The bus made several stops in Ramona then headed to Julian where it made a few stops as well. As it neared the intersection of Highway 79 and Highway 76 Jane had remembered Lake Henshaw and the small cafe and cabins across the street from the lake. She had asked the driver to stop and let her off and had been grateful when he complied. She had walked along Highway 76 in the fading light. In the cafe she had asked to rent a cabin with cash and no ID. She had told the woman she was fleeing an abusive relationship. Her swollen eyes, pale skin, and shaking hands had been convincing enough, not to mention her pants which were torn and dirty from her fall off the rocks when she was trying to reach Daisy.

Jane sat up straight with a deep sigh. She picked up yesterday's newspaper and re-read the short article describing the house fire in Carlsbad and the body found in the home which was, as yet, unidentified. Jane was pretty sure it was Tyler. His truck had been in the driveway and she hadn't seen him in the small crowd that had been watching from a safe distance. She set the paper back down and stood. She thought about the conversation she had had that morning with her neighbor Harold. She had called him from the cafe phone and he had told her about the man who had been looking for her and about the search of her home. She had assured him that she was safe, though she did not tell him where she was, and had asked him not to tell anyone that he had spoken with her.

. . .

Jane folded her arms across her chest. The description Harold gave of the man looking for her sounded like Loyal. The police searching her house was not good news. She closed her eyes and brought up an image of her office. What would the police think about her information wall or about the photo of the Timmerman family with her image inserted into the broken frame? Was she a suspect in the house fire or Tyler's death? She thought about the things she had done. Certainly her finger-prints were in Leisel's home. And on the trackers which were both linked to her phone. Jane rubbed her hands over her face and through her hair. She didn't even know herself anymore. Why had she done all those crazy things? She deeply regretted ever submitting her DNA to genomecestry.com. Yes, her life had been uneventful prior to the DNA test, some might argue boring and predictable, but it had been safe. All the stupid test had done was make her feel that there was an emptiness in her life, that she was missing out on something. She knew that it was a bell she couldn't unring. Her birth family existed and if Tyler's death was not accidental it was very likely suspicion would fall on her. A good lawyer could probably prove her innocence but the Timmerman family would never accept her after they became aware of her unhinged behavior.

Jane felt a hot tear track down her left cheek. Another joined it and several rolled down her right cheek as well. She brushed them away angrily. She was frustrated and scared and didn't know what to do. She couldn't stay in the cabin forever. If she returned to Escondido would she be arrested? Being sent to jail was one of her greatest fears. Just the thought of being incarcerated for a day or two caused her to tremble. She'd give it another day or two, she finally decided. Maybe by then the newspaper would have more information about the cause of the fire and the identity of the body and the manner of death. Jane took a deep breath in and let it our slowly. Yes, she thought, staying here was best. It was Friday. She would wait it out over the weekend and hope for information. At least while she was at the cabin she was safe.

117

JANE GRAY

lthough this was technically only her third day at Lake Henshaw Jane had already developed a few habits. The first was a mid-morning visit to the cafe for a late breakfast. She had become friendly with the owner, Shelly, who would often sit with Jane and chat if she had the time. Before she left the cafe Jane would order a meal to go. This she would keep in her kitchen in the cabin and eat for dinner. She spent the bulk of her day in the cabin reading. Someone had left two books by Barry Eisler behind and she was enjoying them immensely. His books were thrillers about a group of assassins who had somehow ended up working together. Jane had already finished The Killer Collective and was about halfway through The Chaos Kind. When she was back to her real life she planned to read all of his previous books in order, starting at the beginning, so she could learn the backstories of all the characters. Her favorite was Livia Lone, a bad-ass Seattle sex crimes detective who was also a black belt and not afraid to take matters into her own hands when the legal system wasn't doing the job of stopping the bad guys.

. . .

One of the things the characters in Eisler's stories were very good at was being situationally aware. Jane thought this was an important habit for her to practice as well. She checked the parking lot of the cafe each time she was there and memorized the cars that were parked in it. She watched all the patrons of the cafe and tried to imagine what their backgrounds and life stories might be. So when she saw the man and woman approaching the cafe as she was eating her breakfast on Friday morning she did a double take. The first thing that caught her attention was that there was not a new car in the parking lot. Where had they come from? The second thing she noticed was the way they carried themselves. They strode toward the cafe with purpose but at the same time appeared to be trying to act casual. Their heads swiveled as they checked out the environment and they each wore a loose jacket that would be perfect for concealing a weapon. As they reached the cafe's steps Jane stood and walked toward the bathrooms at the back of the cafe. She caught Shelly's eye and gave a slight shake of her head. She hoped Shelly caught her meaning, that if they asked about her Shelly should say she wasn't there.

Jane entered the bathroom and turned to lock the door. Her hands were shaking so hard it took her a few tries to accomplish the task. Once it was locked Jane leaned against the door and strained to hear any bits of conversation. She heard nothing until there was a soft knock on the door.

"It's me," said Shelly softly, "you can come out Jane. They are gone."

Jane unlocked the door and opened it slowly.

"They had a picture of you Jane," Shelly said. "It looked like a driver's license photo."

"Who were they?" asked Jane.

"The woman said she was your sister and that they were looking for you."

"She's not my sister," said Jane. An image of Leisel popped up in Jane's mind for a brief moment.

"I told them I'd never seen you before," said Shelly, "but I'm not sure they believed me. They left though," she added.

"Thank you Shelly," said Jane. She pulled a twenty dollar bill from the pocket of her pants and handed it to Shelly.

"Here's for the breakfast," she said, "I'm going to head back to the cabin."

"You can go out through the kitchen," said Shelly. "Feels safer to me."

118

JANE GRAY

J ane slipped out of the back door of the cafe and hurried to her cabin. Who were they, she wondered, and why were they looking for her? How could they possibly have found her? She opened the door to cabin 116, stepped inside, and turned to lock the door. Before her hand could reach the lock she heard the distinctive squeak of the back door being opened. "Shit," she thought. She hadn't locked it when she left for the cafe. She turned without locking the front door and hurried to the bathroom. She eased the door closed as quietly as possible and turned the lock. She could hear quiet footsteps as someone walked through the cabin. Jane looked around the tiny bathroom searching for any type of weapon. "Think like Livia Lone", Jane whispered to herself, "act like her." Jane wasn't a black belt but she was strong. Her gaze fell on the toilet. It was an old fashioned one with a heavy and removable tank lid. Jane walked quickly to the toilet and lifted the lid. It was heavy and solid. She heard a noise and turned to see that someone was trying to turn the bathroom doorknob. In that instant Jane knew that they were going to kick the door in.

She positioned herself on the side opposite where the door would swing and raised the toilet tank above her right shoulder and slightly behind her. Her breath came in slow short bursts and her whole body was trembling. There was a loud kick and the door burst open. Jane swung the tank lid with every ounce of strength she had. The woman from the parking lot stepped into the bathroom and the tank lid connected. It hit her just under her jaw. There was a loud crack and the woman slumped to the floor. The gun she was holding fell out of her hand. Her head was at a very unnatural angle and Jane knew without checking that the woman was dead. Jane was reaching down to pick up the gun when she heard a male voice say, "Freeze."

119

LOYAL TRUESDALE

Loyal steered through the curves. As the oak trees covering the road began to thin out and the road straightened Loyal could see shrinking Lake Henshaw on his left and the small fire station and the Lake Henshaw Cafe and Cabins on his right. He pulled up to the cafe and parked. He glanced at Trinity.

"How do you want to play this?" he asked.

"Follow my lead," said Trinity.

Loyal nodded and slid out of the truck. He walked around to the passenger side and together he and Trinity approached the steps to the cafe. They walked up and through the front door. There were quite a few patrons sitting at tables and a woman in a leather cowboy hat was serving food and chatting with the diners. She approached Loyal and Trinity.

"Table for two?" she asked.

Trinity held out a picture of Jane.

"Actually I was wondering if you have seen this woman," she said.

The woman took the picture and looked at it for a moment then handed it back to Trinity saying, "Nope, sorry."

Trinity took the picture then reached in her pocket and pulled out her badge.

"My name is Agent Glass, ma'am," she said, "it is imperative that I find this woman. Her life is in danger."

The woman studied the badge for a few seconds then reached out for the picture again. She held it for a moment then gave a short sigh and handed the picture back again.

"She's here," she said, "cabin 116." She paused then added, "Is this about her husband?"

Trinity glanced at Loyal then back at the woman.

"Jane's not married," she said.

The woman seemed to consider this statement for a moment.

"A man and woman were here asking about her less than ten minutes ago," she said. "Jane saw them approaching and something spooked her because she hid in the bathroom. I told them I had never seen her before. I'm pretty sure they believed me. When they left I had Jane go back to her cabin through the back door in the kitchen."

"Where is cabin 116," asked Loyal, "and what is the layout like?"

The woman walked to a small counter and picked up a paper which she handed to Loyal.

"Here's a map of the property," she said. "Jane's cabin has two doors, one in front and one in back. The front opens into a small living room, the back into the kitchen area."

Loyal and Trinity studied the map for a moment then handed it back.

"Thank you," said Trinity, "we'd like to go out your back door as well."

120

JANE GRAY

Jane stopped all forward movement.

"Stand up slowly," said the male voice.

Jane straightened slowly. The man from the cafe was standing less than ten feet away from her. He held a gun in his right hand. He didn't even bother to glance at his dead partner.

"Kick that gun over to me," he said, "no sudden moves."

Jane looked at the gun in his hand then down at the gun on the floor. Both looked strange to her. The barrels seemed too long somehow. She knew very little about guns; she had never actually held one in her hands. Looking down the barrel end of the one the man was pointing at her was terrifying.

"Do it," he said, "now."

His voice was calm and controlled. He spoke quietly but with great authority. Still clutching the toilet tank lid Jane reached out her leg and gave the gun a push with her foot. The gun slid easily along the floor and stopped moving about a foot away from the man's feet. Without taking his gun or his eyes off of Jane he bent at the knees, picked up the gun in his left hand,

and stood up straight again. He slipped his partner's gun into some type of band he had around his waist.

"Good," he said, "now put that tank lid back on the toilet. Nice and easy," he added, "don't get any crazy ideas."

Jane took a step towards the toilet. The tank lid was in front of her body and she was holding it with both hands. As she stepped forward on her right foot and leaned slightly down toward the toilet she moved the tank lid to her right. With a sudden burst she swiveled to her left and flung the tank lid at the man, much like one would throw a frisbee. The lid sailed through the air. Jane heard a quiet popping sound and the bathroom mirror exploded behind her. The man folded forward as the tank lid made impact. His hands flew backwards and the gun clattered to the ground. As he was straightening Jane let loose a loud growl and launched herself at him. She was several inches taller than him and had momentum and surprise on her side. She slammed her body into his and they fell to the floor. Jane landed on top of him. She struggled to stand, intending to run out the door but the man was much stronger than he looked and obviously well trained in fighting techniques. Before Jane realized what had happened he had flipped her onto her back and was now on top of her.

"Fucking bitch," he growled. His face was inches from her and she could smell coffee on his breath. His eyes were dark green and hard. His right hand encircled her throat, his left hand held her right arm pinned to her side. His legs pinned hers to the ground. Jane was immobilized and out of options.

121

TRINITY GLASS

Trinity and Loyal approached cabin 116 from the east. Both had their guns drawn. Trinity signaled that she would take the front door and motioned to Loyal that he should take the back. He nodded silently and veered toward the back of the cabin. Trinity angled toward the front. The man and woman who had been looking for Jane were a problem. The woman in the cafe was sure they had left but Trinity doubted it. The woman in the cafe had been easy to read and if Trinity could see that she was lying about not having seen Jane then so could any other professional. If the government had sent contractors, and Trinity was convinced they had, they would be highly skilled. No, she thought, they hadn't left. It was highly likely that they were in the cabin with Jane right now.

She reached the front door and eased it open. It took her three seconds to analyze the scene and react. In the first second she recognized that Jane was on the floor with a man on top of her. He had her body pinned to the ground and his right hand encircled her neck. His face was mere inches from hers and he was speaking quietly but menacingly. In the second second Trinity saw the silenced gun on the floor just inches from her feet. In the third second, during which the man had become aware of Trinity's presence and started to move, Trinity passed her own gun to her left hand, picked up the silenced gun in her right, and placed two neat shots into the man's skull. A pink mist followed the bullets as they exited the man's head. His body slumped to the right as he collapsed. His torso and legs remained on Jane.

Sensing movement in the small hallway Trinity raised her head. Loyal was standing in the hall. His gun was raised and Trinity guessed that she had beaten him to the shot by mere moments. He stepped out of the hall and toward Jane who was whimpering and struggling to get out from underneath the dead man.

"It's Loyal Jane," he said as he lugged the dead body off of her. He helped her sit up. She scooted away from the dead man as fast as she could. Loyal looked up at Trinity.

"There's another one in the bathroom," he said, "dead."

Trinity nodded. She eased her own weapon back into her belly band with her left hand then used her shirt to wipe the silenced gun clean. It was a Glock 19 9mm with a suppressor attached. Once she was sure her fingerprints were not on the weapon she set it on the floor then turned to Loyal and Jane. He had helped her stand up and had one arm around her waist. She was shaking so hard she looked like she was having a seizure.

"Take her out of here Loyal," said Trinity. "Get her in your truck. I'll be right behind you." Loyal nodded and led Jane out the front door of the cabin. Trinity went through the dead man's pockets and found nothing but what she assumed was a burner phone and a small vial that contained three small white pills. The phone was password protected. Trinity wiped both items and returned them to his pockets. He also had another suppressed Glock in his belly band.

Trinity stood and walked to the bathroom. She stepped over the toilet tank lid that lay in the entry to the bathroom and looked at the woman on the floor. Her head was laying at a very unnatural angle. The bathroom mirror had been shattered by a bullet. Trinity went through the dead woman's pockets and found nothing. Contractors, she thought, traveling clean. She suspected that the pills in the dead man's pocket were to make it look like Jane had committed suicide. Anger at Caldwell bubbled to the surface and she tamped it down. She'd have time to be angry later. Right now she had to ensure Jane's safety. Trinity wiped down the tank lid and replaced it on the toilet. She had no way of knowing what Jane might have touched so she wiped the door handles on both the front and back doors, closed them both, and walked swiftly to Loyal's truck.

122

JANE GRAY

Jane had been shocked when the man's head had jerked to the side and he had crumpled down on top of her. She had known in an instant he was dead and had immediately begun to struggle beneath his weight. Then she had heard, "It's Loyal Jane," and the man had mercifully been lifted off of her. She had scuttled as far away from the dead body as she could then Loyal had helped her stand up and had kept his arm around her waist to support her. The woman, Jane had no idea who she was, had instructed Loyal to take Jane to his truck and he was in the process of doing that now.

"Are you injured?" Loyal asked.

Jane shook her head. She was shaking so fiercely she wasn't sure she could trust her voice to work properly. Loyal still had his arm around her waist and she knew that he could feel her trembling.

"The worst is over Jane," he said quietly, "you're safe now."

Jane nodded again and slid into his front passenger seat

when he unlocked the door. She watched as he walked around the front of the truck and slid into the driver's seat.

Jane took a deep breath in and let it out slowly. She followed that long breath with two more and felt the shaking ease up a bit. She saw the woman from the cabin approaching the truck.

"Who is she?" Jane asked. Before Loyal could say anything Jane added, "She killed that man."

Loyal remained silent and Jane watched as the woman slid into the back seat.

"Jane," she said. Jane swiveled in her seat so she could see her. "I'm a federal agent. You can call me Trinity. I want you to tell me everything that happened in that cabin and then I want you to forget it all. Can you do that?"

Jane nodded.

"Good," said Trinity. "Start with everything that happened after you left the back of the Timmerman property on Tuesday. Leave nothing out."

Jane didn't question how they knew she had been at the Timmerman property. She explained her rage and desire to confront Tyler, her arrival at his home to find it engulfed in flames, the sense of sheer panic that overtook her, and her bus ride to Lake Henshaw.

Trinity and Loyal listened without interruption. When Jane paused after explaining her bus ride Trinity prompted her to tell them everything that had happened in the cabin. Jane took a long breath then described seeing the man and woman approaching the cafe and her sense that they should be feared. She recounted her actions in the cabin, explaining how she had hidden in the bathroom and hit the woman with the tank lid. She told about the man demanding that she put the tank lid down and how she had flung it frisbee style at him then rushed him as well.

"He was stronger than I thought he'd be," Jane said, " when we fell to the floor he flipped me easily. I couldn't move. Then you came in."

Trinity was quiet for a moment then she said, "Take us to the Carlsbad Sheriff Department Loyal."

"Okay," he said.

"Jane," said Trinity, "I want you to give them a complete statement up until your arrival at the cabin. No one broke in or attacked you. You didn't hurt that woman and I didn't hurt that man. Loyal and I tracked you and found you. That's all. Can you do that?"

"I think so," said Jane, "but those people in the cabin. Shelly's going to have to call the police."

"I spoke with Shelly," said Trinity, "she's not going in the cabin until tomorrow. I'll make sure things are cleaned up by then."

123

LOYAL TRUESDALE

Loyal listened to Jane and Trinity's conversation without commenting. Jane's trembling had subsided significantly and she seemed more in control of herself. He was impressed with the way she had handled herself in the cabin. Not many civilians would be so brave and take matters into their own hands the way she had. When they reached the roundabout at the base of Palomar Mountain he turned to look at Trinity.

"There's a sheriff substation in Valley Center," he said. "It's about five minutes from here. Do you want to take Jane there?"

Trinity shook her head.

"No, I'd rather go to Carlsbad," she said. "I'm fairly confident those were the only two assets sent after Jane. And they weren't the best if Jane could get the drop on them. The immediate danger has passed."

"Won't someone be waiting for them to report back?" Loyal asked as he steered the truck through the roundabout and continued west on highway 76.

"Yes," said Trinity, "but there's a window of time. Just get us to Carlsbad so we can get Jane's statement recorded."

"We should call Maynard and have him meet us there," said Loyal. "There's no way Captain Williams is going to let one of us take her statement."

"True," said Trinity, "hand me your phone and I'll call him."

They pulled into the Sheriff Department's parking lot just under forty minutes later and all three slid out of the truck. Maynard Lily was standing at the entrance and gave a wave when he saw them. Trinity put her hand on Jane's upper arm and turned her so that they were facing each other.

"I'm going to request that they video your statement Jane," she said. "I want you to tell them everything that has happened since you took the DNA test. Leisel's house, the trackers, everything. I'll make sure no charges are pressed."

Jane was quiet for a moment then said, "How do you know about all those things?"

"There's no privacy anymore," said Trinity. "Remember that in the future. Someone's always watching."

Jane absorbed her words silently then gave a slight nod.

"You ready?" asked Loyal.

Jane nodded again and they walked across the parking lot to where Maynard Lily was standing. Trinity took five minutes to brief the lawyer then they opened the door and entered the building.

124

TRINITY GLASS

Trinity took Maynard, Jane and Loyal straight to Captain William's office. The door was open. Trinity gave a light knock then walked in. Captain Williams looked up from his computer.

"Agent Glass," he said, "I'm surprised to see you."

He nodded at Loyal and Maynard. "Truesdale," he said, "surprised to see you Lily."

"Captain Williams," said Trinity, "this is Jane Gray."

"We're off the Timmerman case," said Williams, "you know that."

Trinity nodded.

"I'd still like you to take her statement," she said. "There are things going on that I can't tell you about but it's very important that she goes on record about everything that has happened."

Captain William's eyes narrowed.

"Why don't you record it?" he asked. "Take her down the street to the FBI building."

Trinity took a deep breath in and let it out slowly. She knew Captain Williams was angry about the case being taken away.

She understood that anger. The case had been taken away from her as well. Getting mad at Captain Williams was not going to help the situation.

"Captain," she said, "I apologize for the situation. All I can tell you is that until we have an official statement on the record Ms. Gray is in danger. Please. Will you take her statement? Loyal can wait in the lobby and I'll stay out of it. Maynard will represent her."

Captain Williams sighed and stood up. He motioned to Jane.

"Come with me," he said.

Trinity left the building and, having neglected to ask Loyal for his keys, found herself sitting in the bed of Loyal's truck. The day was cool and he had parked near a tree which provided a bit of shade. Trinity leaned her back against the rear window and stretched her long legs out in front of her. Now that Jane was safe she allowed the anger she had pushed back to reemerge. She pulled out her phone and called Caldwell. He answered on the fifth ring which was very unusual. She wondered if he had been debating whether or not to take her call. Skipping any greeting or niceties she got right down to business.

"Did you pass the Timmerman case up the chain of command already?"

"I told you I was going to," he said.

"You didn't think to wait for the external hard drive?"

"You had given me enough over the phone to move forward without it," he said.

"You included Jane Gray in your report?"

"Of course," he said, "she's part of it."

"You set her up Doug," Trinity said.

"I'm not read in on any decisions being made at this point Trinity."

"Maybe not," said Trinity her anger growing, "but you knew what would happen."

"Hard decisions are made every day Trinity."

"Listen Doug," Trinity said, "we've had this conversation. Some people need killing, and I agree. But Jane? An absolute innocent? Suiciding her? Its wrong."

"There's a bigger picture here," he said, "you know that."

"I told you flat out that I was going to continue to look for her," said Trinity. "You sold me out. You put me in danger. If I was there when they arrived they would have done me too."

Caldwell was silent.

"I'm taking a leave of absence," Trinity finally said, "three months minimum, maybe more. I'll get the paperwork to you by tonight. I'd advise you to sign it."

"Come on Trinity," Caldwell began but she interrupted him.

"Sign the damn paperwork Caldwell," she said. Her voice was hard and angry. "And tell whoever ordered this mess that they need a clean up in number 116 at the Lake Henshaw Cabins before sunrise tomorrow."

125

LOYAL TRUESDALE

Captain Williams summoned Detective Hammond and had him lead Jane through her statement. Maynard Lily sat in and advised her. It took just under an hour. Jane detailed everything that she did up to arriving at Lake Henshaw. As per Trinity's instructions she left out the assets and the events that took place inside cabin 116. Detective Hammond wanted to detain Jane for breaking into Leisel's house but Captain Williams let her out on bond. When they were through Captain Williams provided Maynard with a copy of the video on a small external hard drive. He slipped it in his pocket, thanked the captain again, and led Jane out the front door.

Maynard gave Loyal the copy of Jane's statement and told him to call if he needed any more help. Loyal thanked his friend then he and Jane walked across the parking lot in silence. He supposed she was still trying to wrap her brain around everything that she had done since the previous Sunday. He knew he was. He wanted to share the details of Tyler's death with her but knew that he could not. He wondered how the powers that be would spin the situation now that Jane couldn't be used as the fall guy. As they approached his truck he saw that Trinity was sitting in the truck bed. Her back was against the back window of the truck and her legs were stretched out in front of her. A single ray of sunlight had found its way through the leaves of the tree he had parked under and was illuminating her hair. Her eyes were closed. Loyal couldn't help but be struck by her beauty. The world was going crazy but he felt that if he could just hang on to Trinity everything would end up ok.

"All done," he said. Trinity opened her eyes and smiled at them.

"How did it go?" she asked as she drew her legs in and stood.

Loyal slipped the hard drive out of his pocket and held it up.

"When we are back at the house we can see for ourselves but Maynard said that Jane did great."

Trinity stepped over the tailgate and dropped to the ground. She looked at Jane.

"I'm going to send a copy of your statement to my boss," she said. "I don't think you are in danger anymore. Where would you like us to take you?"

"I think I'd like to go home," said Jane.

Loyal thought back to the search of Jane's house as he unlocked the truck.

"Your front door locks are broken, he said. "You are going to have to get that fixed. There is a notice on your door about filing a claim but in my experience you'll get better results if you just fix it yourself."

126

TRINITY GLASS

Trinity's eyes opened abruptly. A glance at Loyal's bedroom clock, a digital relic from the 1990's, told her it was 3:57 am. She lay still for a moment listening for a sound that might have awakened her but heard nothing except Loyal's steady breathing. She closed her eyes for a moment to see if she could fall back to sleep. It only took a minute for her to realize that she could not. As gently as she could she disentangled herself from Loyal's arms and slipped out of bed. Rather than getting dressed, she walked to the bathroom and pulled Loyal's well worn bathrobe from its hook and slid her arms into it. She knotted it around her waist and walked out to the kitchen.

Within ten minutes she had brewed coffee and opened her computer on the kitchen table. She accessed her office email account and read a short email from Caldwell. *3 month leave of absence approved* was all it said. He was obviously angry with her but she didn't care because she was easily as angry as he was, probably more so. Trinity leaned back from the computer and closed her eyes. She had been an agent for so many years and had only taken a handful of vacations. She wasn't exactly sure what she would do with a three month break but knew that she desperately needed it. What had almost happened to Jane filled her with such outrage and disgust. The fact that Caldwell had passed along Jane's information knowing what was likely to happen was distressing as well. It was true, as she had said to Caldwell on the phone the previous day, that some people needed killing. Trinity knew full well that the United States government condoned the removal of threats to the security of the nation and she didn't disagree with the process. But an innocent like Jane? She couldn't get behind something like that.

Trinity sat up and returned her focus to her computer. She exited her email account without replying to Caldwell. He would get a notification that she had read the email and that was good enough for her. Her thoughts moved on to the Bombardier. She needed to know what entity owned that plane. She took a deep breath in and slowly let it out. She wanted to know, needed to know, who was behind the murder of innocent Americans and the harvesting of their organs.

127

LOYAL TRUESDALE

Loyal's eyes opened slowly. He had slept deeply and didn't remember a dream if he had even had one. He looked at his arms and saw they were wrapped, not around Trinity, but around her pillow. Her side of the bed was empty. He felt the sheets and they were cool. She had been up for a while. He glanced at his bedroom clock. It was 7:18. Loyal slid out of bed and walked to the bathroom for his robe. The hook was empty so he slipped on a pair of sweatpants and an old T-shirt, picked up Boo, and walked into the kitchen. Trinity, wearing his robe, was sitting at the kitchen table with her computer open in front of her. There was a pen and a pad of paper next to the computer. The pad was filled with hand-written notes. Trinity was tapping the keyboard and obviously deep in concentration.

Loyal cleared his throat gently so he wouldn't startle her when he approached the table. Trinity raised her head and turned to look at him.

"Morning," she said, "I hope I didn't wake you."

Loyal shook his head.

"How long have you been awake?" he asked.

Trinity glanced at the clock on the computer.

"A little over three hours," she said. "I made coffee but it's probably cold by now."

Loyal walked into the kitchen, poured out the old coffee, and started a new pot. He glanced out the window and saw thick tendrils of fog swirling outside the glass. He fed Boo while the coffee brewed then filled a mug and sat at the table with Trinity.

"What are you up to?" he asked.

Trinity raised her head again and met his eyes.

"Research," she said, "I found the owner of the Bombardier."

Loyal tilted his head a bit and smiled.

"I knew you would," he said.

"That was the hardest part," said Trinity, "After that I just looked at Wikipedia to learn about the company. It's not good news Loyal. The company is called MGI. Have you ever heard of them?"

Loyal shook his head.

"Tell me," he said.

"MGI is a subsidiary of a company called BGI. It was formed in 1999 in China as a genetic research center to partner in the Human Genome Project."

"I remember that," said Loyal, "wasn't that an international project?"

"Yep," said Trinity, "but BGI has evolved since then. There have been allegations of collaboration with the Chinese military and the PLA. They are affiliated with the China National Gene Bank, and apparently they developed a prenatal test that allowed them to compile a huge DNA database of not only Chinese women, but women worldwide."

Trinity paused then said, "It wouldn't be much of a leap for them to jump into organ harvesting."

"And Americans have willingly given their DNA up," said Loyal. "I think I read somewhere that one in five Americans have submitted DNA to direct to consumer DNA testing centers."

"Yes," said Trinity, "that's a good estimate. It might even be more than that. And then there are digitized medical records and all the products that are connected to the internet. That data has to go somewhere. People are giving themselves away."

Loyal stood up and walked to the large window in his living room. The fog was dense outside the glass. He couldn't even see the street. He closed his eyes and brought up the image of his grandson, Mason, that Stella had texted to him. The little guy, fast asleep, with a bootie on his foot monitoring him. He turned back to Trinity.

"So a billionaire needs a new organ and they contact MGI. MGI goes through all their databases and finds someone compatible who is in excellent health. They send the plane over, take the organs, light a fire, and head back to Shanghai for the surgery."

He ran his hands over his face.

"This can't be real Trinity."

"I think it is," said Trinity. She stood up, walked over to him, and took his hands in hers. "I think it is very real Loyal. And the scariest thing of all is that there is no way to stop it. We can't predict where they will go next or who they will target."

"We can track the plane," said Loyal.

"Yeah, but that won't help," said Trinity. "Besides, BGI is a multi billion dollar company. I'm sure they have more than one plane at their disposal."

Trinity wrapped her arms around Loyal and pressed her face against his chest.

"It's happening Loyal," she said, "and there is absolutely nothing we can do."

128

TRINITY GLASS

Trinity kept her head pressed against Loyal's chest. His arms had found their way around her and he was holding her tightly. Her mind was spinning, trying to process all the information they had gathered. She had never felt so helpless. All her life Trinity had been a problem solver and this was a problem she simply could not solve. People would die and there was no way for her to prevent it. After a few minutes she pushed away from Loyal and looked up at him.

"You can't tell anyone what we've discovered," she said.

"I've at least got to tell Stella to get that stupid monitoring bootie off Mason."

Trinity nodded. "I agree, but you can't tell her why Loyal. This is a matter of national security. I read you in on everything when I was specifically directed not to. It's my ass on the line here."

"People need to know Trinity," said Loyal, "we can't keep this to ourselves."

"That's how it works in my world," said Trinity. "You agreed to it when I let you in the SCIF."

"It's different now," said Loyal, "people need to be warned."

"No," said Trinity. She pushed away from him. "First, no one would believe you. Second, our government would shut you up immediately. Tell Stella to take the damn monitor off but keep your mouth shut. These things are solved through channels you don't know about."

Trinity turned away from Loyal and walked back to the bedroom. She slipped out of the robe and returned it to its place on the hook. She dressed in leggings, a tank top, and running shoes. A quick run of the brush through her hair pulled it back so that she could pull it into a pony tail. She returned to the living room. Loyal had not moved.

"I'm going for a run," she said. "Think about what I said."

129

LOYAL TRUESDALE

L oyal followed Trinity out the door and watched her disappear into the swirling fog. He didn't like the idea of her running in this thick fog. His personal trainer, Lacey, had been on a run in similar circumstances and had ended up dead on a trail in Carlsbad. He started to follow Trinity to ask her not to go but she was already gone, enveloped by the thick fog, impossible to see. He considered going after her but decided against it. Instead he picked up the newspaper that was on his front step and returned to his living room. His coffee mug was almost empty so he refilled it and took it, and the newspaper, to the couch and sat next to Boo. He took a long sip then pulled the newspaper from the plastic bag and opened it.

Loyal did not usually read the A section of the paper. Nothing good was happening around the world and there was nothing he could do to stop anything anyways. He did, however read the local section. It interested him. He used to be intimately involved in all the local action and felt slightly removed now that he was retired and out of the loop. The headline he saw on the top half of section B took his breath away.

Homeless man arrested in murder/arson case

Loyal read the article quickly. A homeless man had been arrested for the murder of Tyler Timmerman and the burning of his Carlsbad home. Detectives had solid evidence, they weren't revealing what, that tied the man to the crime. No motive was suggested. Loyal was shocked. Trinity was correct he thought. He had no idea how things worked at her level. The powers that be had quickly moved from Jane's suicide to a help-less homeless man. As Trinity had said, nothing could be done.

Loyal set the paper down, stood, and walked to the living room window. The fog was slowly lifting and he could see to the end of his driveway now. Trinity was still a ghost in the mist. He tried not to think about her out there alone in the fog. As he stood there, his gaze fixed and unfocused, he considered what Trinity had said about not sounding the alarm on BGI and MGI's illegal and terrifying organ harvesting project. He recalled Trinity jokingly saying "what happens in the SCIF stays in the SCIF". He realized now that she hadn't really been joking at all. His hands were tied; he could not say a word.

Loyal's thoughts turned to Jane. He hoped she was okay. He considered calling her but decided instead to call Maggie and let her know that they had found Jane and she was safe. He returned to the kitchen counter, picked up his phone, and placed the call. Maggie answered on the sixth ring and sounded out of breath.

"Did I catch you at a bad time?" asked Loyal.

"No," said Maggie, "I left my phone in my bedroom and had to hurry back here to grab it." She took a deep breath in and let it out. "Have you heard from Jane?"

"Yes," said Loyal, "we found her yesterday at Lake Henshaw. She had rented a cabin there to take some time to think things through."

"So she's ok?" Maggie asked.

"Yep," said Loyal.

"Did she ever meet her birth family?" Maggie asked.

"Not yet," said Loyal, "I think she's still processing everything."

"So what's next for you," Maggie asked, "any big plans?"

"Trinity is taking a leave of absence from her work," said Loyal. "Maybe we'll get away for a while."

"Loyal," said Maggie, "my neighbor is selling his Lazy Days motorhome. You should buy it. He's the original owner and it's in perfect condition. He just put the sign up yesterday. He only wants $3500. I'll send you a picture."

Loyal laughed. "Ok Maggie," he said, "send a picture but I seriously doubt I'll buy it."

They talked for a few more minutes then said goodbye. Loyal returned to his living room window. He could see across the street now. The fog still hung in the air but it was thinning out. He looked right and left but still saw no sign of Trinity. He ran his hands through his hair and let out a small sigh. At that moment his phone pinged, indicating a text message. He still held the phone in his hand so he raised it up and opened the text that he saw was from Maggie. It included several pictures of the Lazy Days motorhome she had mentioned. Loyal studied the pictures. Maggie was correct, the motorhome looked to be in perfect condition. Loyal lowered the phone and closed his eyes. He imagined himself and Trinity in the motorhome driving around the country with no absolute destination in mind. Suddenly the idea of an extended road trip seemed a hell of a lot more appealing.

130

TRINITY GLASS

T rinity knew it was not smart to go running in fog that was so thick she could barely see her hands if she held them up in front of her face. She didn't want to get lost or hurt; the memory of Loyal's personal trainer's murder on a foggy morning such as this was still fresh in her mind. Still, she needed to move and think so she just kept running laps around Loyal's block. She ran the block in front of his house then made two right turns and ran the alley behind his house. As she was making her fourth turn into the alley she nearly collided with a black van that was parked along the side of the narrow road. The van hadn't been there on any of her previous laps and it caught Trinity by surprise. She studied it from the back as best she could through the swirling fog. She was pretty sure she could make out camera housings near the corners of the roof. She knelt and looked at the tires which were brand new and all terrain. Trinity remained in her kneeling position and considered what she was seeing. This was undoubtedly a surveillance van. The odds that it was here for Loyal and herself were astronomical, who else could they be watching?

A slight click caught Trinity's attention. The van door was sliding open. She could sense, more than see, a person slipping out of the van's side door. She reached for her gun then reconsidered. If this was another asset, here for Loyal and possibly her, it wouldn't be smart to kill them with her own gun. The person was standing still beside the van. They hadn't said anything to anyone else who might possibly be in the van and they hadn't closed the door. Trinity quickly ran through scenarios in her mind. Would they send one person or two? They had sent two after Jane, likely because she was an unknown and those two clearly hadn't been their best. Taking out a government agent was a big deal and Caldwell's superiors would likely want to keep the action as contained as possible. One asset, Trinity decided, but certainly one of their best. She ran through possible jui jitsu rear takedowns and decided on the broomstick take-down. Trinity took a moment to visualize the move then moved forward with surprising speed. She wrapped her right leg around the asset's right leg and snaked it between their legs until her ankle was hooked around their left leg. Simultaneously, she pulled on their shoulder with her right hand and pulled them down with her. They landed together, almost like a loving couple cuddling, and Trinity snaked her right arm around the assets neck and applied as much pressure as she could. The asset struggled in her grip but she had them immobilized. Trinity kept the pressure up and gradually the struggling ceased. She kept the pressure for a full two minutes more before releasing the asset and looking at them.

· · ·

It was a woman. She was younger than Trinity by about ten years. She was dressed all in black. In her gloved left hand she still gripped a Glock 19 9mm suppressed pistol. Although the woman was clearly dead, Trinity kicked the gun away as she stood. Her body was shaking from the adrenaline dump and she took a minute to take some calming breaths before grabbing the woman by the armpits and manhandling her back into the van. She picked the gun up and placed it under the driver's seat then climbed in and started the engine. She inched the van along, struggling to see through the blanket of fog. She knew that if she was involved in an accident or was pulled over she was dead in the water. No help from Caldwell would be forthcoming on this one. She supposed that there had been some transfer of trace evidence from herself to the asset during the takedown but there was nothing to be done about that. Trinity reached the end of Robles Rd. and turned right on Cannon. She went one block then made another right onto Avenida Encinas. She drove past the Carlsbad Suites Hotel and pulled into the southern end of the hotel's parking lot. She parked the van in the far corner and wiped down the steering wheel. Trinity searched through the van and found the emergency kit. She removed a flare, struck it on the cap, and stuck it under the driver's seat. As she did this she retrieved the suppressed weapon, locked the van, and started jogging back to Loyal's.

131

TRINITY GLASS

T rinity rounded the corner of Loyal's street and stopped. She had no idea how long she had been gone. She considered whether to tell Loyal about the asset and decided it was better if he didn't know. She leaned forward and placed her hands on her knees for a moment then straightened and walked toward Loyal's house. She tried to remember what she and Loyal had been discussing before the run. It came back to her slowly. She had told him he couldn't tell anyone about anything they had learned. She hoped he had considered what she had said. She knew she had been clear with him from the very beginning that he could not divulge anything that they discovered that had to do with national security. How could she possibly have guessed the enormity of what they would uncover? She was still having a hard time coming to terms with it. Tyler Timmerman had been selected for organ harvesting, most likely from the DNA sample, but she also had to consider how connected he was. He could have been monitored through his Whoop, his smart TV, his Ring doorbell and associated cameras, his electronic medical records, and more. It was a terrifying prospect and the fact that there was seemingly no way to stop it was even more frightening.

Trinity opened Loyal's front door and stepped in to the house. Loyal was standing in the living room looking out the window. She could only see his profile but it appeared that his eyes were closed. He opened them and turned toward her when he heard the door opening.

"You're back," he said, "I was worried about you in the fog."

"Sorry," said Trinity as she wiped some sweaty tendrils of hair that had escaped from her ponytail out of her face. "Did you think about what I said?"

Loyal nodded. "I did," he said, "and you did tell me from the beginning that I was sworn to secrecy." He walked across the room and stood in front of Trinity, their faces were just inches apart. She reached out for his hands and they stood like that for a few moments. Loyal sighed then said, "I'm not going to say anything. I'm going to tell Stella to ditch the owlet bootie. She's against the DNA testing so I don't have to worry about that." Loyal pulled Trinity into his arms and lay his cheek against her damp hair for a long moment then pulled back and looked in her eyes.

"I saw something this morning that I want to show you," he said. He let go of Trinity and walked to the kitchen table. She followed. He picked up a newspaper that was on the table and turned it so that she could see the headline. Trinity's eyes widened slightly as she read it. She took the paper from Loyal's hand and quickly scanned the article then set the paper back on the table.

"Looks like they found a work around," she said, "I knew they would."

Trinity showered and dressed in jeans and a T-shirt. Her thoughts were on Caldwell and everything she wanted to say to him. His superiors had sent an asset to kill Loyal and probably her as well. He had to know that is what they would do. Certainly he had given them Loyal's information. But he had done nothing to stop it. Her loyalty to Doug Caldwell was gone. To keep Loyal from guessing that anything other than a run had occurred she sat down at her computer and began searching to see if she could find any information about the framing of the homeless man. Loyal was sitting on the couch. He had a small fishing pole with a wine cork attached to the end of the fishing line. He was tossing it out and reeling it in while Boo tried to catch it. The little cat was jumping and pouncing, practically doing back flips to try to catch the cork. Trinity watched, a smile on her face, for a minute or so then turned back to the computer. Within two minutes the smile had disappeared from her face.

"Damn him," she muttered under her breath.

Loyal must have heard her because he stopped playing fishing pole with Boo and turned to look at her.

"What's wrong?" he asked.

"Caldwell blocked my security clearances," Trinity said, "I'm locked out of everything."

Loyal set the pole down, stood, and walked to the kitchen table.

"Is that standard procedure?" he asked as he sat down beside her.

"Honestly," said Trinity, "I don't really know. I've never

taken a leave of absence before. But it never happened when I took vacations."

"Sounds like he's punishing you," said Loyal.

Trinity looked at Loyal, then at the newspaper headline about the homeless man, then at her computer, then back at Loyal.

"Yeah, it does," she said. "He may live to regret that decision."

132

CHARLES TIMMERMAN

C harles was sitting in a recliner in his den. His eyes
were closed. In his hand he held a framed picture of
himself and Tyler. It had been taken some years
previously following a lacrosse game. Tyler's hair was mussed
and sweaty, his smile wide, his eyes shining. Charles had his
arm around Tyler's shoulders, his face reflecting the love and
pride he felt for his son. In his mind Charles was replaying the
memories from that day. The depth of his sadness regarding
Tyler's death was profound. Charles had never experienced
feelings such as these. The pain he had felt when they had to
give up their first child was tempered by his knowledge that she
was out in the world somewhere, alive and hopefully thriving.
Tyler was dead. He would never walk through their front door
again. Charles would never hear his son's contagious laugh,
never give his son a hug, never see the love in Tyler's eyes that
he had for his family. It was all gone. Tyler was gone. And for
what? Doug Caldwell had called the previous evening and told
Charles about the arrest of the homeless man. Apparently
someone had turned him in to get the reward money being

offered. When arrested, the man had had something, Caldwell wouldn't say what, of Tyler's in his possession. Details were being withheld until the trial.

Charles was finding that he didn't care about the trial. He could easily predict the outcome. The man would be found guilty and sentenced to prison. He would serve his time and eventually he would be released and allowed to re-join the general public. Tyler would still be dead. Charles opened his eyes and looked at the picture again. He ran his pointer finger over Tyler's face and felt his own eyes fill with tears. Just as he was setting the picture frame back on the end table his phone rang. He pulled it out of his shirt pocket and answered.

"Yes?" he said.

"Mr. Timmerman," a female voice said, "it's agent Glass."

"Doug Caldwell already filled me in last night," said Charles, "he called me immediately after the arrest."

"I was wondering if we could meet," said Trinity.

"If you have something to tell me you can just tell me over the phone," said Charles.

"I'd prefer a face to face," said Trinity. "I'm staying in Carlsbad. Can you meet me at Terramar Point."

"I'm not sure where that is," said Charles.

"Drive north on Carlsbad Boulevard," said Trinity. "When you see Cerezo Drive park and walk west. You'll see me. Meet me there in an hour."

Charles sighed. "I've got a lot going on right now Agent Glass," he began but Trinity cut him off saying, "You'll want to meet me Mr. Timmerman. I'll see you in an hour."

Before Charles could respond the connection was cut.

. . .

Charles went into his office and looked at a real estate map he had of the area. Terramar Point was a lookout just above the beach off Carlsbad Blvd and just south of Cannon Road. He wondered what Agent Glass could possibly want to talk to him about. Caldwell had told him the previous evening that Glass was off the case. Charles had assumed that she had been assigned to something else since Tyler's case appeared to have been solved. Now he wondered if perhaps she was removed for another reason. This thought sparked his interest. He walked into the living room where Daisy's nurse, Phyllis, was sitting on the couch reading a book. She looked up when he walked in.

"She's sleeping," she said. "We took a walk around the back portion of your property and she's exhausted. It's an improvement though."

Charles nodded.

"Thank you Phyllis," he said. "I have something to attend to. I shouldn't be gone more than two hours."

Phyllis nodded and smiled. "I'll keep a close eye on your wife Mr. Timmerman.

Charles nodded. "Thank you," he said as he walked out of the room.

133

TRINITY GLASS

Trinity cut the connection with Charles Timmerman and set her phone on the kitchen table. She turned to look at Loyal. He was watching her carefully, his eyes full of curiosity.

"I need the external hard drive you have in your safe," she said.

"What are you going to do?" asked Loyal.

"It's better that you don't know," said Trinity as she pushed back and stood up. Loyal stood as well and grabbed her upper arm gently.

"I'm in this with you Trinity," he said quietly, "we can't go back and do things over."

Trinity sighed. "I know that Loyal," she said, "but this is something I have to do on my own. It is better if you are out of the loop. Can you please get me that hard drive?"

Loyal nodded without saying anything else and left the room. He was back in under three minutes with the hard drive in his hand.

"You sure you don't want me with you?" he asked. His

concern for her was apparent on his face. Trinity nodded then leaned in and gave him a gentle kiss.

"I'll be back before you know it," she said. She met his eyes for the briefest of moments, gave a small smile, then turned and walked out of the house.

It took Trinity less than ten minutes to walk from Loyal's house to Terramor Point. While she walked she pulled up Caldwell's contact information and placed the call. She was furious. She had tried to hide it from Loyal. She didn't want him anywhere near what had happened earlier this morning. The coastal fog had finally lifted. Trinity could see a thick layer of haze in the distance, far out over the sea. The springtime sun was gentle and warmed the skin on her arms. Seagulls flew above her and pelicans skimmed the crests of the waves, their giant wings spread wide, searching the ocean for food. Trinity stood at the edge of the bluff and looked out to sea. She loved the ocean; the sight, scent, and sound relaxed her and helped her feel grounded. What she was about to do had the potential for catastrophic outcomes but she felt she had no other choice. She had made the decision and now she had to follow through with it.

Caldwell answered on the first ring.

"Glass," he said, "you coming back after all?"

"What the fuck did you do?" Trinity said.

"I'm not sure what you mean," said Caldwell.

"Another asset?" said Trinity. "At me and Loyal?"

"It's out of my hands," said Caldwell. "I don't know what you are talking about."

"At the very least you gave up Loyal's address Doug," said Trinity, "don't bother denying that."

There was silence on the line.

"You've got another clean up," said Trinity, "black van in the southeast corner of the Carlsbad Suites Hotel."

Trinity paused a moment then added, "Don't contact me Doug. I'm in the wind. You keep sending assets you'll keep having clean ups."

When Caldwell didn't say anything Trinity ended the call.

Trinity slid her infrared necklace out of her T-shirt and let it lay on her chest. This necklace would create an unidentifiable image of her face if any hidden cameras happened to catch her meeting with Timmerman. She had picked this spot because it was fairly remote but wasn't taking any chances. She had been standing on the bluff for about fifteen minutes when she heard footsteps approaching behind her. She turned and saw Charles Timmerman making his way along the trail toward her. He was dressed very casually in faded jeans and a dark blue wind-breaker. A black baseball cap was sitting atop his head, the brim pulled down close to his eyes. He walked steadily toward her, his hands in the pockets of the windbreaker and his head tilted down to avoid the breeze. He stopped when he was less than three feet from her. She could see now that he was wearing dark sunglasses which he reached up and removed. His eyes were swollen and there were dark circles under them. It was clear that Charles Timmerman was suffering.

They stood, just looking at each other for a long moment. Finally Charles cleared his throat and said, "I'm here."

"Mr. Timmerman," Trinity began speaking then paused for a moment, softened her voice, and began again.

"Charles," she said, "there are two things that I have for you."

Trinity held out her left hand and opened it. The external hard drive with all her research and notes lay in the palm of her hand. Charles looked at it but did not reach out his hand to take it.

"You haven't been told the whole truth about your son Charles," said Trinity, "you are going to want to look at this. What you choose to do with the information is up to you. I simply feel that you deserve to know."

Charles reached his right hand out and gingerly lifted the external hard drive. Trinity lowered her left arm to her side.

"Do not involve me in any of it," said Trinity, "I'll deny this meeting ever took place."

Charles looked at the small drive for a long moment then slipped it into the pocket of his windbreaker. He gave Trinity a small nod indicating his agreement.

"You said there were two things you wanted to give me," he said.

Trinity nodded.

"Jane Gray is your daughter," she said. "I have her contact information if you want it."

Charles' eyes filled with tears. He blinked them back and swallowed then said, "Give the information to Leisel. My first duty is to protect Daisy."

"I can't reach out to her," said Trinity, "just take the information and pass it to Leisel."

LOYAL TRUESDALE

Loyal stood at the living room window the entire time that Trinity was gone. Boo was making figure eights around his ankles and Loyal leaned down periodically to pet his cat. Nearly forty minutes had passed before he caught sight of Trinity walking back to his house. She had her hands in the front pockets of her jeans and her head was tilted toward the ground. The tension she was carrying in her body was obvious even from a distance. Loyal walked to the front door and opened it for her as she neared it. She raised her head as she walked through the doorway and their eyes met. Loyal was unable to read her expression which was quite unusual. Once she had passed by him and entered the house Loyal closed the door and turned to face her. Trinity was silent for a beat then she said, "A shit storm is going to be coming Loyal. We need to disappear."

MAGGIE MACPHEARSON

Maggie was feeding the quail that gathered every day in her front yard. She tossed handfuls of bird seed out on the driveway and smiled as the cute little birds bobbed their heads and pecked at the seed. Feeding the wild birds had been her late husband's hobby and by continuing the tradition Maggie felt a connection to him. She was just turning to walk back into the house when her phone rang. She answered in her usual fashion.

"This is Maggie," she said.

"Maggie, it's Loyal."

"Hi Loyal, what's up?"

"I was wondering if your neighbor had sold that Lazy Days motorhome yet?"

"I don't think so," said Maggie, "it was still parked in their driveway this morning. Are you interested in buying it?"

"Yes," said Loyal, "if you give me his contact information I'll reach out and come pick it up today."

"Sure," said Maggie, "I'll send you the contact when we hang up. Will you stop by my place and say hello?"

"I'm wondering if there are back roads to your house," said Loyal, "I'm driving the buggy."

Maggie gave Loyal directions through Hidden Meadows then through Cougar Pass. Once they were on Betsworth they could turn on Lilac and get to her house easily.

She disconnected the call and sent Loyal her neighbor's contact information then tucked her phone back in her pocket. Something in Loyal's voice had sounded off. She wasn't sure what it was but it worried her. She hoped that Loyal hadn't gotten himself mixed up in yet another "adventure".

136

LEISEL TIMMERMAN

L eisel found a coveted parking spot along Carlsbad Boulevard and squeezed her car into the tight space. She slid out of her car, adjusted the baseball hat she wore on her head, and walked slowly to the sand. She slipped her sandals off and carried them in her left hand as she walked south toward lifeguard tower 37. It was just after 10:00 am. Joggers, walkers, and bicyclers crowded the sidewalk and bike lanes on Carlsbad Boulevard but the beach was relatively quiet. She could see a few surfers in the water. They appeared to be waiting patiently for waves that didn't seem to be forthcoming. The ocean was gray and flat, which matched Leisel's mood. Her father had called the previous evening with the news of the arrest of a homeless man for Tyler's murder and the burning of his house. It made no sense to Leisel. Tyler had lived in an upscale area. Leisel had never seen a single homeless person in his neighborhood. Not even in the park that backed up to Tyler's house. And with all Tyler's security cameras surely he would have noticed if someone had taken up residence in the park. It made no sense.

. . .

Leisel approached tower 37 and climbed up. She sat with her legs dangling off the edge of the platform and set her sandals beside her. She brushed the loose sand off of her feet by rubbing them against each other then focused her gaze on the endless sea. She attempted to clear her mind but images of her brother kept returning. She remembered the day her parents had brought him home from the hospital. Leisel had been angry and jealous at first but Tyler had been such a sweet little guy that she couldn't help but fall in love with him. All these years she and her brother had been each other's advocates and best friends. She felt lost without him. Leisel thought she couldn't possibly have any tears left but her eyes filled and a few tears trickled down her cheeks. She didn't bother to wipe them away. Instead she let them fall from her face into her lap. She glanced down at the tiny little water marks they left on her jeans. As Leisel lifted her gaze and refocused it on the ocean her phone vibrated in her pocket. She slid it out and looked at the text. It was from her father. Leisel tapped the text and opened it. It was short and to the point.

Jane Gray is your sister. Here is her contact information. What you do with it is up to you.

Her father had listed a phone number and an address in Escondido. Leisel read the text several times. She took a deep breath in, held it for a few seconds, then slowly let it out. With a shaking finger she tapped Jane's phone number and listened to it ring.

137

TRINITY GLASS

L oyal drove his buggy to Valley Center. They took Cougar Pass through Hidden Meadows to avoid possible surveillance and cameras. Trinity sat to his right in the passenger seat. Their suitcases were in the back seat along with a cat carrier containing Boo. They had stopped at the bank on their way and pulled out a significant amount of cash. Their phones were sitting on the kitchen counter in Loyal's house. Trinity always carried a burner phone and she had activated it when they left the bank. They pulled into Maggie's neighbor's driveway just past 11:00 am and parked next to the motorhome. Loyal had called the owner, a retired dentist named Dr. Webb, and he was standing next to the motorhome waiting for them. Maggie was there as well.

Trinity and Loyal slid out of the buggy and approached Dr. Webb. He was a large man, at least 6'2", with a balding head and a wide smile. He reached out his hand and Trinity shook it then Loyal did as well. Maggie gave Loyal a hug and shook Trinity's hand when Loyal introduced her. Trinity had not yet met Maggie but had heard a lot about her from Loyal. She was glad to finally meet her. The motorhome looked it's age, 1984, from the outside. The blue and white paint was faded and scratched. Trinity could imagine it parked in the corner of the local Walmart and housing some homeless folks. Dr. Webb opened the door and they all stepped up the two stairs. The inside of the motorhome was a completely different story. It was in pristine condition.

Two narrow steps led into the vehicle. To the right were the driver's seat and the co-captain passenger seat. A sleeping or storage area was above these seats. Directly in front of Trinity was a dining area with two bench seats and a small table. A large window provided a nice view of the outside. To the left was a small kitchen with a sink, oven, and stove. Beyond that was another couch that folded down into a bed. Trinity turned to the left and walked down the length of the motorhome. She saw now that there was a large closet space opposite the fold down bed and a bathroom and shower were tucked in the very back of the vehicle. The floors were light brown laminate and the cabinets were a slightly darker brown. She turned and saw Loyal just behind her. Dr. Webb was showing him how the built in generator worked. He flipped a switch and it burst to life with a throaty growl. Even in profile she could see that Loyal was smiling widely. Beyond Loyal and the dentist Maggie stood on the top entry step and peeked around the corner. Maggie was smiling and when Trinity turned and caught sight of her face in a wall mounted mirror she was surprised to find that she was smiling as well.

. . .

Fifteen minutes later Loyal was the proud owner of the 1984 Lazy Days motorhome. Maggie offered to lend him her buggy trailer so he and Trinity could tow his buggy behind them as they traveled. Loyal drove the motorhome over to Maggie's house and Maggie drove his buggy. Trinity knew how to drive a stick shift vehicle but deferred to Maggie's expertise. She would have plenty of time to drive the buggy while they roamed across the United States.

"Where are you planning on going?" asked Maggie as she helped them hook up the trailer.

"Not sure yet," said Loyal.

"You sure you want to take the cat with you?" asked Maggie.

Trinity looked at Loyal.

"Don't really have anywhere to leave him," said Loyal.

"I'll keep him if you want," said Maggie, "he'll be a good friend for Storm."

Loyal looked in the cat carrier at Boo.

"It would probably be easier without him," said Loyal, "we don't really have a plan."

"We just want to disappear for a while," added Trinity.

"You should check out Slab City at the Salton Sea," said Maggie, "it's close and probably one of the best places to disappear in the entire country."

Trinity pulled out the burner phone and looked up Slab City. Loyal looked over her shoulder as she played several YouTube videos. It certainly looked like an eclectic crowd lived in Slab City. When the videos were over Trinity slid the phone back in her pocket and looked at Loyal.

"Might be a good place to stay for a few days," she said, "just to get our bearings and make some decisions."

Loyal nodded. "Agreed," he said.

Twenty minutes after that Loyal and Trinity hit the road. They had removed all the license plates from the tailer, and buggy and left Boo with Maggie. With their computers and phones still at Loyal's house and the motorhome still registered to Dr. Webb they were virtually untraceable.

CHARLES TIMMERMAN

Charles ejected Agent Glass' external hard drive and shut his computer down. Other than running his hands through his hair he did not move. His anger over what he had just read and watched was immense. If Agent Glass' information was correct, and he did not doubt for a moment that it was, the United States government, specifically OSI, was covering up his son's death to avoid an international incident and allowing other innocent Americans to be slaughtered for their organs as well. He understood now that Agent Glass could not be the person to bring this evil to light. She had given him this information for one simple reason; with his connections, money, and power Charles could be the person to expose the atrocities being perpetuated upon the American public.

EPILOGUE

Riley Gable completed the last two reps on her Tonal machine folded in the arms of the exercise machine and powered it off. She used a towel to wipe the sweat off her face and neck and dropped it in the laundry room as she headed for the kitchen. As she walked through the new home she shared with her husband of three years Riley couldn't help but smile. They had designed the home together and only recently moved in. It was a true "smart" home, totally wired and connected to the internet. The house was located in Florence, Oregon, a small town with less than 10,000 residents located on Oregon's central coast. Her husband, James was an airline pilot based out of Eugene which was about an hour and a half from Florence.

Riley entered the kitchen and poured herself a glass of water. She had recently stopped drinking coffee and really missed it, but she and James had decided to have their first child and she wanted her body to be in pristine condition for the baby. They had submitted DNA tests to genomecestry.com and the results had indicated no problems genetically for their future child. Riley washed out the glass and was setting it on the counter when she heard the unmistakeable click of the front door opening. She wasn't expecting James for another two days but called out his name anyway.

"James," she said, "is that you?"

There was no answer. Riley stepped into the dining room, intending to check the front door but stopped in her tracks when she saw an Asian woman standing in the entryway.

"Who are you?" asked Riley. "How did you get in here?"

"Riley Gable?" asked the woman.

"Yes," said Riley suddenly feeling very unsure of herself. "How did you know that?"

At that moment Riley felt a tiny pinch in her neck, almost like a bee sting. She raised her hand to the spot and turned slightly. There were two Asian men standing behind her. One held a syringe in his gloved hand. Riley felt a wave of dizziness wash over her. As her body crumpled to the ground she felt strong hands catch her to break her fall. As she was placed gently on the ground she thought she heard the Asian woman say, "I'm sorry Riley Gable, but you have something that we need."

AFTERWORD

I received a phone call from my brother Mark, to whom this novel is dedicated, about 9 months ago. He'd had a dream and he couldn't get it out of his head. He thought it might make a good start for a story. Boy, was he ever right. Mark said, "There's this woman, let's call her Jane, who is trying to find her birth family. She enlists Loyal's help somehow." That little nugget is what brought this novel to life. I'm not sure Mark will recognize his dream, but I guarantee it is in here.

On the subject matter that the book deals with....all the statistics on DNA testing are accurate, it did take me two and one-half hours to read the privacy policy of one of the most popular direct to customer DNA sites, and the Chinese Communist Party does have a proven history of organ harvesting from prisoners. The part about them coming to the USA to harvest healthier organs for the supremely wealthy was formed in my imagination. But, as I said in my dedication, *when dreams become reality...*

ACKNOWLEDGMENTS

Writing a book, creating characters and bringing them to life, imagining scenarios, plots, events...all these things bring me great pleasure. But in the end it is you, the reader, who gives life to the novel. So thank you, dear reader, for taking the time to give life to the characters in this book.

As always, I owe so much to my cold readers. These folks take time out of their busy lives to read and critique what I have written. Terry Coker, Madison Cooper, Hayley Helms, and Mark Palmerton, I am forever in your debt. Thank you for the honesty.

Once again Terry Coker, LASD (ret) made himself available for any questions I had about police procedure and guns. He also provided, through HAM radio, a few "Terry-isms" that make Loyal so real.

My deepest appreciation to Marta Palmerton, Mother and dear friend, for editing the proof with me.

I can't say enough about Kym McNabb, a dear friend, unexpectedly found and truly treasured, who creates my covers.

A tip of the hat to Hannah LaVine. Always first in line to order a copy of the new book.

In the creation of a book there is always one person who stands out, who is always there to listen and share feedback. My husband Brett is that person. Brett, you are deeply loved. None of this would exist without you.

ALSO BY KATHLEEN HELMS

A.I. Smith

Loyalty

Mistrust

Deception

Made in the USA
Middletown, DE
09 April 2023